Readers lov
by T

"Tender and sweet, but still with some very realistic touches, this story had me captivated, and I can't wait to see what Ms. Lain will do with the next story in the series."
—(un)Conventional
Book Views

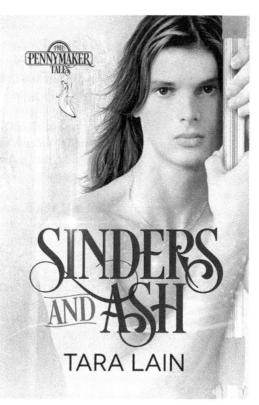

"…an enjoyable, sensual story, full of charm, wit, age-old wisdom, and, of course, as with all fairy tales, a happily ever after ending."
—Rainbow Book
Reviews

"If you're feeling in the mood for a bit of an enchanting romance; put the kids to bed, get under the covers with your Kindle and read this one to yourself...but not out loud!"
—Sinfully… Addicted to All Male Romance

By Tara Lain

LOVE IN LAGUNA
Knight of Ocean Avenue
Knave of Broken Hearts

LONG PASS CHRONICLES
Outing the Quarterback
Canning the Center

PENNYMAKER TALES
Sinders and Ash
Driven Snow

TALES OF THE HARKER PACK
The Pack or the Panther
Wolf in Gucci Loafers
Winter's Wolf
The Pack or the Panther & Wolf in Gucci Loafers (Series Anthology)

Published By DREAMSPINNER PRESS
www.dreamspinnerpress.com

TARA LAIN

Published by
DREAMSPINNER PRESS

5032 Capital Circle SW, Suite 2, PMB# 279, Tallahassee, FL 32305-7886 USA
www.dreamspinnerpress.com

This is a work of fiction. Names, characters, places, and incidents either are the product of author imagination or are used fictitiously, and any resemblance to actual persons, living or dead, business establishments, events, or locales is entirely coincidental.

Driven Snow
© 2015 Tara Lain.

Cover Art
© 2015 Reese Dante.
http://www.reesedante.com
Cover content is for illustrative purposes only and any person depicted on the cover is a model.

ISBN: 978-1-63476-618-0
Digital ISBN: 978-1-63476-267-0
Library of Congress Control Number: 2015947598
First Edition November 2015

Printed in the United States of America

This paper meets the requirements of
ANSI/NISO Z39.48-1992 (Permanence of Paper).

To the Beautiful Dream Team—Thank you for your wonderful support, enthusiastic help, and just being great pals! And thank you for encouraging me to keep writing fairy-tale romances.

CHAPTER 1

SNOW CRINGED back toward Professor Kingsley as the group of visiting students glanced at him and giggled.

"—face like a girl."

"Doesn't look all that formidable."

Snow turned away. Yes, he looked different. Well, different since he happened to be a guy. Yes, he hated it.

The visiting professor, Jacobs, frowned at his protégés, but didn't seem to be trying very hard to make them act better. They stared, whispered, and laughed.

Professor Kingsley leaned down. "Wipe up the floor with this guy. He's an arrogant son of a bitch." Turning to the crowd, he clapped his hands and raised his voice. "Thank you all for coming. Today's exhibition match between Grandmaster Professor Herman Jacobs and Grandmaster Snowden Reynaldi is about to begin."

A chessboard and two game clocks were set up on a table raised on a small platform. The hundred or so people in the room pressed toward it. Professor Kingsley leaned over to Snow again. "Have fun, but don't take too much time. We need to start practicing for the Anderson Tournament, and you need your rest."

"Yes, sir." Snow walked over to the table. Jacobs already occupied the chair in the "power" spot with the best lighting and view from his seat. He faced the black pieces. Snow flipped his hair over his shoulder and slipped into the chair opposite. A tall guy, probably twenty or so—about Snow's age—walked over to Jacobs. He glanced at Snow and cocked a half smile. "Get this done fast, Prof. We all want to go out for drinks to celebrate."

Jacobs laughed. "I'll keep that in mind." He nodded his head. "Grandmaster."

Snow nodded.

The referee stepped up and held out his closed hands. Jacobs tapped the left. The referee opened his hand. Black. That meant Snow moved first.

2

A little rumble from Jacobs's group of students showed their displeasure.

Snow gazed at the board, vaguely aware the timers had started. In his brain, pieces floated on a sea of white, every move possible. His hand drifted into the storm and shifted the king pawn two spaces to e4. *Measured and therefore absolute.* His hand slapped the game clock.

Jacobs shifted in his chair. He glanced up. The muscles around his mouth tightened as he slid his bishop pawn two spaces to f5.

Snow kept his face placid. *Trying to tempt me. So silly.* His fingers snaked out. Capture at f5. *Bam.* He hit the game clock.

Jacobs frowned ever so slightly. Snow caught the movement, and his eyes flicked up—

And froze.

Oh my. Oh. His breath caught. What a sight.

There *he* stood behind Jacobs, like a statue, one hand under his chin, the other supporting his elbow, eyes as golden as a chess trophy gazing at the board. His slim mouth curved upward as if he saw perfectly what Snow would do next, as if he saw Snow himself, saw through him. *Prince. Riley Prince.* His body was as tall, hard-muscled, and lean as the fairy tale his name suggested.

Here. He's here.

His ever-present critic sniped *You don't think he came to see you, do you?*

Snow's hand reached out like it wanted to touch the prince.

Someone gasped.

What? Wake up!

Snow blinked and saw Riley's golden brows draw together and his eyes flick up to Snow. *Wide-eyed. Worried.*

Snow took a breath and looked over to where his opponent stared at him with a little smirk. A glance at the board showed the man had moved his pawn to g5. Snow glared at his own hand, still suspended in space. Dear God, he'd nearly touched the piece. At their level, an illegal touch would have required a penalty and a possible loss. Wouldn't every one of Jacobs's students love to tell the story of how Snowden Reynaldi made a rookie mistake and lost to their professor? The game didn't count, but his reputation did.

Get this over with.

But his eyes wouldn't focus on the board. They wanted to look at Riley Prince again. Snow glanced up toward Riley.

Riley gazed at him, a tiny crease between his brows.

Don't worry, my prince.

Every one of Jacobs's students had a broad smile. Professor Kingsley looked neutral, which often meant he was worried.

Snow turned his head back to the board. *Enough.* He reached out a fingertip and gently persuaded his lovely lady to the edge of the board. Queen to h5. King trapped. He nodded. "Checkmate."

He sat back, finished. All he wanted was to gaze at that perfect face.

The students gasped. Jacobs's eyes widened. "No." He stared at the board.

Riley smiled and applauded with the others in the small audience, which made Snow's heart beat harder.

I could go over there. Say hello. Introduce myself. His stomach knotted.

His stupid inner critic, which had been his constant companion since childhood, said, *Don't be an idiot. Why would he want to talk to you?*

Snow tried to look at Jacobs, who was still staring at the board, but his eyes drifted back to that beautiful face. A profile reminiscent of an ancient coin.

As he watched, a pretty girl stepped up beside Riley and slipped her hand through the crook of his arm. She stretched up to whisper something in his ear. Riley chuckled. Snow sighed. *The golden girl to go with the golden boy. Courtney Taylor, yearbook queen.* Of course, what his prince deserved.

Snow blinked once, twice, then looked down to the chessboard again.

Don't want to watch.

What did you think? He just came here to see her.

"Son of a—" Jacobs swallowed and plastered on a smile. "In three fu—flaming moves. You got me." He shrugged. "I guess I came to get beat, Reynaldi."

Snow nodded but stared at the board. "I was just lucky."

Jacobs snorted. "Cut me a break, Grandmaster. You haven't been 'just lucky' at this game since you were three. Your modesty doesn't become you."

Snow's head felt heavy. He didn't look up. Jacobs's hand thrust into his field of vision. "Thanks for the game. I'm sorry I wasn't able to give you more of a go."

Smile. Turn up your lips. "It was fun."

Another snort. "Yeah, easy for you to say. Thanks again."

As Jacobs walked away, someone patted Snow's shoulder. "Good job, Snow. Guess you showed him not to mess with NorCal University."

Snow ducked his head but really smiled this time. Hard to understand, but a lot of the students didn't mind that he was shy and weird. They liked that he helped make NorCal famous.

Jacobs's students had quit whispering. They stared at him now like he'd turned into a giant reptile. Was it better to be feared than ridiculed?

Just part of the game.

I suppose.

Professor Kingsley's voice rang out over the large room. "Special thanks to Herman Jacobs for participating in our exhibition challenge today. Anyone wishing to join the chess club, we have sign-up forms on the table by the door, and there are refreshments in the connecting room."

Snow craned his neck, staring around. No giant golden gods anywhere.

Gone. Damn.

Dreamer.

Bitch.

A hand grabbed his arm. "Hey, Snow, I knew a three-move checkmate was possible, but how did you know you could use it on him?"

Snow tried to refocus his eyes to stare at the guy. Didn't remember his name. "I, uh, I don't know."

"But you must follow a string of logic."

Snow shook his head. "No, all moves are possible. Until they aren't."

"I don't get it."

Professor Kingsley's voice came from behind him. "It's okay, Barry. Snow's a physicist. He plays chess based on fundamental quantum theory."

Snow glanced around the room. *Where did Riley go so fast?*

Barry frowned. "But if you look at the Fisher game versus—"

The professor slipped an arm around Snow's back, dislodging Barry's hold. "Sorry, son, I need to borrow Snow right now. We'll discuss it at the next club meeting, okay?"

"Oh, sorry. Sure, no worries."

"Not a problem." He led Snow away and into the room where people gathered to drink punch and eat cookies. "You doing okay?"

Snow smiled. "Yeah, fine."

"Good game."

"Thank you. He walked into it."

The professor patted his arm. "I'm sure." He grinned, which gave his handsome face an impish quality. "I must confess to a certain delight at your decimation of Jacobs. He was so sure he could bring his chess club here and at least play you to a draw. He's such an ass."

Snow smiled and nodded. Making the professor happy. Definitely a top five favorite thing.

"But no more Mickey Mousing around with exhibitions. Starting next week, we'll go into serious training for the Anderson."

"Yes, sir."

"We need to work on your confidence in front of people too. The big prize at the Anderson and the quality of the competitors will attract a lot of press and fans. You're going to have to survive it."

Just the idea made him sickish. Snow glanced at the big table laden with every kind of sweet thing, which the students were decimating. "Oh look. All your favorite desserts." He laughed.

Professor Kingsley made a face. Nobody hated candy more— especially marshmallows. He said they were a waste of air.

"Harold." A hand descended on the professor's shoulder.

Snow sucked in a little breath. Coach McMasters. The football coach. *Did he bring Riley?*

Kingsley turned and shook the big man's hand. "Kurt, good to see you. Not exactly your usual hangout."

"Actually, I knew I'd catch you here. I've got a problem you can help me with."

Snow took a step back. "I'll leave you—"

"No, no, this will only take a second. Don't mean to disturb your celebration. It's just that I need a physics coach. Uh, tutor, I guess. One of my boys is struggling in physics. He needs the credit to graduate, so he can't drop it, but if he falls below a C, he's not eligible to play, so he'll have to pull out. I thought you might have someone who could help him."

"I'm sure I can find someone to help. Who's the boy?"

"Riley. Riley Prince."

Snow felt his mouth open and forced it shut.

Professor Kingsley chuckled. "What? Your prince of the gridiron isn't infallible?"

McMasters shrugged. "He's smart enough. The best on the field, as you know. He just doesn't get physics."

The words popped out of Snow's mouth. "He understands chess. Physics shouldn't be hard. He must be approaching it wrong."

The professor cocked his head. "How do you know he understands chess?"

"Oh, uh, I don't, I guess. It's just that he was here, and I thought I saw him anticipating my move."

McMasters frowned. "He was here?"

Kingsley got a funny little smile. "Is that when you almost missed the move?"

"Oh, I—"

"Who almost missed a move? Not my Snowball." An arm slipped around Snow's waist, and he glanced back to see Winston. Snow stepped forward to avoid the embrace, but the professor standing beside him gave him no place to go, and Winston managed to kiss his cheek. "Hi. What did I miss?"

The professor smiled. "Only Snowden wiping out Jacobs in three moves, that's all."

"Well, of course. So how could he have missed a move if he only made three?" Winston laughed.

"Not important. He won handily."

Winston gave Snow a little hug. "So are you ready to go celebrate your victory?"

Snow shook his head. "It was nothing special. I don't need to celebrate."

"That's okay. I don't need a special reason to party." Winston laughed again, and Professor Kingsley nodded approvingly. As the only two out gay men in the physics department, they'd been pushed together, and the professor strongly approved of Snow having "companionship." Probably because he was lonely himself since his wife died. Snow liked Winston okay. Still, his heart yearned elsewhere.

Stupid.

Bitch.

Suddenly the double doors that led from the classroom into the courtyard beyond burst open. Snow looked up. *Who?*

The beauty of the woman who stood in the doorway inspired a few gasps, even from Winston, who didn't like girls. He whispered, "Wow."

Something about her seemed like a reverse image of Snow. Her long hair was as red as his was black, her skin as deep olive as his was pale white. The professor sucked in a noisy breath, and as he exhaled, he whispered, "Anitra." He walked quickly to where the woman stood, his hands extended. "Welcome, my dear."

She flashed white teeth and spoke just loud enough to be heard through the room. "Hello, Harold."

Amazingly, the professor leaned over and kissed her cheek; then he turned toward the people still mingling in the room, most of whom were members of the chess club. "Everyone, I have a wonderful surprise. This is Anitra Popescu. She's just joined the university staff as Assistant Dean of Students, and she's a chess master in her own right, so I've persuaded her to assist me as advisor to the chess club. Since our club is growing and I'll be devoting substantial time to preparing Snowden for the upcoming international tournament, I think you'll all benefit from Anitra's assistance." He grinned. "I'm sure the volume of new members will also increase exponentially."

Anitra smiled, and her dark eyes swept the room, then connected with Snow's just for a moment. A shiver traveled from his tailbone to his head.

As if in slow motion, the professor's fingers intertwined with the woman's. "By the way, I should also announce that Anitra is my fiancée." Kingsley beamed, the room erupted in applause, and for some weird reason, Snow felt sick.

Winston leaned over. "That's great for the professor. He's been so lonely for the last couple years, don't you think? Man, she's quite a catch for an old dude." He laughed.

"Yes, that's great. Just great." The whole room spun.

The professor accepted congratulations all around, but his head rose as he looked toward Snow, while still holding Anitra's hand.

Snow tugged at Winston. "Let's go."

Winston looked confused. "But I think he's coming this way."

"I want to go." He looked up at the football coach, who stared at Anitra's full-bosomed beauty like she'd just descended from *Penthouse* heaven. Snow took a deep breath. "Coach, I'll help you, okay?"

The coach's eyes widened. "But—"

Winston clasped his arm. "Help with what?"

Snow nodded toward McMasters. "I'll do it. I'll contact you. Come on, Win." He started walking, pulling Winston after him, which must have looked funny since Winston stood six five of skinny while Snow barely made five eight.

Winston stutter-stepped to catch up. "What was that all about?"

"Nothing. Just the coach needs someone to explain physics to some of his players."

"I can help with that. How do you have time?"

"It won't take much." He made it out the door of the room and down the hall. *Move fast.*

Winston glanced at him sideways. "If it was anyone else, I'd say you just wanted to stare at some football player ass, but I can hardly get your attention enough to look at mine."

"Don't be silly."

"Why are we moving so fast? Don't you want to go back and meet Professor Kingsley's fiancée?"

Snow shook his head.

"Why?"

"I don't know."

"Did he tell you about her?"

He shook his head again. Why hadn't the professor told him? Why was he just finding out now?

"It sounds like she's going to be a part of your life, so get over it. He's your mentor, and she's going to be his wife."

His wife. "Yes, I'm so happy for him."

CHAPTER 2

WINSTON GRABBED Snow's arm again. "Forget about it. Let's have some fun."

"What fun? Where?" His idea of fun seldom matched Winston's.

"We're going to a party."

Snow pulled back. "I'm not much for parties."

"Oh come on. You've got to loosen up sometime. The Zetas are just the guys to do it."

"Zetas?"

"Yeah. One of the brothers is in my history class. He invited me."

Do not think about who you might see at the Zeta house. "The Zetas don't want me in their house or at their party." He didn't have the heart to say they didn't want Winston either. The Big-Men-On-Campus jock fraternity did not do nerds. Especially not gay nerds.

"Sure they do. Come on."

Hardly any motivation on earth could have gotten him through the doors of that frat house—except one thing. What were the chances of seeing Riley? He swallowed hard. "Okay."

His feet kind of wanted to go faster, until they got within half a block of the Zeta house. There the sight of giant dudes and dudettes in letter sweaters guzzling beer on the front lawn while two of them arm wrestled and the others threw money on the grass stopped him in his tracks. "Win, we can't go in there."

"Sure we can. Come on, I was invited."

"I'll bet the guy who invited you doesn't remember—even if he was serious to begin with."

"We'll blend in."

"You're kidding." But a flash of golden hair from the open front door of the frat house captured his gaze just as Winston pulled his arm, and he wound up being propelled into the mass of humanity on the lawn.

They made it slightly farther than he'd predicted. Most of the Zetas were so drunk they wouldn't have noticed a hippopotamus. Still, two hopeless physics nerds stuck out more than large river horses to guys like the Zetas. It was actually a girl who leaned over the arm of a football player approximately as big as Delaware and slurred, "Who the hell is that?" She pointed directly at Snow.

The guy shook his head like a great, confused lion. "Don' know. Pretty girl. Thought I knew all the cheerleaders?"

"Junior." She slapped his arm, missed, and tried again. "That's no girrr-lll. That's some kind of freaky guy."

"Wha? Wha's he doing here?"

The domino effect began. Junior the giant leaned over to Cyclops number two and asked who they were. Cyclops passed it on until heads started turning, forming a phalanx of frowns. Dark frowns.

Snow pulled hard against Winston, who had stopped to stare in horror at a girl removing her double-D cup bra in order to use it as a slingshot. "We have to get out of here."

"No way, man."

"I'm serious."

A hard hand slammed onto Snow's shoulder. "What the hell are you doing at a Zeta party, fag?"

Snow shook his head. God, he hated talking in front of people. "Mistake. Sorry. Going."

The hand whirled him around until he stood face to chest with a guy he'd seen on the football team catching stuff from Riley. Not so big, but his face radiated one clear message. Hate. "Where the fuck do you get off crashing our party?"

The giant who had mistaken him for a girl cocked his head. "Hey, Rog, don't hurt him. He's prettier than any fuckin' cheerleader I ever saw."

Rog tightened his grip. "All the more reason to rearrange some of those faggy features, don't you think?"

Winston took a step forward. "I was invited. Honest."

The guy didn't even look. He just slammed his hand against Winston's chest and sent him flying backward into a tree.

Snow ripped his shoulder from Rog's grasp and raced to Winston's prostrate body. "Are you okay, Win?"

A hand clamped on his shirt collar and flew him backward into space, legs splayed in the air, arms flailing, headed for God knew where. His heart pounded in his throat as he prepared for pain. Totally out of control. *Try to relax so it doesn't hurt so bad.* Slam! He plowed into something slightly softer than the ground and landed in a pair of strong arms as surely as if they'd been a circus act. "Gotcha." Snow looked up into golden eyes, slightly narrowed, with crinkles at the corners.

"Hey, Prince, what the fuck?" Rog charged toward them.

Riley set Snow on his feet and pushed him behind his big body. He extended a hand toward the fuming Rog. "Enough, man. Do you not know that this guy is the school's giant chess champion, for Christ's sake? You hurt him, and you'll lose your scholarship and be expelled so fast they won't even notify your parents first. Shit, man, he probably makes more money for the school than the football team."

"This fag?" Rog scowled over Riley's shoulder. "Get serious."

Riley crossed his arms and didn't budge.

"Well, hell. Get him away from me." Rog spun and headed for the keg.

Winston had managed to struggle to standing with no help from any Zetas.

Courtney appeared at Riley's side and wrapped an arm around his waist. He pulled her closer and kissed the top of her head.

Some piece of Snow's heart chipped off and lay in the dirt. He stepped around Riley and gave him a glance. "Thanks." Crossing to Winston, he grabbed his arm and power-walked away from the whole Neanderthal bunch. Blood pounded in his ears, and nerves in his brain fried as laughter drifted after them.

Two blocks away, Winston sagged to the grass and dropped his head to his knees. "I'm so sorry I got you into that mess."

Snow frowned. "Just learn that guys like that have zero interest in guys like us except to bloody our noses."

"Thank God that big hunk was more of a gentleman."

"Gentleman? My ass. He was just protecting the eligibility of his damned football team." Snow leaned against a tree. Some bubble in his brain—or maybe his heart—went *poof.*

Winston shook his head against his knees. "I thought he seemed nicer than that."

Snow blinked fast. "Don't kid yourself." Good advice as long as he was paying attention. He blew out a long stream of breath. "I have to tell the coach I'm not going to help with the tutoring."

Win looked up. "Why? I don't think this should be the deciding factor. Hell, it makes no sense for you to take time to be a damned physics tutor, but two hours ago you were all hot to do it. The big hunk saved you. He saved both of us. Maybe if you help the team, they won't be so obnoxious in the future."

"We shouldn't need saving." Snow kicked at the sidewalk with his sneaker.

"True, but facts are facts."

"It was a stupid idea." He crossed his arms.

"Yes. But I get the feeling you're just being pissy, not sensible."

"Then you do it."

"Okay, I will."

"What?"

"I'll do it. Tell the coach I'll help his stupid players."

"You just want an invitation to a Zeta party."

"Yes, and I'm not too proud to admit it."

"But—"

"Snow, do you or do you not want to tutor the football team?"

That was the question of the damned century.

ANITRA PULLED her lips back from Harold's. "Everyone seemed very happy for us."

He smiled and the wrinkles popped out around his eyes. "Of course. They know that somehow I ended up with the fairest one of all."

"Thank you, my dear."

He leaned in for another kiss, but she stepped back against the door to her apartment. "Have you thought any more about the tournament?"

He frowned. "I'm so sorry to disappoint you, but you know that I'm already dedicated to training Snowden for the Anderson tourney. Perhaps we can find you another coach to assist you."

She stuck out her lip. "But you're the best. And the Anderson is the highest profile tournament in the US this year. I have to be there."

"There are a number of other good coaches I can recommend."

"What will people think? I'm your fiancée, and yet you won't coach me. Won't people assume I'm not as good as Reynaldi?"

"They won't assume anything. They know that I've been Snow's coach since he started at NorCal."

She smiled tightly. "But if you coached me instead, they'd assume I'm better. That I have the superior chance of winning."

He sighed. "They would only assume that I'm a turncoat coach who isn't dedicated to his students."

"But—"

He held up a hand. God, she hated that gesture. Who did he think he was? "Anitra, you know I think you're an exceptional player. I've never suggested that you're better than Snowden. Few people are. If you continue to apply yourself, you may be his equal someday."

Her nails dug into her palms. "But how can I get better if you won't help me?"

"I will help you exhaustively, my dear, but after the tournament." He smiled benignly. "I'm sure Snowden himself will be more than happy to assist you in your training, once he's won the tournament and has more time available. After all, didn't you say his presence at the University—" He smiled. "—along with my own, was the main reason you applied for the position? Just be patient. You'll achieve everything you desire."

What the hell did he know about what she desired? She ran her hands across the lapels of his suit jacket. "It's hard to control my dreams, Harold, when you're right here and I know you can propel me forward so easily."

He kissed her forehead. "It's my goal to make you supremely happy. We'll achieve all your dreams—together."

She shivered. "I'd best go in. I'm still not used to your California drops in temperature."

He pulled her a little closer. "I'm happy to take on the task of keeping you warm."

She shook her head and pushed away. "It's such a bother having these religious scruples about sex before marriage, I know. But you wouldn't want me if I wasn't true to myself."

"That's so, but we are engaged."

She smiled. "All the more reason to get us to the altar quickly."

"Once the tournament is over, the wedding will be my top priority."

She controlled her frown. "I hate playing second fiddle, you know that."

"You're never second fiddle, my dear. But I must be true to my commitments—or you wouldn't love me."

She forced out the word. "Yes."

"See you tomorrow."

"I look forward to it."

He stood watchfully while she unlocked the door, then waved, stepped off the porch, and glanced at her once as he walked to his car. Probably headed back to work out a strategy for Reynaldi. *Dammit. Dammit. Dammit.*

She stepped inside and slammed the door.

"Uh-uh-uh, temper, temper." Hunter leaned forward in the chair where he sat reading the newspaper in front of the fireplace.

"Were you spying on me?"

"Of course not. What do I care what you do with the chess loser?"

"Nothing, I suppose." She crossed into the living room of the townhouse and collapsed on the sofa. "Dear God, this is so damned tedious. And so frustrating."

He leaned his big body forward. "Nothing ventured, nothing gained."

"Spare me the dime-store slogans."

"Then focus on what you've got to win."

"Yes. There is that. Once I've won the tournament, I'll have a perfect platform from which to garner sponsorships and commercials. Perhaps films from there. It's all within grasp. They've hardly ever had a female chess champion, and never a beautiful one. I'll be a sensation." She gazed into the fire, but all she saw was the future.

"You'll surprise a lot of people because, right now, not many predictions think anyone can beat the kid."

She raised an eyebrow. "Oh? What have you read?"

He handed her a copy of the *Daily Mirror*. The paper gave far more space to chess, both in the print and online versions, than most publications, since the NorCal Chess Club was so famous. The story, headlined "Reynaldi Virtually Unbeatable," went on to blah-blah about how experts agreed that, even at this late date, no real competitor had emerged for Reynaldi. The Russian was the only possible contender, according to this reporter. "Bullshit."

Hunter smiled. "They say he's number one. The best of the best."

"Won't it be fun changing their stupid, narrow minds?"

"You go, girl." He laughed.

"And, of course, I don't intend to play him."

A quick frown flashed across his handsome face. Anitra narrowed her eyes. "I don't think you take our enterprise seriously enough. After all, if I profit, you might also."

"I take you very seriously, baby." He stretched and grinned.

She raised a brow. "On the other hand, you can be replaced."

"By Dr. Chess Face? Right. Not bloody likely. Besides, where else are you going to find a guy with a ten-inch cock?"

She glared at him, then burst out laughing. "Well, there is that."

THE FOOTBALL flew in a high, arcing parabola and landed perfectly in the hands of Rog, just as if Riley had thrown it from a few feet away rather than half a field. All around Snow and Winston, the fans went crazy, yelling and stamping their feet. A few days ago, Snow would have been happily cheering too. Now all he saw was the anger and revulsion on the football player's face. As the other fans began to file out, Snow grabbed Winston's arm and moved toward the steps from the bleachers. Had to get to the coach's office.

As they walked across the tarmac, the knots in his stomach felt like they could easily rise and choke him.

Winston stretched his long legs to keep up. "What's your hurry? We'll only end up waiting until the coach gets there."

"Just want to get this over with."

"What are you going to tell the coach?"

"The truth. I don't have time. You do."

"Are you feeling okay?" He stared down at Snow.

"Of course."

"You're acting kind of weird."

"I just don't like getting beaten up by subhumans. I guess I didn't think they could be that mean."

"You warned me."

"I know, but I didn't quite understand."

You're an idiot.

That I do know.

Seeing Riley in his natural habitat felt like a strange kind of death. Death by unrequited desire. Snow swallowed. Maybe that was overstating the case. Not like he'd ever really had a boyfriend. Winston didn't count. Win had an unrequited desire for Snow. Of course, he had an unrequited desire for a lot of guys. Karma, right? Snow paid the price of leaving Winston unfulfilled by yearning for a prince who didn't know he existed, wasn't even gay, and now proved he was just like all the others. *So much for your damned fairy tales.*

The coach had said to come right after the game. They walked slowly to give him time to get there from the locker rooms. Snow pushed through the double doors of the huge athletic building that housed the gym, locker rooms, training facilities, classrooms, and offices. He knew because he'd looked it up. A few steps in, a man the size of a tree trunk moved in front of him. "Sorry, no visitors until two hours after the game."

"Uh, Coach McMasters is expecting me, uh, us."

The big man looked at a clipboard. "What's your name?"

"Snowden Reynaldi."

The guy glanced at Snow like he must have made a mistake about his identity. He nodded at Winston. "Who's this?"

It wasn't as if they were planning an assassination. "Another physics tutor. That's why the coach asked us here."

The guy frowned in suspicion but finally nodded. "Okay. Down the hall, second door on the right."

"Thank you." They skirted around Tree Trunk Man and followed the hall. Even this far from the locker rooms, the air had a tinge of sweat. At the door, Snow took a breath. *Here you go.* He plunged inside.

A handsome young guy wearing sweats lounged on the edge of a reception desk in the outer office, flipping through what looked like a sports magazine. He glanced up, and his eyes widened slightly. "You the physics guy?"

"Yes, I suppose I am."

He nodded at Winston. "Who's this?"

"Another physics guy."

He cocked a half grin at Snow. "Jesus, man, they should put you on the cheerleading squad. You're prettier than most of the girls." He held up a hand. "Sorry. No offense. Coach says I got no filters. Name's Danny."

"Hello."

"Hope I didn't embarrass you. Sorry."

"No. Others have said the same." Snow forced his eyes from his shoes.

Danny pointed toward a door in the back wall. "Coach is waiting for you inside."

"Thank you."

Snow managed to cross the few steps to the door without passing out. Just what he'd needed. Someone to remind him what a freak he was. He glanced back at Winston at his heels, pushed down the door handle, and walked into the inner sanctum.

CHAPTER 3

SOMEWHERE IN the background, he heard Coach McMasters say, "Hey, Reynaldi, thanks for being on time." But he didn't see him. All he saw was the blazing glow of golden light that was Riley Prince.

Riley sat on a chair in front of the coach's desk, still wearing his uniform pants but no top, with only a towel around his neck, his golden hair plastered to his forehead with sweat, his cheeks pink as roses, and two strips of black on his cheekbones emphasizing the blush. His chest. Dear God, did humans really look like that? Carved as if from alabaster. Riley leaned forward, but still no fat bunched at his waist. Snow had heard of six-packs, but this was some amazing expansion of that idea. Twelve. Maybe sixteen-pack.

"Uh, Snowden."

"Snow."

Snow looked up at the coach, then at Winston, and blinked. "Yes?"

The coach nodded. "I was saying, this is Riley Prince. You volunteered to tutor him in physics, right?"

"Oh. Yes. Yes, I did." He tried to swallow the mouth full of cotton. "I mean, actually, no. I mean—"

Winston kind of snorted and stepped forward. "I'm Winston Erhlinger. Snow doesn't have time to do the tutoring, so he asked me. I'm an honors student in physics."

Coach McMasters half stood and shook Winston's hand. "I see. Yes, I guess that makes more sense. I was wondering how Reynaldi could manage it with his practice schedule and all. I appreciate you doing this, Erhlinger."

Riley stared at his hands, and for just a second it looked like he frowned. Then he stood up. Funny to say stood up, since there was no other direction to stand, but in Riley's case he stood up and up and up. Snow's eyes followed the motion until they landed on the guy's face. He was smiling. Not some phony, polite, arrogant, football-star smile, but a real one, with dimples and everything. He extended a large, long-fingered hand to Winston. "I sure appreciate you doing this for me, man." Sweet Jesus, Snow actually felt jealous of Winston getting that smile instead of him.

Winston about cracked his face with his grin. "Hey, my pleasure. I didn't realize it was a one-on-one. Thought it was more of a class."

The coach said, "Is that a problem?"

"No. Not at all. I'm a big fan."

Snow's knees gave way, and he sank into the other guest chair in front of the desk. Fan. Winston didn't know a football from a watermelon, but he sure liked handsome hunks.

It felt like heat touched his face, and he glanced up to find Riley's golden eyes staring at him. Riley stretched out a hand. "Good to see you again."

Sweet Jesus. Snow stared at that big paw, then extended his own and watched it get swallowed. Heat traveled up his arm to his chest and then his brain. Like looking into the sun. He shook slowly, one, two, three times. The shake ended, but Riley kept holding; then he kind of shook his head and dropped Snow's hand like it was hot. A little extra pink seemed to attack Riley's cheekbones. "Sorry I won't get to work with you. I'm a fan."

Snow caught his breath. "You, uh, you like chess?"

The coach leaned forward. "Yeah, I didn't know you were a chess player."

Riley shrugged. "I looked it up to help me with strategy on the field. I don't understand it very well, but I sure like watching you play the game."

The coach looked confused. "Is there much to see?"

Riley's cheeks got brighter. "Hard to explain."

The words fell out of Snow's mouth. "Because you know what I'm going to do next, don't you?"

"Yeah."

McMasters looked back and forth between them. "What the hell are you talking about?"

"Riley has an innate grasp of quantum reality."

"I do?" Riley's eyes widened.

"He does?" The coach looked just as shocked.

"Yes, that's why he's so good on the field. It's why I know he can learn physics." He had to get out of here. Snow stood. "So, you're in good hands with Winston. Good luck passing your exams." He practically ran to the door and heard the coach say, "Thanks again, Reynaldi." He escaped into the outer office, waved at Danny, who managed to look like he was lying down in his chair, and gasped for breath as he made it into the hall. Riley Prince might be the most beautiful human ever generated, but he hadn't said a word about Rog's attack on Snow and Winston the night before. Clearly, the man had his priorities, and the top of his priority list was football.

SNOW CURLED on his rug and stared at the ceiling instead of his chessboard. Focus! He sighed. No use. His brain conjured images of Riley Prince wrapped in erotic embraces with Winston. *Stupid. Totally.* Riley was far more likely to be having sex with Courtney at this moment than Snow's tall, skinny friend, but Snow's brain refused to create that picture. *Jealous. Simple truth.* No matter how much he told himself that Riley qualified as a small-brained homophobe, he still wanted to be the one teaching him, the one Riley smiled for, and the one he felt grateful to.

Snow flipped on his stomach and rested his cheek on his hand. His cell chimed in his pocket, and he practically knocked himself out, he rolled back over so fast. He pulled the phone to his ear before he hit the green button and had to try again. "Hello. Uh, hello."

"Hey." Winston sounded weird.

"What's wrong?" Maybe they did have sex and Win felt embarrassed. *Good grief, you're nuts.*

Winston sighed. "Crashed. Burned."

"What are you talking about?"

"He can't learn physics."

"That can't be right."

"Never spent a more frustrating three hours in my life." Winston grunted. "Or with better scenery. Man, that guy is hunky." He sighed. "But he gives new meaning to the term dumb blond."

"No. Riley Prince isn't dumb."

"You weren't trying to shovel shit into his brain all afternoon."

"You just couldn't teach him."

"Hey, thanks a lot."

Winston didn't deserve his disdain. "Sorry. I just mean that he can't learn physics from the standard curriculum. His professor's probably tried that all year. He needs a different approach."

"Hell, I tried everything."

Snow sat up. "I know. Thanks for taking it off my hands."

"By the way, he apologized for what happened at the Zeta house. Said something about that Rog dude having a lot of emotional issues because of family stuff, and Riley's trying to get him some help."

"That's something, I guess. Still, seems like he cared more about the football team than our lives."

"Yeah, well, I'm sorry I didn't save the football team. I sure would have loved all that free beer." He laughed.

"I'll buy you your own kegger."

Win laughed again, then paused. "Seriously?"

Snow smiled. "Sure. If that's what you want."

"Nah. So, want me to come over and tuck you in?"

"I'll be up plotting chess moves all night."

Win chuckled. "I'd like to mate your king."

Snow sighed real softly. "Sleep well."

"Okay, okay. You know how to hurt a guy. See you tomorrow."

Snow clicked off the phone and stared at it. Was he giving Winston false hope?

I never told him I wanted to be his boyfriend.

You never said you didn't either.

He slipped the phone into his pocket again. *Maybe I just want someone to care about me.*

You're a desperate mess.

So true.

What was he going to do about Riley Prince and physics?

Nothing. It's not your problem.

Feels like my problem.

Add it to the list.

He sighed, faced his chessboard, and tried to concentrate more on the Ruy Lopez opening than on how to get a prince into his castle.

OH NO. How can it be morning?

Stare at a chessboard for enough hours and the sun comes up.

Snow dragged his body out the door of his condo and hurried to Campus Coffee. Millie waved as he walked in. "Hey, sunshine. I've got it all made."

He smiled and grabbed his tea latte from the counter. "Bless you."

She laughed. "That bad, huh? Did NorCal's chess master have a bad knight? Get it? Knight?"

He glanced around and felt heat climb his neck. "Didn't sleep well."

"Hey, I'm just kidding. Enjoy your tea." She cocked her fuzzy-haired head at the pastry sitting on a napkin beside where his large tea had stood. "Hang on." She picked it up and inspected it carefully, then tossed it in the trash. "Sorry, sweetie. I told Carol to give you a croissant, but I forgot to say no nuts. That one has almonds. Let me get you a plain."

He held up a hand. "I'm not actually very hungry, so I'll just go with the tea. But I really appreciate you looking out for me."

"Can't have my favorite chess master dying on the floor of Campus Coffee."

He grinned. "There are worse places."

"Would you actually die if you ate the nuts?"

"I've got one of those pens for extreme allergic reactions, but if I forgot it or collapsed too fast, I imagine I could die." He patted his pocket where he always kept his epinephrine pen.

"Glad we didn't test the theory."

"Me too. Thanks again for the tea. Just how I like it."

"Kiss kiss, luv." She swept back to serve the line of caffeine-deprived college students. Snow slid ten dollars into the tip jar—they billed him for all his purchases—and slipped out the door, dragging on his tea. Life was short and he was busy. Why couldn't he let go of his sense he had to teach Riley Prince? Like he'd be responsible if the guy failed? *Sick.*

Even though his class on particle physics was a favorite, he barely heard the lecture. When the professor gave them an assignment, Snow wrote it down, but the teacher stopped him on the way out. "You okay, Reynaldi?"

"Yes, sorry, sir. Had a bad night." He shuddered at Millie's awful joke.

The professor gave him a friendly pat on the shoulder. "I know the responsibility of chess has to be crushing, but you're going to be a great physicist. Don't lose sight of your priorities."

"Thank you, sir. I won't."

But what were his priorities? He wandered out of the physics building into the bright fall day. He loved chess and he loved physics, but the old adage about those kind of things not keeping you warm at night felt deeply and sadly true. It had been a long time since anyone had held him or warmed him. Since his grandmother died.

Whose fault is that?

Mine.

Winston would be happy to hold you.

Don't want Winston.

Dreamer.

Bitch.

"Reynaldi?"

Snow looked up. Coach McMasters sat on the bench outside the building. "Hello, sir."

The coach stood. "I'm sorry to lie in wait for you, but I can't let this go without trying. You know your friend failed with Riley. He didn't feel like he got much out of the tutoring."

Snow stared at his feet. "They didn't give it much of a chance."

"I know, but Riley was really discouraged. He said he got the same thing from Erhlinger that he gets from his professor."

"Maybe that's because it's physics."

"But you said you knew he could learn. You said that."

Snow glanced up. The big, strong coach looked like someone had drowned his puppy. *Damn.* "Yes, I said that."

"Why did you think it? How could you have been so wrong?"

You can say Riley's dumber than you thought and call a halt to this whole mess.

No, I can't.

Because you're a mess.

True.

He sighed long and loud. "Many people teach physics as if it were a game of logic. Nothing could be further from the truth. Riley understands that innately. He just has to be taught from a field he understands."

"Can you do it?" The coach sounded so hopeful.

"Maybe. Probably."

"Oh man, if you can do that, I'll send the whole cheerleading squad to root you on at your big game."

Snow stared at the floor. "That won't be necessary."

"I guess I didn't ask the right question. Will you do it?"

Slowly, Snow nodded. "When would you like to begin?"

"Riley's professor has given him two weeks to get his scores up or he'll declare him ineligible. That would throw him out of the final regular-season game that decides the standings in the championships. Without Riley, we're toast. Start this minute, as far as I'm concerned."

Snow looked around as if Riley might appear out of a bush. "Where is he?"

"He's in class, and then he has practice. Any chance you could meet him at his apartment after that?"

Snow swallowed. "Okay."

"Oh man, I don't know how to thank you. Here." He handed Snow a sheet of lined paper with an address on it. "This is where the kid lives. Six p.m., okay?"

"He doesn't live at the fraternity house?" That was a blessing, anyway.

"No. He likes it off campus. I'm really relieved. If anybody can bail him out of this mess, it's gotta be you."

"No guarantees. You understand that? And I don't have much time, so if my theory doesn't prove true, I can't keep going. Professor Kingsley's going to be upset as it is."

"I'll talk to him."

"Riley just may not have a brain for physics."

"I can't believe that. He's smart. Honest."

Snow nodded and looked at the address. Riley might be smart, but Snow was dumb as dog shit.

CHAPTER 4

"SNOWDEN, WHY are you doing this? We need to practice. Study. When I told Coach McMasters I could help him, I certainly never meant for you to volunteer."

Snow packed another notebook into his backpack. "I think I can help him. Maybe no one else can. Winston already tried."

"Please. Physics is physics."

Snow shrugged and kept packing.

"Maybe you have a crush on this big jock?"

Snow snapped his head up to find the professor smiling fondly at him. Snow shook his head. "It's for the good of the school."

"Of course—"

"Who has a crush on whom?" The silky, husky voice wormed its way up Snow's spine. He tensed all over.

The professor laughed, but at least he said, "Nothing. Just teasing Snow. How are you, my dear?"

Snow kept staring at his backpack.

"Lovely, darling. But I'm so happy to have arrived in time to meet Snowden."

The professor tapped Snow's shoulder. "I forget you haven't met Snow yet. Snow, come, meet Anitra."

Snow looked up slowly, then looked back down.

Are you afraid she'll turn you to stone?

Maybe.

He stood in front of her but couldn't quite meet her eyes.

She reached out a slender hand with pale pink nails and grasped his chin. "Aren't you adorably shy?" She tipped his face up until his eyes were on a level with hers, but still he looked down. "Whoever heard of a shy chess master? But there's no need to be so with me, is there?" She squeezed slightly until his eyes flipped up, met hers, and held. A tremor started at his tailbone and wriggled its way up until he had to control the shiver. She smiled, showing perfect white teeth that gleamed against her smooth skin. "After all, I'm on your side."

He wanted to rip his chin away. He wanted to run. Everything inside him turned to cosmic mush, and he did neither of those things.

"My God, Harold, you never told me your protégé was so pretty."

The professor smiled. "Surely you've seen pictures of Snow."

"They barely do him justice. That skin. Those lashes. Women would kill for them."

She still held his chin like she was examining a cow. He didn't want to be rude, but damn. "Excuse me." He moved his chin to the side and out of her grasp.

She raised a brow. "Oh, I'm sorry. I was carried away by your charms."

Not likely.

"I hope you'll allow me to participate in your coaching a little. Sometimes an outsider's view can make all the difference. I'm not blinded by my own strategy."

Snow felt his eyes widen.

The professor touched his arm. "Thank you so much, my dear, but Snow has a very particular approach to chess that doesn't lend itself to traditional coaching methods."

An instant flash of annoyance crossed her beautiful face before she smiled sweetly. "Why would I ever be traditional about anything?"

"I'm familiar with both your styles, and one is not better than the other. They're simply different."

"That difference might give me the superior perspective."

The professor looked at Snow.

Don't do it. Don't do it.

"No, I think I'll go with the 'if it ain't broke' approach and use our usual methods. But thank you so much for the offer."

Relief made his head feel cottony. "Yes, thank you."

Her bright smile came nowhere near her eyes. "Oh my, you even sound like a girl."

A small crease appeared between the professor's eyebrows. "No, he doesn't, Anitra. Snow has a musical but perfectly masculine voice."

She hooked a hand over his shoulder. "Of course, that's what I meant. The music."

Must get out of here. Snow grabbed his backpack. "I'd best be going. Good to meet you." He headed for the door.

"Don't commit too much time to this enterprise, Snow. We have work to do, remember?"

"I won't."

Her voice stopped Snow. "Oh, what's he doing?"

Don't tell her. Don't tell her.

"A bit of tutoring to help a fellow student."

"How compassionate. To jeopardize his championship for another."

Jeopardize? He glanced back to see the woman hanging off the professor like an ornament. Did she really care about him? But what could she gain from pretending? She must love him. "I won't spend too much time. We can work later."

"Good. See you tonight, then." The professor gave him a wave.

Snow scurried out the door like dogs were chasing him. On the other side, he stopped and leaned back against the painted wood. Why was he reacting this way? Her wanting to coach him should flatter him, not scare him to death. Okay, so she was angry, but more at the professor than at him. Why did he feel like he could throw up?

He pulled his phone from his pocket and glanced at the time. *Get moving. Riley expects you.* God, that made him want to throw up too, but in a different way.

He started jogging across the campus. He hadn't told Coach McMasters that he couldn't drive, so he had to get to Riley's apartment some other way. By cab, if he could find one. Not many cabs roamed the streets in a college town. Still, the address was close to campus. He could walk. Well, run, actually.

A half hour later, he hadn't spotted anything yellow except an old cat, and he rounded the corner of the street Riley lived on. He slowed to a walk and took a few deep breaths. Hopefully he wasn't sweaty. Not that he ought to care. Of course, what he ought to do didn't seem to count for much.

He looked for the numbers on the row of older, two-story homes that lined the street. Most looked a little run-down. One stood out for the riot of flowers in the beds and bright white paint on all the trim. Sure enough. Number 557. But an old lady sat on the porch in a swing, rocking back and forth. Snow double-checked the number. It was definitely the one the coach had given him. He stood outside the white picket gate. Should he bother her?

"Don't just stand there, cutie. Come on in."

Was she talking to him? He took a quick glance over his shoulder.

"Yes, you, young man. You must be here to see Riley."

Funny how he almost always knew if he liked a person immediately. Her he liked. "Yes, ma'am." He pushed open the gate and walked up the flower-lined path to the porch.

She cocked her head at him as he stood at the edge of the top step. "Well, good. He needs more nice friends. I'll bet you're a smart friend too."

What did he say to that?

"I'm Eudora Wishus." She stuck out her hand, and he took it gladly. Her skin felt as thin as tissue, but warm, and her grip let him know she was no frail flower. "Riley lives upstairs. Just go through the front door and straight up the stairs. My apartment is on the left as you go in. Drop by anytime."

He had to smile. "Thank you, ma'am."

"Just call me Eudora."

"I'm Snow. Snowden Reynaldi."

"Of course you are."

He didn't know what to say to that either, so he smiled and walked into the house. As promised, there was a door on his left. Brilliant blue, it featured a picture of a cat with its leg extended saying "Talk to the paw," and a brass knocker shaped like a bird. The stairs stretched ahead of him, and he climbed briskly. Somehow Mrs. Wishus had sucked some of the fear out of him. If Riley lived in a house with such a charming character, he couldn't be that scary. Maybe Snow should sit down and ask her why he felt this stupid responsibility for a guy who only cared about stupid football. Oh well. He trudged up the stairs. Still, when he got to the door at the top, his hand paused in midair while he sucked in some oxygen.

The door flew open, and Snow staggered backward toward the staircase. He took a step, and it landed on air. *Oh no.* His arms flailed. A big hand grabbed his arm and pulled him forward, which succeeded in lifting him off his feet. He flew, slammed into Riley's body, and got wrapped in his arms—which mostly made him think about being hurled through the air by Rog at the frat party. That just made him mad again.

Gasping for breath because he'd hit Riley's chest with full force, he gazed up into golden eyes that crinkled at the corners as Riley smiled. "Hi. Glad you found me." Then he laughed, which vibrated Snow in places that really needed the attention but could be very embarrassing if they decided to respond at this moment. He wriggled a little to get his groin out of contact with Riley's thighs. "Put me down, please."

Riley's eyebrows rose. "Oh, sorry." Slowly, he put Snow down.

Did he notice anything? Damn. Snow hung the backpack in front of his crotch. "Hello." *Best defense is a good offense.* "We'd best get started." He walked briskly into the big, bright room full of comfy-looking, if a little worn, furniture.

"Oh, sure. Sure."

Snow stopped. The room was even kind of neat. "What a nice place."

"Thank you."

"Why don't you live in your fraternity house? Aren't you the king of the Zetas?" Snow frowned when he said it.

A little cloud floated over Riley's face. "No. I like having my own place."

"Oh. Can I ask why?"

"I don't really feel at home at the frat house."

Words spilled out before he could grab them. "Seemed to me you fit right in." Snow sucked in his breath. "I'm sorry. I didn't intend to be as mean as your fraternity brothers."

"I deserve it. I should have told them they were wrong. Sometimes peer pressure sucks."

"At least you kept them from killing us. That's something, I guess."

"Honestly, a lot of them are good guys. Roget has issues. He's kind of pretty, you know? And he got taken for gay a lot when he was a kid. In his neighborhood, it's more than hard to be gay. So he takes it out on the world. I really am sorry. I'll report him to the administration if you want me to."

Snow felt his lips tighten. "It's hard to be gay in any neighborhood."

"I can imagine."

"No, you can't."

"But you told the coach you'd tutor me anyway, and I'm so grateful." He cracked a half smile. "I really am sorry. For their behavior and my own."

Snow crossed his arms and hugged himself. He needed it. "Yes, well, for some reason I feel like I'd be letting down the school if I don't try to help."

"I'll take whatever reason you've got."

Snow stared up at the handsome face. Was there any way to say no to Riley Prince? "Okay, let's get started." He'd been pretty mean when Riley really had saved them. "This honestly is a nice place."

Riley's dimples flashed. "My landlady lives downstairs. She furnished it and everything."

"Mrs. Wishus."

"Oh, you met her. Wild, isn't she?"

"Yes, amazing. You're lucky. My apartment's owned by a foundation. Not much personality."

Riley gave Snow kind of a long look. "You see that, do you?"

"See what?"

"How special she is."

"I'm sure anyone would."

"Not really."

"She invited me to drop by anytime."

His eyebrows shot up. "No kidding? Man, she doesn't warm up to everyone. She really doesn't suffer fools gladly, as the saying goes. She must get how special you are too."

Heart. Stop. For a second, he didn't breathe at all. Sucked into a vortex of Riley Prince's dimples.

Riley clapped his hands, and it effectively woke Snow up. "I'm so excited about this. Never thought I'd look forward to physics. We can work at the table by the window. I love the light there."

The guy never seemed to say anything that sounded like a football player or a frat boy. Well, not since the night of the party. "Okay." Snow hauled the backpack to the table and pulled out a notebook. Riley sat opposite him with the aforementioned light shining off his perfect cheekbones. *Sigh. Try to work in this state.* Snow took a breath. "Let's get oriented. What do you know versus what you need to know?"

Riley sighed. "I know all the proofs and stuff. I've memorized laws and theorems until I'm blue. But then I stare those formulas in the face, and they make no sense. It's like gibberish floating in a sea of confusion."

"You're just not looking at it in the right light."

"Clearly, but truth is, I'm not really the brightest bulb in the chandelier."

"Who the hell told you that?" Snow's frown actually hurt, it was so deep.

Riley shrugged. "Nobody. Everybody." His breath hissed out in a long arc. "My physics professor. Hell, I think Winston wanted to say it too."

"Nonsense. Who's your professor?"

"Jenkins."

"Why didn't you ask for Kingsley?"

"Stupidity. I thought he'd be harder, so I changed my schedule to take Jenkins."

Snow crossed his arms. "Jenkins is a pretentious snob who doesn't know anything about physics you can't memorize from a book." He caught his breath. "Sorry. I didn't mean to be so critical."

"Where were you when I was wrecking my own life by taking Jenkins?" Riley laughed.

"The truth is, Professor Jenkins doesn't like jocks and doesn't like anyone who's better looking than he is. That means he's likely to count you out before you even start. I'll bet you're not doing any worse than other people he's passing, but he's patting himself on the back for making a football star ineligible."

Riley shook his hanging head. "But what can I do about it now? It's too late in the semester to drop the class. I need it to graduate."

Snow patted the notebook in front of him. "Exactly what we planned. You study like crazy, and we'll blow him away so he has to pass you. I just want you to know that his opinion of your intellect is skewed. You're very smart."

Riley pursed his mouth in a half grin. "How would you know that?"

"Because anyone who can anticipate my moves in chess has to be brilliant." Snow flashed his teeth.

"I don't know how I do that."

"How do you know where to throw the ball so that one of your fast runners can catch it?"

"We have plays. We practice them."

"Do you ever vary from the play?"

"All the time."

"Why?"

"I see what's happening on the field, sense what will probably happen next, and do what feels right."

"And that, my friend, is physics."

"What?"

"Physics simply explains the natural world. Well, 'explains' is probably the wrong word. It embraces the realities of the natural world. Particles and waves, the absolute of probability, the delineation of measurement."

"I don't know what you mean."

"When you throw the ball, do you try for a spiral or end over end?"

"Spiral."

"Why?"

"It goes farther."

"Why?"

Riley shrugged.

"You know the answer."

"Air drag?"

"Yes, good. What determines the speed of a punt?"

"How hard he kicks it."

"What principle is that?"

"Force."

"Which determines…?"

"Uh, acceleration."

"Yes, good. Let's plot horizontal and vertical velocity of the football." Snow began to write in the notebook, and Riley stared with wide eyes. "The parabolic path of a football can be described by these two equations." Snow wrote:

$$y = V_y t - 0.5gt^2$$
$$y = V_y t - 0.5gt^2$$
$$x = V_x$$
$$x = V_x t$$

"y is the height at any time. V_y is the vertical component of the football's initial velocity. g is acceleration due to Earth's gravity, 9.8 m/s^2. x is the horizontal distance of the ball at any time. V_x is the horizontal component of the football's initial velocity. Does that make sense?"

Riley nodded and never took his eyes away from the page.

"To calculate the hang time, peak height, and maximum range of a punt, you must know the initial velocity of the ball off the kicker's foot and the angle of the kick. The velocity must be broken into horizontal and vertical components." Snow wrote them out.

Riley opened his mouth, closed it, and tried again. "Holy shit, I could use this to find out a lot of important stuff."

"Yes, like how far a pass will go given a certain amount of force. You know that instinctively, but this could prove it." Snow smiled. "And proving it could help you pass your course."

Riley scooted even closer to Snow's chair, which made goose bumps travel up his arm. "Show me some more."

Snow smiled. *Got him.* "Okay, so let's calculate maximum range. I'll bet that would be good to know."

"Man, it sure would." Riley picked up a pencil and started doodling numbers beside the formulas Snow notated. A half hour later, he was solving the problems himself, his broad forehead lined with concentration. "If we change the angle of the kick to 60 degrees, we get a hang time of 4.84 seconds, a maximum range of 72 yards, and a peak height of 179 feet." He looked up. "Is that right?"

Snow nodded. "Now, this is pretty basic, but we can get a lot more sophisticated." He scratched out a slightly more complex set of calculations, and Riley seemed absorbed.

"Man, this is so dope."

"Glad you like it."

"Wish Jenkins could make physics so interesting."

"You have to create the excitement for yourself. See the potential."

Riley looked up. "You make it exciting." He smiled slowly. "You make everything exciting."

"M-me?" Snow's brain froze.

"Yeah. Why do you think I come see you play all the time? It's like plugging into the solar system and catching the stars in my hand."

"S-stars are gas."

"The planets, then. I've wanted to tell you this for a while. I think you're—"

The sound of a key in the lock brought both their heads up.

Nooooooo.

Like some cosmic joke, the apartment door opened and beautiful, perky, perfect Courtney Taylor walked in. "Oh, hi. Are you two still studying? Oh my gosh, Snow, you must be magic or something. No one could ever get him to study physics before. I told him, 'You have to do it, baby. The team can't do without you. Find a way to learn this shit.' And what do you know? He found you. Amazing." She walked over, pushed

Riley's head back, kissed him on the lips, and plopped down in his lap. "Did you learn a lot, baby?"

Her knee bumped Snow's thigh, and he leaped up like he'd been shot. "Oh gosh, look at the time. Better get back to work myself. Have to study for the tournament and all." Sweet God, he had to get out of there.

Riley stood Courtney on her feet and stepped over beside Snow. "When can you help me again? I've only got two weeks. I made so much progress today. I know you're busy, and I hate to ask, but could you please—"

"Yes, of course. Just text me, okay?" He ripped out the pages they'd been working on, shoved the notebooks into his backpack, and headed for the door. He seemed to be running from everyone these days. "Bye. Bye, uh, Courtney."

Outside the door, he clambered down the steep staircase and stopped at the bottom just to breathe.

What were you thinking, you idiot? That somehow his girlfriend had magically transformed into a teapot?

He started to tell me something. He said he's wanted to tell me for a long time.

What are you dreaming? That he suddenly quit being straight and is attracted to a wimpy little queen like you? Spare me.

Okay. Okay.

The door to Eudora's apartment flew open, and a hand emerged, holding a glass. "Hey, cutie. Have some water."

Like it was perfectly normal to accept water while standing in hallways, he grasped the glass and drank the liquid down. Amazing how much better he felt.

She took the empty glass. "Lessons for the day. Don't sell yourself short. And don't believe everything you see. Got it?"

"I… I guess so."

"Good." She patted his cheek, and then the door closed behind her. If a caterpillar suddenly appeared saying "Who are you?", he wouldn't be even slightly surprised.

CHAPTER 5

SNOW STARED at the board with a frown.

The professor walked back from the cabinet where he kept the chess supplies. "Let's not use the Kasparov/Topolov Netherlands game. You know that one by heart. I'm going to set up another one of their games, and you see if you can intuit Kasparov's moves, knowing what you do about his play."

"You want me to play like Kasparov?"

"Yes. It will increase your ability to anticipate an opponent's moves."

"All right."

The professor arranged the pieces. "I'll make your first move for you to launch the game, and you can proceed from there." He moved Snow's pawn to d4.

Snow grinned. "Since that's Kasparov's favorite opening, it doesn't tell me much."

"Ah, true." The professor moved his black knight to f6.

Snow breathed out. *I'm Kasparov.* He slid his pawn to c4, Kasparov's most likely follow-on. "Let's see what game you're playing."

E6. The professor moved the black pawn beside the knight.

Knight to f3. *There. That white knight looks harmless enough.*

The professor nodded. "Good. So how did your tutoring session go?" He moved to b6.

Snow caught his breath. *Hope he didn't hear that.* "It went well. I used some formulas he'd relate to. By the end of the time, he was doing the work on his own." Snow responded with a3. Petrosian Variation.

"Excellent. I'm sure the coach will be eternally grateful." Bishop to b7.

The giant elephant in the room sat on his lap. Was he going to ask? "Uh, Professor?" He tapped the knight to c3.

"Well done. Yes?" The professor stared at the board.

"Why didn't you tell me about your engagement?"

A slight pause in his hand was all that showed Kingsley's reaction. Knight to e4. "I must confess, it all happened so fast."

"How *did* it happen?" *Try not to frown.* Knight takes e4.

He cleared his throat. "I went to that conference of educators, remember? Anitra was there as well and introduced herself. She told me she'd applied for the assistant dean's position largely because she wanted to be on the same campus as me. Call me an old fool, but I was flattered." His bishop snatched up the knight at e4.

"I imagine."

The professor kind of giggled. "One thing led to another, and we found ourselves with much in common. I hadn't felt that way in—well, a long time. By the end of the week, we were both smitten."

Smitten. Interesting choice of words. "Fast work." Knight to d2.

The professor gave him a startled glance. "Uh, yes. I'm sure it seems that way. But when it's right, it's right." Bishop to g6.

Snow swallowed. Obviously the professor saw nothing strange about the woman. Snow pushed back from the table. "I know this game."

"Yes, Kasparov's Grandmaster game. I thought I might be able to fool you. But you're way ahead, as always."

Maybe his feelings were just jealousy? "Are you going to coach Ms. Popescu?"

"Yes, after the tournament. I thought you might like to help. She could benefit from your intuition. She's such a logical player."

"So she's not entering the Anderson Tournament?"

The professor shook his head. "She has the rating, but I've told her she's not ready."

"How can she be rated and yet we've never played?"

"I will confess, she's played in many obscure and lower-level tournaments. That's kept her below the radar. Quite a clever strategy, really, but that's also why she's not prepared for the Anderson. Never really been tested."

"Does she agree with you? About not being ready?"

He smiled tightly. "No. But she'll do as I say."

Snow felt his hand tremble, and he stuck it in his lap. Why did he feel this way about a woman the professor clearly loved? "That's good, I guess."

The professor grasped his arm with a warm hand. "Don't worry. Nothing will change in our relationship. Anitra will learn to love you as much as I do, and you'll just have another mentor."

Snow turned up his lips, but it was hard.

The professor's hand tightened. "Confession time. Don't you have just a teeny crush on the football hero?"

He blew out his breath. "That would be stupid. He's straight."

"We don't always want who and what we should."

Snow shrugged.

"Does Winston know?"

He gave in to the frown. "Professor, I know you'd like Winston and me to pair up, but it's not realistic. I don't feel that way about him. It would be very convenient if I did."

"I understand. I just don't want you to be lonely. I know how painful that can be. Not having any family is hard for a young man."

"I'm not lonely—" *Not exactly.* "And you've always been like family to me."

"Yes, but I see you getting these romantic fantasies, and I worry. We need to find you a realistic partner. After all, you're almost twenty-one. Life should be about more than chess moves." He smiled goofily. "I've found that out for myself."

Snow's stomach twisted.

The professor rocked back in his chair. "Let's try one more game, and then I want to get home. I'm meeting Anitra for a late cocktail." He started setting up the board.

Forty-five minutes later, Snow walked down the tree-lined street to his apartment—the place he'd inherited from his parents. He would have rather had the family. He sighed. At least it was a place to sleep and practice chess. In the entry, he checked the mail. Flyers for chess magazines, a few fan letters—most went to his post office box—and two invitations to tournaments. Most of those went directly to the professor.

He climbed the stairs to the top floor like at Riley's place, but there the resemblance stopped. This building was all stainless and glass, shiny, new, and cold. No worn, friendly carpet or worn, friendly landlady. His family's trust owned the building, which meant he'd own it once he turned twenty-one.

He tossed the mail trash on the table inside the front door and walked over to sit in the rocker he kept by the huge front picture window. He might not like the inside of the place, but he loved the view—well, usually. Now, dark storm clouds roiled over the treetops and blocked the far-off vistas he usually enjoyed. A rumble vibrated the window glass. Yeah, just the way he felt. Why couldn't he get over the terrible fear? He'd always trusted Professor Kingsley, respected his judgment. Why not now?

He dropped his head in his hands as a flash burst across the sky and vibrated—in his pocket.

Wait, that was his phone. He grabbed for it, glanced, gasped, and clicked all in one move. "Uh, hi."

"Hi, Snow." The smile in Riley's voice warmed the phone.

"Hi."

He chuckled. "You told me to call, remember?"

"Oh yes." He'd said text, but this was better.

"I'm so sorry we got interrupted. When can we get together again?"

Just tell him no. Say no. "Uh, tomorrow?"

"Great. Perfect. I worked on some more formulas, and I think I got them right. I'm really excited for you to see them."

"Oh. Sure. Me too."

"How about I come to your place this time?"

"My place?" He swallowed hard.

"Yeah, you said you have an apartment. That way you don't have to get all the way over to my house."

Snow glanced around frantically. "I guess so—"

"I don't mean to impose. I just thought, you know, if I come to your place, maybe that way we wouldn't be interrupted again."

A soft stream of breath rushed out of Snow's mouth. "Oh yes, that would be good."

"Great. Text me the address, okay?"

"Okay."

"What if I bring some food and we eat while we study? I mean, I know how much I'm putting you out, and at least you wouldn't miss dinner."

"That, uh, that would be good too."

"Great. See you tomorrow."

"See you." He hung up and texted the address before his hands started shaking so hard he couldn't find the keys. He looked again at the vast open space that was his apartment. Where could he buy furniture and dishes in one day?

ANITRA SET the green apple martini next to Harold's seat in his most comfortable recliner. The chair was as old and worn as the man. "Enjoy, darling."

He picked it up and sipped between his smiling lips. "Ah. You're so good to me. I've been looking forward to our time together all day."

"We could have had so much more time." She oozed onto his lap.

He took one more sip and set down the glass, then wrapped his arms around her. "We both have our responsibilities. Let's not discuss it."

"Of course, dear." She kissed his cheek and wriggled her butt against his lap. Bingo. His erection poked up between her legs. She suppressed a shudder. His arms tightened, and he pressed the bulge harder against her thighs. She wriggled a little more, then slid off his lap to the footstool. He sighed, and she smiled. *Suffer.* She handed him his glass.

He sipped. "Aren't you having one?"

"Yes, mine's over there." She pointed to the end table opposite.

He held out his glass. "Here. I can share."

"Oh no." She stood quickly and crossed to her own drink. "You've had a hard day and earned every mouthful." She sat and sipped her own drink. "I need to go soon. Early day tomorrow."

"I suppose you must. I'm pretty tired too."

"I'm sure." She glanced up. "Between teaching, coaching, and all your administrative duties, I don't know how you do it." His eyes drifted closed, and she smiled. "I'd best go, dear. See you tomorrow."

She let herself out and drove to her place in record time. To hell with the campus cops. She pulled up into her garage, rushed in the back door, and walked straight to the living room, where she could hear the TV.

Hunter sat facing her in the easy chair, his huge cock erect in his lap, the sounds of porn playing on the TV across from him. With a curve of his lips and a long stroke of his dick, he welcomed her. "Hi, baby. Just keeping it warm for you."

SNOW POINTED toward the wide back wall of the bedroom. "Put it there, please."

The two burly deliverymen hauled a bedframe in, then went back for the mattress. Snow leaned against the wall.

What the hell are you thinking? That you're going to need this thing?
No. It just looks weird for a grown-up to sleep on the floor.
You've been doing it most of your life.
Maybe it's time I stopped.

Dreamer.

Bitch.

"Is that okay, sir?"

"What? Oh yes. Fine, thank you. Put those two tables on either side, and we're done in here." Snow glanced at his phone. Just enough time to make the bed and wash the set of brand-new dishes so they didn't catch something lethal.

A half hour later, he signed the delivery papers and handed a tip to the two men.

"Thanks a lot. You just get married or something? Man, I never saw a dude get so much furniture at once. And not even a Foosball table." He grinned.

"Oh, should I have one of those?"

"No. Most girls don't like it. But you could use a TV."

"Damn, I forgot."

"That's usually the first thing a guy gets." The man grinned and handed Snow the receipt.

"I guess so, but I play chess. No time for TV."

"Hey, jeez, I thought you looked familiar. You're that chess champion. Good luck in the big game. Hey, George, this here's that chess guy. Snow, right?"

Snow smiled. "Yes. Thank you. And I'll remember about the TV in the future."

The man held up a big, callused hand. "Hey, no way. I wouldn't want to be the one to get you hooked on football or porn or something and make you lose your edge."

Snow laughed. No use saying he was already hooked on football.

When the deliverymen left, he made the bed really quick with the sheets and the "bed in a bag" thing he got at the department store. Could he sleep on that? He sat on the edge. Felt really cushy, even though he'd asked for a hard mattress.

He took a fast shower, then looked at his clothes. Five pairs of khakis did not a wardrobe make. Oh well, who the hell would notice? At least he had that nice silver-gray sweater the professor had given him. Everyone said it made his dark eyes pop.

Dreamer.

Bitch.

He wiped off the brand-new table with the brand-new dishcloth, and set it with some brand-new flatware. At least the rug under his feet had been there longer than a few hours. The rug, the rocker, and the table inside the door had constituted his entire interior landscape until today. Even his multiple chess sets lay on the floor.

Man, had his lawyer been surprised when he asked for five thousand dollars. He'd never used anything beyond his food allowance since he started school three years before.

Dreamer.

Bitch.

He sat on the floor and stared at the chess set. One of his many games in progress. *Think of an original move.*

Nothing.

He interferes with your concentration. He's bad for you.

Go fuck yourself.

Yeah, because that's the only person who's going to fuck you.

CHAPTER 6

THE KNOCK on the door sounded like an answer to a prophecy. Snow looked around. *A lot of work for a lot of silliness. Teach him physics and let it go.*

He opened the door and nodded at Riley. The guy smiled from ear to perfect, shell-like ear. Snow stepped back. "Hi. Welcome."

Riley walked into the apartment carrying two large white bags. "Hey, it smells new in here."

Yeah, stupid and silly newness. "I got a new couch."

"It's really nice."

"Thanks."

"I brought Chinese. Maybe we can work a little and then heat everything up in the microwave."

Oh crap, did he have a microwave? "Uh, sure." Probably most kitchens had one, right?

Riley pointed in the general direction of the kitchen. "I'll just put it in there, okay?"

"Okay."

Watching Riley walk across the rug to the kitchen was like observing a perfect chess match or listening to Bach—everything worked together. He moved with a relaxed efficiency that made him a star on the football field and an excuse for grown men turning gay. Not that Snow needed any turning.

Don't look. You could turn into a unicorn or something. Snow stared at his feet.

"Where shall we work?" Riley stood in front of him, smiling, holding his notebooks.

Since he'd bought a new table and chairs just so they'd have a place to sit, Snow nodded toward the dining area, where he'd had the movers put the set.

"Great." Riley walked from the kitchen and dropped the random pages Snow had left for him on the table. He cocked his head and fingered the delivery tag still attached to the chair.

Well, damn.

"Looks like you did some serious shopping. Nice stuff too."

"Thanks."

"You must not be a starving student like some of us." Riley laughed.

"My parents left me some money."

"Left?"

"Yes. They died when I was little. My grandmother raised me." Snow moved the carefully laid flatware aside and sat in one of the new chairs. Felt kind of weird.

"I'm really sorry."

He shrugged. "I barely knew them. I miss my grandmother a lot. She was pretty eccentric, but I loved her."

"Shit. That means you've got nobody?"

"No. I mean, the professor is kind of like family." Snow didn't mention the voice in his head.

"Kingsley?"

"Yes."

"He seems nice."

Snow nodded.

"I'm really sorry for your loss." Riley gently rested his hand on Snow's arm. It should have been so light Snow could barely feel it, but every blood vessel in his body sent its full complement of cells rushing to that one small touch. Snow's whole being wanted to curl up around those fingers.

He swallowed. "Thank you." He stared at the spot where their skin connected. If he never moved again, could he just stay here and feel like this?

Suddenly the hand and the warmth vanished. "So, let me show you what I did."

Sigh. "Okay."

"Honest to God, I never thought this stuff would make sense to me, but when you related it to something I understand so well, it just clicked, you know?"

"I'm so glad." Did he dare put his hand on Riley's arm? No chance. Instead he flipped through the pages Riley had done on his own. "This is good. You really are getting it."

Riley rocked back in his chair and threw his arms over his head, a move that should have dumped him on his butt but instead made him look like Thor. "Yahooo!"

Snow had to laugh. "Okay, let me show you a few more tips, and I think you could be ready for Jenkins." Riley leaned in, which raised all the hairs on Snow's arm, but soon he was engrossed in his teaching.

An hour later he leaned back. "So you understand how the two forces propel the running back in the opposite direction?"

Riley grinned. "Yeah, I get it."

"So do you want to—?"

"I got it. Let's eat. And talk."

"Are you sure—?"

"Yes. I got this. Now sit in your favorite spot—which I have a strange suspicion isn't at this table—and let me serve you some food."

Snow opened his mouth, then closed it.

Riley stood all the way up to his six and a half feet of perfection. "So where do you usually sit?"

Snow cleared his throat. "Either in the rocker or on the floor."

"Well, we can't both sit in the rocker and still eat, so I'll set us up on the floor. We'll have a Chinese picnic."

Riley walked into the kitchen, but Snow was still back on the thought of both of them sitting in the rocker. *Good Lord, what a fantasy.* He sat mesmerized as Riley walked back and forth to the living room with some of Snow's place mats, flatware, and dishes. Then he carried two glasses. "Hope you don't mind. I got us some wine."

"I, uh, I'm not old enough until later this year."

"I won't tell if you won't." As Riley walked back to the kitchen, he said, "If I pass the exam, I'll bring you champagne. Deal?"

"Yes." No more words came out of his throat, but he really loved the idea of a future reason to celebrate—together.

Finally, Riley walked back to the living room, carrying two dish towels and several Chinese food carryout boxes. "I guessed at what you might like." He set the food down and made a sweeping gesture with his arm. "Your feast, my lovely."

What could he say? Snow got up and walked to his now-defined spot on the rug, where he sank down cross-legged.

Riley flopped down opposite him. "See, I knew you'd look comfortable somewhere." He folded his legs, and even though they were very long legs, he still managed to look graceful.

Snow peered at the boxes. "What did you guess I'd like?"

Riley opened a container and poured liquid into two bowls. *Whew, glad I bought the bowls.* "I thought you'd like egg flower soup, since it's warm and nourishing, and full of sunshine, just like you."

Was it possible his heart stopped beating entirely?

Riley opened a carton and removed two crisp-looking cylinders. "And spring rolls, since I bet that is your favorite season."

"It… it is."

"Then I got some cashew chicken and prayed you weren't a vegetarian. But it's my favorite."

Snow squinched his lips. "I can eat chicken, but not with the cashews. I'm allergic to nuts."

"I'll remember that in future. Meanwhile, it's a good thing I got some moo shu vegetables too." Riley carefully laid out plum sauce on thin pancakes and loaded them up with veggies, placing two on Snow's plate and one on his own. "That will help make up for the chicken." Funny. He didn't take any of the cashew chicken for himself either.

Snow shook his head. "I really don't eat that much."

"We need to keep you fed. You're only as big as a bird."

Yeah, a turkey.

Riley raised his wineglass and held it out. "To physics."

Snow picked up his wine and stared at the almost clear liquid. "To physics."

"And the laws of affinity and attraction."

He swallowed. "The laws of affinity were replaced by the laws of quantum chemistry and chemical thermodynamics some time back."

"Oh?" Riley handed Snow a bowl of soup and a spoon. "You'll have to explain that to me in detail sometime."

He tried to chew the moo shu without getting plum sauce on his khakis. "Are you planning on taking more physics next semester?"

"No." Riley sipped a little soup. "But I'm very interested in chemistry." He grinned until his dimples looked like tiny craters in a satin surface.

Dear God. Snow grabbed his spoon and scooped. The too-hot soup hit his tongue. *Ow!* He dropped the spoon and coughed, spewing chicken broth and bits of egg a foot in front of him, including on Riley's knee. *Ow. Ow.*

Smooth move, lover boy.

Riley grasped his arm. "Are you okay? Are you hurt? I'm so sorry. I heated it in the microwave. I should have warned you it was so hot."

"So sorry."

"Did you burn your tongue? Let me see." He came up on his knees and pulled Snow to kneeling in front of him.

Snow stuck out his tongue.

Riley leaned in. "It's kind of red. But not too bad. Maybe I should kiss it and make it better."

"Wh-what?" His tongue popped back in his mouth.

"Definitely think I should—if you wouldn't mind." Riley's big hand traveled from Snow's arm to his neck. "But I have to see it if I'm going to administer first aid."

Snow just stared at the gold eyes getting closer and closer to him.

"Come on. Let me see the wound."

In a year he couldn't show Riley Prince all his wounds. Slowly he slid out his tongue.

Riley stared at the throbbing tongue, his breath warming Snow's nose. Then, gently, ever so gently, he took the tip between his lips and sucked.

Oh my God, what's happening?

If you don't know, idiot, you don't deserve it.

Like the answer to a prayer, Riley pulled Snow's tongue deeper into his own mouth and sucked harder.

Every function in Snow's being shut down—except sound. That was definitely a moan pouring out of his chest. No, wait. A similar sound came from Riley as he wrapped his arms around Snow and pulled him closer. *Wow.* He'd never even dared to dream this far. Was he making Riley Prince moan?

Stop thinking, you idiot. This has to be some kind of mistake, so don't miss it while it's here.

Still, Snow didn't know much about kissing, so it took a little thought. His tongue was now officially inside Riley's mouth, a position he wouldn't mind having continue for, maybe, ever. So what should he do to encourage that eventuality? What was his move?

Tentatively he slid his tongue against the soft heat of Riley's. *Oh, nice.* Riley seemed to think so too, because he opened his mouth wider, tightened his arms, and pressed a very large, hard bulge in his jeans against Snow's midsection. *Hmm, being taller would be good right now. Even lying down, there's no way to get the mouth and private parts into close proximity simultaneously.* Still, he rubbed his abs, such as they were, against Riley's lovely protuberance, and got a very satisfying gasp against his mouth.

Riley kind of fell down to the rug with Snow under him. *Oh my, yes.* Lots of hot parts pressed against him in wonderful places. *Oh God.* He about lost consciousness when Riley's hardness pushed down on his own throbbing penis and particles of fire zipped from his groin to every nerve ending. Cities could get lit just from the waves of joy washing through him—

And just like that, it was gone.

Riley kind of levitated and landed next to Snow. "Oh man, I'm so sorry. I got carried away. I never meant—"

Clearly, he'd never meant to kiss Snowden Reynaldi. Snow sighed and sat up slowly. "That's okay. I know, sometimes any port in a storm."

"What? What does that mean?"

Snow shrugged. "Maybe you got turned down by Courtney, and I look kind of girlie, and it's easy to get confused and—"

"Hang on!" Riley came straight up to sitting and grasped both of Snow's forearms. "You're not *any* port, as you say. You're *the* port for me. I just never meant to enter that port quite so fast." He grinned.

Snow frowned. "Okay. What does that mean?"

"Let me back up." He wrapped Snow's hand in his big palm. "Hi. I'm Riley Prince. I'm gay, and I've had the hots for you since the first time I ever saw you."

"What?"

Riley smiled softly and gazed into Snow's eyes. "I'm crazy about you. I've been trying to figure out a way to meet you and get to know you for over six months. And suddenly you volunteered to tutor me. Jesus, I almost passed out. I don't know why you did it, but I hope it's because you like me a little too."

His brain wouldn't keep up. "But Courtney?"

Riley pulled Snow's hand to his lips. "Yeah, she's a great girl. It's so hard for athletes to come out. I didn't have anyone I was interested in, so my coach suggested that I find a girl willing to pretend to be my girlfriend. Courtney was kind enough to agree."

"But, but—"

"I know she got a little carried away the day she came over to my place. She was putting on a show for you. I hadn't told her that I wanted to make exactly the opposite kind of impression." He laughed.

Head exploding. Snow shook it to see if it rattled. "Makes no sense."

"What doesn't?"

"You being in any way interested in me."

"Now why would you say that?" He leaned in and kissed Snow's cheek.

With Riley's lips that close to his, he couldn't think of many reasons. "Just doesn't make sense."

Riley kissed an inch closer. "Really? Doesn't make sense that I should get all hot and bothered over the smartest, sweetest, most beautiful guy I ever met?"

He could not be saying that. "I'm not any of those things."

"What mirror have you been looking in, my lovely?" He leaned back, which took his lips away, which was clearly a crappy idea. "Look in the Riley mirror."

"What?"

He pointed at his own face. "Here."

Snow raised his gaze slowly and stared into Riley's golden amber eyes. *Whoa.* He shied away.

"Uh-uh." Riley raised Snow's chin until his eyes rose too, and he stared at Riley. Riley's grin disappeared, replaced by an expression that sent shivers of pleasure up Snow's spine—respect, affection, and—his breath caught—desire. Riley smiled slowly. "Like what you see?"

Snow nodded.

"I wanted to kiss you so much, I didn't even eat any cashews."

Snow shook his head. "I wondered why."

"Now you know. So, do you believe I'm interested?"

Snow nodded slowly.

"Good, because the quarterback of the NorCal football team is about to pass physics and then shock the world of sports by coming out as gay. At that point I'd be honored if you'd be willing to date me and, if you like me, consider being my boyfriend."

"I—I already like you."

"How do you know?"

"I just do. I'm intuitive."

"I know."

Some seed Snow barely recognized exploded in his heart, becoming a twining vine of joy. "Besides, I'm your tutor. You have to accept what I say."

Riley's laugh burst out, and he fell back on the rug. "Yes, sir. I promise to accept your advice, counsel, teaching, kisses, hugs, and anything else you want to give me."

Snow wrinkled his nose. "I don't know much about what I could give you. I say I'm gay because I've only ever been attracted to boys, but I don't really have much experience."

"Good. That gives me a chance to be a tutor too."

Snow's eyes widened. "So you have experience, uh, I mean, being gay?"

Riley nodded and stared at the big sneakers on his big feet. "Yeah. Chickenshit, right? I've known I was gay since I was eleven or twelve. I came out to my parents when I was sixteen, but then I got scouted by NorCal. Since I'd never made any public declarations about being gay, like on social media, I turned a yellow tail and went back in the closet. I mean, I told the coach, but nobody worked hard to change my mind. There are rumors here and there, but I'm a big guy, and nobody says it to my face."

Snow shrugged. "So why change now? You're a senior. You can do what you want next year."

Riley leaned his head back against the couch. "Because it's chickenshit, like I said. People are always going to give gay guys crap when they don't know anyone who's gay. I can change that. A lot of people think they know me. I mean, look at you. Chess champion. Much bigger than I'll ever be. But you never claim to be anything but gay."

"I'm so weird, nobody's surprised."

"No, you're not. You show the world that gay guys can be brilliant geniuses and beautiful. I can show them that gay guys can be big and strong and well coordinated. We all have a part to play." He chuckled. "I have to confess, I practiced that speech, but I'm hoping it's true."

Snow's heart beat so loud he could barely hear. Could this really be happening? "Umm, so you said you have enough experience to teach me." He stared at his moo shu.

Riley sat up and got a very serious expression. "You see, Mr. Reynaldi, it's all a matter of physics. Your quantum physics says that electrons can be in two places at the same time." He leaned forward and pulled Snow across his lap, somehow managing to not spill any Chinese food in the process. "It's like my tongue can be in my mouth—" He ran his soft tongue across Snow's barely parted lips. "—and inside your mouth at the same time." He insinuated inside and kissed Snow slowly and thoroughly. *So that's how it feels. Invasive and completing at once.*

Riley pulled his lips back from the kiss but kept them close to Snow's so his breath warmed Snow's wet mouth. "And just as particles can be waves and waves particles, so I can feel completely relaxed and completely excited simultaneously."

Snow grinned. "I knew physics could be fun, but this is far beyond my expectations."

"You didn't have enough faith in your subject matter."

"Clearly." He smiled and whispered, "What happens now?"

"First, I want to know if you're interested in me, or am I just living in fantasyland?"

Snow's eyes widened. "Oh, did I not show enough interest?"

Riley laughed. "Yes, but I don't want to take anything for granted. You're too special."

My, that moo shu is interesting. "I've been dreaming about you ever since the first time I saw you. I didn't think you were gay, so I never even hoped it could be more than a dream."

Riley caressed Snow's hair. "Think of all the time we wasted dreaming about each other."

"In quantum physics, particles in contact become quantumly entangled. Perhaps we simply needed more time for the entangling to occur." Snow smiled softly. This had to be a dream.

"I really like this physics stuff."

"And I look forward to your tutoring." The blush heated his ears and cheeks.

Riley leaned back against the new couch, taking Snow with him. "As much as I'd love to continue your lessons this minute, I don't feel I have the right. I want to come clean and be free to take you out and be seen as a proper boyfriend for you. No sneaking around. So let's finish our meal, get to know each other a little better, I'll take my test, talk to my coach, and we'll have our official first date. I hope that might be the homecoming dance."

Snow swallowed. "That could be too big a statement for a first date. I mean, the chances are great that you'll be homecoming king."

"That gives me more reason to get this all done fast. I really want to take you to homecoming, Snow."

Holy wow. He shook his head. "I don't understand why you'd pick me. There are so many men, guys, you can have."

"You're beautiful, special, and smart."

"And there are plenty of people who exceed any of my attributes."

Riley curved a soft smile. "I love how I feel when I'm with you."

"How is that?"

His brilliant eyes flashed up. "Smart."

"It's not a question of feeling. You are smart."

"And I love that you really mean that."

"I do."

"I rest my case."

Snow needed to revise his thesis about dreams coming true. "Okay, go see Jenkins and set a day for your test."

CHAPTER 7

RILEY STARED at the computer screen. Courtney's breath warmed his ear as she peered over his shoulder. "Holy shit, you passed."

Riley opened his mouth like a fish. *Un-fucking-believable.* "He did it. Snow found a way to push that shit into my dense head."

"With all due respect to your pretty friend, *you* did it, Riley. You passed that final with such flying colors, Jenkins gave you a fucking C for the semester. This is awesome."

Riley grinned. "Yeah, it really is, isn't it?" He pushed the chair back, causing Courtney to retreat to the couch. "I gotta call Snow. I barely believe I can finally ask him out."

"Oh. Did you already tell the team?"

That stopped his forward motion like three linebackers. "No."

"When are you going to do it? You go out with a guy, and you know somebody's going to notice. Hell, neither of you is exactly unknown on this campus."

"I better tell the team before I go on the date."

She nodded. "Think so."

"Maybe I'll come out to the team and the frat first, which is pretty much the same thing, and then I can tell Snow everything at once."

"Sounds like a plan."

He flopped in his big easy chair. "But that means I need to do it fast, because if I don't get Snowden's cock in my mouth soon, I'm going to wither up and die."

She raised both hands. "TMI, baby." She grinned. "So when are you going to do it? Tell the fraternity, I mean, not suck Reynaldi's cock."

"Tonight. We've got a frat meeting. That includes a lot of the team. Good time. Nobody will be drunk until later. Well, most won't be, anyway. I've got less chance of getting my ass kicked by multiple players."

She shook her head. "I don't envy you. What do you want to do about me?"

He ran a hand through his hair. "Oh hell. My brain didn't get that far. What do you think?"

She leaned back, her perfect breasts pushing against her cheerleader's sweater. "I've got practice tonight. How about I tell the whole squad that we broke up because you're just not doing it for me?"

"Oooh, harsh."

"Yeah, but don't you think it will seem strange if I never once suspected you were gay?"

"Probably."

"So that would explain it, and tomorrow, after the news spreads, all the girls will come running to tell me why you weren't exactly Bradley Cooper."

"Okay. Yeah." Man, this was tough. "It's stupid for me to try to maintain my alpha male status when I come out. It's just going to be hard, you know." He sucked in a breath. *And maybe painful.*

Courtney leaned forward. "You're plenty of alpha for anybody, baby. You just happen to like to fuck guys."

"Yeah. I suppose so. It's weird when gay guys believe their own stereotypes."

"As long as you realize that, you're gonna do fine."

"Thanks, Court. For everything."

She stood and stretched, revealing the body that launched every freshman's wet dreams. "Hey, I've enjoyed being the queen of the school."

"You're still the queen of the school."

"Oh, I don't know. Snowden Reynaldi might give me a run." She laughed.

TWO HOURS later he stood in front of the coach's office, holding his breath and praying not to barf. Step one. Holy shit, he was scared.

He walked into the outer office and found Danny lolling in the desk chair, reading a sports magazine. "Yo, Prince. How's it hangin', man?"

"Good, thanks. I, uh, called the coach, and he's expecting me."

"Sure. Go on in."

"Uh, do you work here?"

"Nah. Just like hanging out around the coach."

Not much could make Riley laugh right then, but he did. Danny was so laid-back it was amazing he could stay upright. *Wonder how he'll feel about me being gay?*

He rapped on the inner door, waited for the "Yeah," and pushed inside. "Hey, Coach."

McMasters nodded. "Riley. I heard directly from your physics professor. Congratulations are in order. You did it, and I'm proud."

"Thank you, sir. I owe it all to Snowden Reynaldi."

"Yeah, when that guy Erhlinger failed, I just couldn't let it go. Reynaldi said you could learn physics, and I believed him. How did he do it?"

"He used football."

"You're kidding."

"No. I'll show you sometime in case you want to use it on the team. Great stuff, actually."

"Well, thank God that's behind you."

"Uh, yes, sir." Riley stared at his shoes.

"Sooooo…."

He took a huge breath and looked up. "I want to come out."

"Out of where?"

"Out of the closet, sir. I want to tell the team that I'm gay."

"Shit."

"I know."

"Is it okay for me to ask why?"

Riley nodded. "I, uh, met someone."

"You're in love?"

"Well, not yet, but it's pretty special to me."

The coach sighed and leaned back in his desk chair. "Is it by any chance Snowden Reynaldi?"

"How did you know that?"

"When I heard you'd been showing up at chess matches, I knew something was up. I guess if you like 'em pretty and very, very smart, he's your guy."

"Yes, sir." He'd never quite known he had a type until he saw Snow.

"I don't want you to think I'm not supportive, but I have to ask if you'd consider waiting until after the championship game."

Riley blew out a stream of air. "Because throwing a shit bomb like 'your quarterback happens to be gay' into the middle of a well-oiled machine could be bad."

"I'd like to think it won't make a difference."

Talk about challenging his newly formed convictions. "I thought about it a lot. I feel like it's not fair to ask Snow to sneak around with me. I want to date him. In fact, I'd like to take him to homecoming."

"I'm sure he'd understand."

"Yes, sir. He's a great guy. But I think maybe it's not fair to me either. I've been living this lie for a long time. Maybe knowing who my real friends are before I graduate wouldn't be such a bad thing."

The coach stared at the top of his desk and suddenly slapped it. "That's a pretty well thought out line of reasoning, Riley. Go for it, son, and let's see how much of a shitstorm it creates."

Riley stood and extended his hand. "Thank you, sir." *Hope that line of reasoning doesn't bite me in the ass.*

"I guess I'll find out tomorrow at practice how it all turns out." Coach McMasters laughed, but it sounded kind of forced.

On the way out, Riley stopped at the reception desk and stared at Danny sleeping on top of his magazine. Should he wake him up and tell him? *Nah.*

He stopped in the cafeteria for some milk and sat out in the sun while he drank it. What he'd told the coach about why he wanted to come out now was all true, but not the whole truth. Actually, he kept noticing that Winston always hung around Snow. Plus, he'd talked a lot about Snow when he was trying to tutor Riley. Obviously Winston had the hots for Snowden. The guy might be geeky, but he was kind of cute, and they had lots in common, while Riley wasn't in the same brain universe as Snow. If Win tried to stake a claim, who knew what Snow would do? No, Riley needed to come out, declare his interest, and try to prove he was the man for Snowden Reynaldi.

Still, the last swig of milk tasted kind of sour going down, and every minute until his frat meeting felt like the last mile of dead man walking.

He didn't drag himself up the steps of the frat house until five minutes before the meeting was scheduled to start. Fighting with himself about maybe waiting until later in the semester had taken all his energy. He felt like he'd been whipped with a stick and didn't want to go in at all.

Inside, the guys sat on every available piece of furniture, plus three of them lay on the floor. "Hey, Prince, how ya doin'?" Weird that Roget should be the first one to say hi.

A couple of his teammates slapped his butt as he walked by. He perched on the windowsill.

The fraternity president, Fred Furness, called them to order. Fred managed to combine the huge strength needed to be a guard and the brains to be premed. People respected him. Still, Fred grew up in South Central LA, not far from Roget. No way of knowing how he'd react to Riley's declaration, and that could make all the difference in the other guys' attitude. Shit, his hands were actually sweating.

Fred led them through old business, then launched into the new business of sprucing up the fraternity house in time for homecoming. "We're gonna have a ton of alums here, so we need to look good, man. We want all the happy alumni support we can get for the chapter."

Oh damn, he hadn't thought about how the alums might penalize the chapter for having a gay guy. *So much to think about.* Hell, why hadn't he just done this when he first got to school? *Chickenshit idiot.*

Fred looked around. "Okay, so if there's no other new business, I guess we can adjourn."

One of the guys in back by the dining room yelled, "I'll get the beer."

Riley's hand flew up by itself.

Fred nodded. "Yeah, Prince, you got something?"

"Uh, yeah."

Bill Ruth, the tight end, slapped a hand on Riley's shoulder. "Don't worry, man, we're all voting for you for homecoming king. Let's drink." He laughed.

"Uh, thanks, but that's not it."

"You have new business, Riley?" Fred piled up his papers.

"Not new, exactly. I just wanted to tell you all something." He swallowed. Jesus, he'd been a lot braver at sixteen.

The tone of his voice must have stopped some of the guys and made them look around, because suddenly it felt like the whole room was staring and the walls were closing in.

"Yeah. What?" Fred smiled, but he obviously wanted to move on.

"I never told, I mean—" *I should have practiced.* "I never told you before, but I'm gay."

The guy next to him slapped his shoulder and snorted. "Funny you're not, Prince."

Someone back near the kitchen door said, "What did he say?"

Another voice replied, "He said he never told us, but he's gay."

"Nooo shiiit."

Fred frowned, a scary sight on his big face. "Are you serious?"

"Yes."

Fred just stared, although the whispering at the back of the group got louder.

However hard he'd thought this would be, his fears had been one tenth of what it actually was. Riley shuddered. "I figured before I graduated you ought to know. You can't kick me out because of the antidiscrimination crap, but I'll quit the fraternity if you want. Since I don't live in the house, that should take care of it."

"Like hell." That icy-cold voice quieted every other sound in the room. Rog stepped out of the group he was standing in and faced Riley. "I still got to get your slimy fag sweat on me every time you pass. Fuck if I'll do it."

LeRoy, the second-string running back, pushed past Rog. "You can pass to me, Riley. I figure you were my friend yesterday, and you still are today."

Bill raised a finger. "Pass to me, man." Riley gave the tight end a nod.

"Outhouse" Oliver Hanson, the biggest damned guard on the team, pushed between two other guys. "For that matter, you can pass to me."

A voice from the back Riley couldn't identify said, "Pass to you or make a pass at you? Fags in the fraternity are bullshit, man."

Somebody else yelled, "Yeah."

Fred crossed his arms. "You just decide you're gay?"

"No. I've known for a while."

"So you been lyin'?"

Shit. Facts are facts. "Yes. I mean, I never exactly said I was straight, but I lied by implication."

"You tell Courtney you're a fag?"

Double shit. "She must have suspected something, because she broke up with me."

"But you lied to her."

"Yeah. I guess."

"Against the honor code."

Riley frowned. "I never lied on a test."

"Still, Zetas aren't liars."

The front door opened, and Danny slouched in. He glanced around. "What the fuck's going on?"

"You're late for the meeting." Fred scowled, but Danny could ignore King Kong.

"Why's everybody look like they want to barf?"

LeRoy said, "Riley just told us he's gay."

"No shit?"

"Yeah."

A smile spread like warm maple syrup across Danny's handsome face. "Hey, man, that's dope. Never knew there was any other gay guys on the team." He walked across the floor and stuck his hand out to Riley.

What the hell? Danny? Riley slowly shook his hand.

LeRoy asked the question for them all. "Are you saying you're gay, Danny?"

"Sure."

"You never said anything."

He shrugged. "Why should I? What the fuck business is it of yours?"

Riley caught his breath, and it came out as a laugh. He laughed some more. A few guys joined in. Some looked confused, and the rest radiated anger. Riley shook his head and wrapped an arm around Danny's neck. "Thanks, man. I think you just summed it up. I'm the same man whether I'm gay or straight." He looked around the room. "You don't want to play with me? Knock yourselves out. You blow the championship? Look in the mirror for somebody to blame. I'm out."

He strode out the door, made it to his car still looking like a bloody movie hero, got behind the wheel, and about passed out. He could so easily have avoided this whole ordeal, and all the shit that was still to follow, but then he wouldn't have deserved Snow. He reached for his phone as he pressed his foot on the accelerator.

CHAPTER 8

SNOW CLUTCHED the phone to his ear. "Of course you can come over."
Calm down, heart, so I can hear.

"I know it's short notice." Riley sounded—what? Upset was an inadequate word. Nervous and excited at the same time.

"I just need time to make a phone call." Professor Kingsley would kill him, but what a way to go.

"I'm interrupting your plans, aren't I?"

"Just come over. I want to see you."

"You're sure?"

"Of course."

"Okay, I'll be there in ten minutes. Or, have you eaten? I can bring food."

"Have you eaten?"

"Uh, no. But I'm not very hungry."

"Don't worry. If we're starving, I can figure out something. We can order pizza."

"Sounds great. See you soon."

Snow hung up. Riley was coming to see him. Wow. He'd called twice during the week to say he was studying like crazy and then taking Jenkins's test. Maybe he'd failed? He sounded so upset. Maybe that was why. *Oh no.* He'd seemed to be doing really well. If he'd failed, he'd lose his eligibility and not be able to play anymore.

Maybe that's good. Especially if he decides to come out. The football team isn't exactly PFLAG.

Hell, he won't come out. Way too much to lose.

I'll date him anyway.

Oh sure. He'll want to be seen with the princess of NorCal chess—not!

He surveyed the apartment. What should he do? Everything looked just the way it had the last time Riley was there a week before—carefully laid table, well-made bed—except for the mess in the middle of the rug where Snow actually lived.

Better call the professor.

He won't be fond of this call.

Tell me about it.

He grabbed the cell and dialed.

"Hi, Snow. You're not talking while biking, are you?" The professor laughed at his own joke.

"No, sir. I'm, uh, not coming."

"We have practice scheduled." He said it as if that meant it was destined.

"I know, but I had something very important come up. I'll put in extra time tomorrow after class."

"I set this time aside for you, Snowden."

"I realize, sir, and I very much appreciate it. I'm so sorry to cancel."

Pause.

He's waiting for you to tell him what came up.

I know.

Kingsley sighed. "Very well. I'll see you tomorrow at 2:00 p.m. sharp, correct?"

"Yes, sir."

Snow hung up and stared at the phone.

See, you didn't burst into flames.

Yeah, yet.

He sprang up and started cleaning his pile of papers, extra chess pieces, leftover sandwich crusts, and glasses of tea. Still, no quieting the racing blur of his mind. Why was Riley coming over? Maybe he'd failed and he blamed Snow for it?

No, he's not like that.

Maybe he'd passed and he wanted to say thank you.

Snow paused the whirlwind and stared out the window. Maybe he wanted to have sex.

Wow, that stopped him. He flopped cross-legged onto his rug. What if Riley did want sex? Jesus, Snow's cock didn't even know what sex felt like, and it still rose like the sun in summer. He stared down at his bulge. *Are you scared?* He grinned. *Not as much as I should be.*

His brain clicked in. *Sheets are clean. Oh dear. Condoms.* Surely Riley would bring them if he had designs. *And lube.* That Snow had. Of course, he'd probably crawl under the rug if Riley realized he only had it to masturbate.

He's going to figure out you're a virgin sometime.

The knock on the door rocketed him to his feet. *Oh God.* He swallowed hard. *Try to look a little cool.*

He bounded to the door and pulled it open. *Whew.* Just the pure physicality of Riley always gave him a shock. So big. So perfect. "Hi."

"Sorry to call you so late." Jeez, he even looked upset.

"Come in."

Riley walked past him, then paused in the entry. Snow closed the door and gazed up at him. "Are you okay?"

"Yeah. Kind of. I passed. The professor gave me a B+ on the test, which adds up to a C for the semester."

"That's fantastic. Amazing." He clapped, then cocked his head. "But you don't seem real happy."

"I just—I came out to the fraternity."

Snow's heart leaped and dove at once. "Oh my God. Come in and sit down."

Riley walked right into the middle of the rug and flopped on the very spot where Snow loved to sit. That spot got just the right light from the windows. It had the most power. Snow folded down into his cross-legged position opposite him.

Riley half smiled. "You have to show me how you sit so easily on the floor. I always feel like a water buffalo."

"Lots of practice. So tell me what happened."

He let out a long stream of air. "I told them I'm gay."

"How did they take it?"

"Some were real supportive, and some were really awful."

"Rog."

"Yeah, he was one of the awful ones. Said he didn't want me to pass to him anymore." Riley hung his head. "Man, this is going to make things hard for Coach."

"Rog is an idiot."

"Yeah, but I'll admit I could have chosen a better time to do this. Like not in the middle of football season."

"Maybe it's a blessing, because they have to play with you if they want to win, so people like Rog will have to get over it fast or compromise their own futures."

He sighed. "But I made them have to do it."

"Did anyone ask Rog or the others to pretend to be someone they're not so they can be on the team? Doesn't Rog get to be as big an asshole as he wants and no one questions him?"

Riley stared at him.

"So how come you're the only one who has to put on an act to play football?"

For a second, Riley stared some more. Suddenly he launched himself at Snow, pushing him down against the rug and winding up with his arms planted on either side of Snow's head. "You're so brilliant. You're even better than Danny."

Snow tried to catch his breath. "That's good, I guess. Who's Danny?"

"Just some guy in my fraternity who told us he's gay after I came out. When our fraternity president asked him why he'd never told anyone, he said it was nobody's business, like the whole question was so obvious. I could have kissed him."

A frown fluttered across Snow's forehead. "I remember him. I met him in your coach's office. Did you—kiss him?"

"Nope." Riley flashed the dimples. "But I sure would like to kiss you."

"You—you would?"

Riley nodded his golden head.

"It appears you're in a good position for it."

"Ever the master of logistics." He lowered his lips until they touched Snow's. Softly he pressed his tongue to the seam between Snow's lips and stroked.

Oh my. Last time, Riley had put that tongue all the way in. *I better open up.* He parted his lips, and Riley instantly took the hint. Warm, wet, and full. *Oh yes, yes.*

Snow sighed and wrapped his arms around Riley's shoulders. Riley adjusted so his hips came down onto the carpet next to Snow's legs, and he kept one arm behind Snow's head for balance.

Darn, kind of want that nice weight he put on me before. But no complaints. Snow sucked on Riley's tongue and got just the reaction he hoped for. A long, low moan. Riley kind of flipped on his side and pulled Snow with him so they were more face-to-face. Oh wow, Snow's khakis looked like a lesson on how to build a pyramid, and Riley's jeans—Jesus! Kong. That thing looked big.

Could I touch it? Want to so badly.

Riley pulled Snow closer for another kiss, which gave Snow the chance to slip a hand down between them under cover of darkness. As Riley's tongue dug deep into the secret recesses of Snow's mouth, Snow's hand slithered to its goal—and stopped.

What'cha gonna do now, big boy?

No idea.

Riley took the decision away from him. He reached down, grabbed Snow's hand, and pressed it hard against his giant bulge. *Holy wow.* Snow stretched his fingers until he traced the outline of a rod with a flared head framed by some nice squishiness.

That got a double moan from Riley—to say nothing of a throb from Snow's penis that half hurt and half felt wonderful. When Snow's fingers rubbed against the zipper in Riley's jeans, Riley slipped his hand around and ripped that sucker down.

Oh God, you got what you wanted. Now what?

Had to explore. Still nibbling against Riley's tongue, he let his fingers slip inside the open gap in Riley's pants. Twining his way through folds of cotton— he froze. Skin! Hot, smooth skin. Had to be cock. Balls would be hairy, right? Oh God, he had his fingers on Riley Prince's cock. *Pass out.*

His lips had frozen along with the rest of him. Riley opened his eyes and stared at him from an inch away. His lips moved against Snow's. "What do you plan to do now?"

"Don't know."

"Why don't you wrap your hand around that guy and let me do the same to you."

"Oh."

"Sound good?" His lips tickled, and his breath smelled sweet against Snow's nose.

"Sounds very good." He might, however, have to give up breathing. He slid his fingers farther—and slid and slid until that big, hot cylinder filled his whole hand and then some. He tightened.

"Oh yeah." Riley bucked his hips, and his penis slid through Snow's hand, dragging the smooth skin over the hard muscle beneath.

Amazing. "Oh, I like that."

"You do?" He did it again, and Snow smiled. "Let me share the wealth." Riley slid down Snow's zipper and burrowed one finger inside.

Panic! "I, uh, I'm not as big as you."

"I'm six and a half feet tall and weigh two fifty. You're what? Five eight and one forty?"

He swallowed. "About."

Riley looked down, grabbed his own penis away from Snow, then held it out as if it were attached to the front of Snow's pants. "That would look pretty funny, don't you think? Out of proportion?" He gazed into Snow's eyes. "I think you're the most beautiful person I ever saw."

"Oh my. Thank you."

Riley slid his hand deeper and grasped Snow's privates. He smiled. "Okay, now this is a pretty impressive dick for a little guy."

"It is?"

"Don't you take gym?"

Snow shook his head.

"You've never seen any men naked?"

"Not since I was little."

"Well, damn. How do I rate?"

"You're you."

Riley's eyes got kind of watery, and he kissed Snow again, soft and deep, but he kept exploring with his hand until he'd fisted Snow's penis and started pumping.

Snow ripped his head back. "Oh God. Oh man."

"Good?"

"Indescribable."

Riley chuckled but got more serious with his strokes. Snow tried to remember to keep squeezing Riley's cock too, but it was hard to concentrate.

Riley scooted back a little. "Hang on."

"No. Don't stop." *Dear God, did I really say that?*

"I won't. I promise." He unwrapped Snow's hand from his own penis and then scooted closer until he had both their dicks side by side. With fingers stretched, he folded both cocks in one big hand, then wrapped his other hand around the package. "See what you think of this." He started pumping like a farm wife making butter.

"Oh wow. Oh God. That's so great, so—oh." Snow's eyes rolled back in his head as his noggin bumped against the carpet. His hips had a mind of their own, bobbing and weaving. A little embarrassing, but who cared. *Too great. Too incredible.*

Riley leaned in but didn't stop stroking. "Snow, have you ever been sucked?"

"What?"

"Has anyone ever given you head?"

Snow's head shook on its own as his brain flew off into space. *Would he? Could he?*

"Want it?"

"Oh God, I want anything from you."

"You're amazing, and I'm dying to taste you. Have been since the first moment I saw you." His strong hands pumped, keeping time to Snow's hips' Virginia Reel.

"I love what you're doing."

"You'll love this more." In one move he slid back, opened his hands, and stuffed Snow's cock into his mouth.

Snow's mouth opened. Wider. A sound like a scream or a wail flowed out. "Ohhhhhh. Ahhhhhhhhh."

Riley sucked the head and then swallowed until Snow's dick felt locked in a lava tube—but in a good way.

"Holy blessed shit!" Every cell in Snow's body exploded like someone had let off the big bang in his groin. Semen might be shooting from his penis, but it felt like his whole body melted. His vision blurred, blacked out, then blazed with light as another pump came out of him. And another. One more. Nothing had ever, ever come close. "Oh God, oh, oh, ooooooh."

It took what felt like minutes for the shudders of pleasure to finally die down, replaced by a warm glow. His lashes fluttered. "Wow."

Riley grinned like a Walt Disney cat, but it only took a brief glance to see his penis stretched—red, hot, and painful-looking—toward Snow.

Snow smiled lazily. "Why did I get all the benefits?"

"Because you've earned them."

"How?"

"By being—you." He smiled as he gave Snow back his compliment.

Snow pushed up to his elbow. "Not fair." With a hop, he made it to his knees. "Wait." He didn't know much, but one thing he could do. Jumping up, he kicked off his khakis, ran into the bathroom and pulled the bottle of lube out of the top drawer, then grabbed a towel. *Sticky stuff.* He squirted it on his hands as he trotted back into the living room, knelt where Riley still lay with his jeans around his knees, and grabbed his penis in both hands. "Does this feel good?"

"You kidding? Just keep that up and you'll have more than lube on your hands."

"Oh, I hope so."

Gazing into Riley's eyes, he tried to gauge how he was doing. Riley's mouth opened and his eyes closed. *Good combination.* Snow squirted a little more lube and went back to work. The smoothness of the skin on Riley's dick caressed his hands. Fascinating, all that ripple of muscle and connective tissue beneath the surface. He'd never enjoyed the feeling when it was his own penis. Just a perfunctory action. Now he understood why. Masturbation didn't even approach what he'd experienced with Riley's mouth. Could he give Riley a blowjob?

Better walk before you can run. Concentrate.

He tightened and released his hands as Riley gasped louder and louder. "Oh God, how can you be so good at this? Oh shit, Snoooooooow." His face contorted as if in pain, and his hips rose from the floor in an arch as a fountain of ejaculate shot out of his penis, rose in the air, then fell back to splat on Riley's abdomen and Snow's hands. *Oh my God.* He'd done it. He'd made Riley Prince come.

Sure. A poodle could make a guy that horny come.

Well, at least I'm on par with a dog.

"Snow?" Snow glanced up to see Riley gazing at him. "Where do you go when you get all quiet like that?"

"Sorry."

"No, I'm just curious."

Snow shrugged and wiped his sticky hands on the towel, then gently patted the spots of wetness from Riley's skin. "I have mental conversations, I guess you'd call them."

"You mean, like, both sides?"

"Um-hmm."

"Hey, if you need good advice, ask somebody smart." Riley smiled.

Should he say any more? "I spent a long time with my grandmother after my parents died." He set the towel aside and ran a finger across Riley's glowing skin. "She was hard of hearing. I was a weird kid who mostly studied and read books, so I didn't have friends."

Riley cocked his head, and his smile was so kind it brought heat behind Snow's eyes. "So you had to talk to yourself?"

Snow nodded. "It became a habit. Two sides of my brain each take a viewpoint in a conversation and argue with each other. It's probably schizophrenia at its most classic."

"Sounds like loneliness to me."

"Yes, I suppose that's true."

Riley slipped his fingers into Snow's long hair. "I'd like to be your friend."

Snow turned a half smile. "I think this might be called a friend with benefits."

"But the friend part is the most important. Okay?"

Snow stared at the etched pattern on the rug. "I'd like that."

"So, my friend, will you go to homecoming with me on Saturday?"

Snow gazed at Riley. This much happiness had to be tempting fate. "Yes. Yes, I will."

CHAPTER 9

"CHECKMATE." SNOW slid his pawn and smiled at Professor Kingsley.

The professor leaned back in his chair. "You devil. Got me again."

Snow suppressed his grin. "Just lucky."

"Yes, the Snowden Reynaldi version of lucky. Brilliant and relentless." He sighed. "I must admit, I've wanted to fault you for your dreamy lack of focus the last week, but it doesn't seem to have hurt you one bit. I'd never want to jinx us by overspeaking, but I don't honestly see who can beat you." He rubbed a hand over his eyes.

"Thank you, sir. Are you okay?"

"Yes, just a little tired. Keeping up with a younger woman is murder." He laughed. "But my love life is not the interest here. Do you feel like telling me what's going on in yours?"

Snow tried not to smile, but it didn't work.

"Ah, so I guessed right? Come on, confess."

"Riley Prince asked me to homecoming."

The professor's eyes narrowed, and his mouth popped open. "Excuse me?"

"Riley's gay. He came out to his fraternity and the team. His coach already knew. He's invited me to the homecoming dance."

"Well, I'll be—that's amazing. And if I'm not mistaken, the happiest thing that could have happened for you. Am I right? Haven't you been nursing a bit of a crush?"

Snow bobbed his head in time to his heart. "Yes, but I never dreamed anything would ever come of it. Then Riley brought me Chinese food and told me he had—had been—was interested in me. He passed the physics test, then asked me to homecoming."

"Good for him. I'm so happy for you, Snow."

"Thank you."

"I'll bet Winston's disappointed."

Dear God, he'd barely thought of Win. "I, uh, haven't told him yet. This all happened so fast."

"I'm sure he won't be entirely shocked. I think he knew you weren't really interested in him romantically."

"I hope you're right."

"So you may be going to the dance with the homecoming king. Will that be awkward?"

Wow. "I haven't really thought much about that either."

Kingsley smiled, but with kindness. "A little less dreamy and a little more forethought would be good. The quarterback of the soon-to-be-championship team declaring he's gay and showing up at a big event with a man is not without repercussions. I don't want you to be caught off guard."

"Good advice, sir. As always."

"So this is our last practice until next week."

"Oh? I thought we'd get in a couple more this weekend."

The professor smiled but quickly controlled it. "No, I have some family obligations. Of course, I won't miss homecoming." He glanced at his watch. "In fact, I need to get going. I'll tell you all about it when I see you at the dance."

Odd. The professor had very little family and never spoke of them. Still, no practice might give Snow a chance for another blowjob. Or two. He smiled and gave the professor a big hug. "Thank you. Have a great time until I see you."

The professor tapped his nose. "You too, son. Remember I love you."

Snow's eyes widened. The professor said that rarely. It meant so much. "Thank you. I feel the same."

"See you Saturday night."

Outside the physics building, the sun warmed him. Or maybe that was just the sweetness of Professor Kingsley's hug. If a guy had to grow up without benefit of much parenting, it sure was great to have a mentor like the professor.

He started toward his bike. Two arms grabbed him from behind. "Hey, Snowball."

"Hi, Win." Talk about fate. From the professor's lips straight into manifestation.

Winston let go and leaned against the tree closest to the sidewalk. "You been practicing?"

"Yes, last session till next week. I guess the professor is busy until Saturday."

"Probably busy fucking that gorgeous creature he's engaged to."

Snow frowned. "You sure you're gay?"

"Hey, who better to appreciate the style of a beautiful woman than a gay man?"

"I suppose."

Win stepped forward and leaned over quickly to peck Snow on the cheek. "But you're lots prettier. And I don't have to be gay to see it."

"Thank you." He scuffed his sneakers. "I really wasn't fishing for a compliment."

"So speaking of beautiful, are you going to get all dolled up and come to the dance with me on Saturday?" Win batted at some leaves on the tree above his head.

Well, damn. Snow stared at his shoes. "Uh, you never mentioned it before."

"No. I figured you didn't even know about it, so why bother you with the idea of having to get dressed up when you've had other things to think about." Finally a frown crept over Win's face. "Why?"

"I, uh, already have a date to the dance."

"What? Who?"

Snow took a deep breath. "Riley Prince."

He snorted. "What the fuck are you talking about?"

"Riley came out as gay. He asked me to the dance." Stillness. Win said nothing. Finally Snow looked up. Winston stared at him like he'd grown an extra head. "I'm sorry. I was going to tell you. It just happened."

"Riley Prince is gay?"

"Yes, apparently so."

"And he asked you out?"

"I told you that, Winston." Snow crossed his arms.

"This is not Snowball wishful thinking or fantasy, right? If I go to that dance, I'm going to see you with Riley?"

"Win, what the hell?"

Winston held up both hands. "Sorry. I just know you sometimes live in your own world. So I guess you can't say no when the prince of the campus asks you out, right?"

"I didn't want to say no, Win. I like Riley. He's a nice guy."

"With a brain the size of a grain of sand."

"Not true. He passed his physics test with a B+."

"You're shitting?"

"No. I told you he could learn. He needed the right approach."

Win's voice got singsongy. "The Snowden Reynaldi turn-you-into-a-gay-boy approach?"

"Come on, Win, that's not fair. I never had a clue Riley was gay until he told me."

"And say you haven't been jerking off to his football posters for the last year. Shit, every time I try to get close to you, you're mooning over Mr. Shoulder Pads. I'll bet you don't say no to him, right?"

"Winston!"

"What about you and me?"

"We've never been more than friends."

Win bent over and stared at Snow's face. "Not from lack of me trying."

Snow stepped back. "Seriously, I don't know much about romance, but I never got the feeling that you'd die without me or anything. We just got thrown together because we're both gay nerds."

"Speak for yourself." Dear God, he looked like he could cry.

"I'm so sorry. I never had any idea you were serious in any way."

"I've walked on eggshells around you since we met." He pranced like a ballerina on drugs, and two girls walking past giggled. "Don't disturb the great chess master. Don't break his fantasy bubble. This is the thanks I get."

"I'm sorry, Win."

"Oh, fuck off." He threw both hands in the air and took off down the sidewalk.

Snow sank down on the first step of the physics building. He hadn't thought anything could dim his excitement about the dance. Wrong.

Come on, this isn't about you.

Yeah, I was a thoughtless asshole to Winston.

Yep. Bad karma, my friend.

Snow shuddered.

ANITRA LAUGHED as Harold staggered across the threshold of his home, carrying her. *Good way to get dropped, but the niceties must be observed.* He lowered her to her feet inside the entry.

"Welcome home, Mrs. Kingsley."

"Thank you, Dr. Kingsley. Won't everyone be surprised when we tell them?" *Yes, especially Reynaldi.* She held out her hand to admire her combination engagement and wedding ring. They were worth a pretty penny. She'd made sure of that.

He kissed her ear. She hated that but succeeded in not shuddering. "Shall we slip upstairs for a little preliminary honeymoon activity before the dance?" He chuckled. "I've waited a long time."

"You've been so understanding of my scruples, but I must make you wait a little longer. After all, this is my chance to put on the red carpet glamour for once, so I need a couple of hours to primp. I want everyone to be so happy at your choice of wife." She glanced up through her lashes. "And once we get into bed, I don't want to have any reason to leave for many, many hours."

"I fear you have a point, because I'd happily forgo the dance altogether for a chance to get you under me finally." He sighed. "And that would be unwise, since I'm expected to help chaperone. Besides, I wouldn't miss Snowden making his appearance with Riley Prince."

Her brows slammed together, and she had to take a breath to smooth them out. "What do you mean?"

He helped her off with her coat and hung it up, then did the same with his. "We've been so caught up in the sudden wedding plans, I forgot to tell you. Our big man on campus, the heroic Riley Prince, has come out as gay and asked Snow to the homecoming dance. This all just happened, so I'm sure it will be a bit of a sensation. I don't want Snow to get hurt in the cross fire. You know how sensitive he is."

"Oh yes, of course." The little shit would steal her big moment at the dance. Damn him. That big hunk of gorgeous was way too good for that little pipsqueak. "Why don't you get comfortable, I'll bring you a cocktail, and then I'll go try out my bathroom for the first time."

Harold removed his suit jacket, loosened his tie, and sat in the disgusting easy chair he favored in the living room. He picked up some tome on the life of Einstein. *Jesus.* "I'll take you up on that, my dear. Enjoy your ablutions. I swear, if this house had only one bathroom, you'd never have married me."

She wrinkled her nose. "Boys pee on the floor. I've always said, the secret to a happy marriage is one bed and two bathrooms." Laughing, she headed for the kitchen.

"There's ice in the bar, dear," he said, waving toward it.

"Oh, I know, but I put some cocktail glasses in the kitchen refrigerator to chill. Plus, we may be married, but I'm not ready to reveal my secret cocktail ingredients to you yet. That's far too intimate."

He leaned his head back and closed his eyes. "Ah, the truth to your power over me comes out. I married you to learn how you make such delicious cocktails."

"Yes, but I won't tell." She laughed. *I'll never fucking tell.*

SNOW STARED out the car window at the country club the college had rented for the homecoming dance. *Wow, this is it.* He'd been scared a few times in his life, but never quite like this. The minute they walked in, they'd be the center of attention. He hated that.

You're not exactly invisible when you're playing chess, idiot.

That's different. I'm not really there.

You're weird.

You ought to know.

"Are you having a conversation with yourself again?" Riley laughed as he backed into the space, shifted into park, and flipped off the ignition.

Snow turned and looked at his golden vision. "Yes, I'm afraid I am."

"Who's winning?"

Snow managed a smile despite the butterflies. *Don't be selfish. Riley's the one who's nervous.* "How are you feeling?"

Riley blew out a long column of air. "More nervous than before my championship game my senior year in high school, when I knew if I blew it I might not get the scholarship."

Snow took hold of Riley's big hand. "I know you must be so scared."

"How did it feel when you came out?"

Snow shrugged. "I never really did. My grandmother didn't think much about it, and as I told you, I didn't have many friends. So when I started college, I just told people I was gay and that was that."

"How did you know?"

He smiled and stared down at his hand, twined with Riley's. "I've never felt the slightest twinge of attraction to a girl. Since I didn't have any peer pressure to date girls or moon over them, I just accepted that for me, boys were the thing."

"No religious stuff?"

He shook his head. "I come from a family of scientists. I didn't know my parents well because they were constantly traveling on research expeditions. Even my grandmother was a mathematician. Never went to church."

"Probably just as well. My parents had to struggle a little with their religious upbringing but came down firmly on my side. I've always been grateful and appreciative."

"So if they accept you, why shouldn't other people? Certainly no one else has more right to judge."

"You do have a clear way of seeing things."

Wish Winston thought so. "Just makes sense."

"Have I told you how beautiful you look in your tux? I didn't think anything could shine like your hair, but that does. Man."

Snow ran a hand over the silk. "I asked the tailor to give me something fashionable. I never could have picked it on my own. They don't make tuxedos in khaki."

Riley laughed. "You'll be the most gorgeous man at the ball."

"Have you looked in the mirror?"

"Thank you. It means so much to me to have you with me. Not nearly as scared. Let's go in and have fun."

Snow opened the car door and stepped out. He wasn't going to say that sometimes, for him, fun could be challenging.

CHAPTER 10

INSTANT AWKWARD. Riley walked up beside Snow and tucked his hand through his arm. As they got closer to the club doors and more and more students and faculty appeared, Riley's arm got tenser, until Snow slipped his arm out and they walked side by side. Inside, they lined up with people waiting to check in at the reception table. People said hi to Riley and glanced at Snow, but no one asked the obvious—until they got up to the head of the English department, Mrs. Ishwood. She beamed. "Riley, great to see you." She looked right past Snow. "Where's Courtney?"

"Uh, I don't know, ma'am." She frowned. "We're not together anymore."

"Oh dear. I'm so sorry. I didn't mean to pour salt in wounds."

"No, ma'am, it's fine."

"So sorry." She passed him his nametag and an envelope. "Your drink and food tickets are in there, for you and—oh dear."

He took the envelope. "Thank you."

She looked up at Snow with a slight crease between her brows. "You're that chess boy, aren't you?"

"Snowden Reynaldi, ma'am."

She searched through her list. "I don't have you down."

Riley took an audible breath. "He's my, uh, guest, Mrs. Ishwood."

"Oh, good. Good." She looked confused, and the man next to her, one of the music instructors, nudged her. She looked at him, then back up at them. "Well, have a good time."

As they walked away, she turned to the music guy, and her face lit up with understanding. Clearly Mrs. Ishwood wasn't high on the rumor tree.

At the door to the ballroom, a group of girls and guys all tried to crowd through at once. The crush pushed Riley against Snow, and he actually jumped. He looked down. "Sorry."

"It's okay."

Inside, music blared and people milled around, some checking the numbers on their tickets with the numbers on the tables. A long buffet lined the walls around the room, but apparently they were supposed to go get the food according to table number. Riley examined the tickets. Snow saw the number four. When Riley glanced around the room, his gaze fixed on table four and his fair skin turned whiter. Of course, he'd been seated with his teammates and fraternity brothers, one of whom was Rog. Rog sat next to a woman who would have stolen the sexy crown from JLo. Sitting next to her was a much bigger African American guy who nodded toward Riley, but he didn't smile or wave him over. Two seats sat conspicuously empty at the table.

From a foot away, Snow could still feel Riley trembling. All around the big room, people whispered and stared. Snow wanted to run. *No way.* He had to be the strong one. He rested a hand on Riley's arm. "Why don't we go use some of those drink tickets?"

"What? Oh, good idea."

Snow pulled him toward the back bar. Suddenly a big hand landed on Riley's shoulder. "Hey, man, those dudes give new meaning to the term spherical asshole, and I don't mean that in a good way. Come on over to our table. I sent Wiznicki and his girl over to hang out with the homophobes."

Snow looked up at the tall, lanky guy he'd seen in the coach's office. Danny.

Danny stuck out his hand. "Hi. I remember you. Hell, I'd want to come out for you too. You are fucking beautiful. I'm Danny. Remember me?"

Snow grinned. "No filters?"

"That would be me."

Riley nodded, though he didn't quite smile. "Thanks, Danny. We're in." They followed Danny to a round table where Snow met Stanley and Esther, Ed and his fiancée, Jennifer, and Danny's date, Carlos Herrera. Carlos was out of college and in dentistry school, and he must have practiced on himself, because his teeth were gorgeous.

While the band played, most people concentrated on food and the nonalcoholic punch rather than dancing. When Riley and Snow got back to their seats, Carlos passed a flask to Riley. "Here, man. That punch needs a lot of help."

Riley held up a hand. "I better not. I'm designated driver. But Snow can have all he wants."

Snow shook his head. "I'm not much of a drinker. Thanks."

They both picked at their food. Riley talked a little football with Danny, but he didn't look comfortable. A rise in noise volume near the entrance made them both look up in time to see Courtney arrive on the arm of a handsome guy Snow had seen on the football team. "Who's that?"

"Second-string quarterback. He's a junior. He'll take over as first-string for me after I graduate. He's good."

Danny leaned over. "Looks like she promoted him to first-string already. Way to get even, I guess."

Snow watched her smile and cling to her date's arm. If he didn't know she'd been a beard for Riley, he'd have thought she was a betrayed woman paying him back.

Another tall, athletic-looking guy stopped behind them, a pretty girl on his arm. He patted Riley's shoulder. "Hey, man, good to see you."

"Thanks."

He held out a hand to Snow. "I'm Mike Henderson. This is my girl, Sheila." She smiled. Mike looked back at Riley. "I heard. Takes guts. I'm proud of you, man."

Riley looked half pleased and half embarrassed. "Thanks."

"See ya." He walked off.

Snow said, "He seems like a nice guy."

"Yeah. Captain of the lacrosse team. We're not close, but I like him."

The music got a bit louder, and more people hit the floor. Carlos took Danny's hand. "Come on, guapo. Let's show them how it's done."

As Carlos and Danny walked to the floor with lots of eyes following them, Professor Kingsley and Anitra danced by. *Wow.* She swooped and twirled, holding her pure white dress out to the side like she was performing in some kind of Viennese opera. The dress outdid everything in the room— so much so that it hovered at ostentatious, but Anitra's bold features and flaming hair beat the flamboyance of the gown into submission. Professor Kingsley smiled, but under the twinkle lights his face looked gray and his cheeks sunken.

Riley whispered, "Is Professor Kingsley okay?"

"I don't know. He's been really tired lately."

Danny cha-chaed up to Riley. "Come on, man. Get out here and show some support for the team."

"Team?"

"The rainbow team. Come on." He danced away.

Riley looked a little ill himself. "You want to?"

"No need. You've made enough of a statement for one night."

Riley stared at the dance floor. "Oh hell, come on." He stood and took Snow's hand. "Might as well go all the way, right?" Three steps later, he turned and held up his arms. "I think I better lead, because that's all I know how to do."

Snow nodded. "Good, because I barely know how to dance at all."

Riley's chest expanded, and then he grinned, the first half-natural smile of the night. "Let's give 'em their money's worth."

Snow stepped into Riley's arms and could practically hear the collective sucking of breath from the crowd. Anybody who might have thought they were just two guys hanging out now knew the worst. Snow stumbled a little. "Sorry. I never really had a dance teacher."

"I'm not that good either, so let's fake it together." Riley smiled and pulled Snow a little closer. Not tight. No big statements. Hell, Riley just being on that floor with a guy exploded most of the heads in the room.

As they rocked tentatively, Professor Kingsley and Ms. Popescu danced by. She grandly swooped her skirt, extended her left hand, and waved. "Hellllooo."

Wait. What was on her hand?

Riley whispered, "Was she wearing a wedding ring?"

"I don't see how. I mean, the professor would tell me, I think." Tell him? Surely he'd invite Snow.

"She actually looks like she's going to a wedding tonight."

"Yes. That's quite a dress."

The band stopped the slow song they were playing and plunged into something up-tempo. Riley stepped back. "Too much for me."

They walked back to the table. Riley leaned in to Snow. "I feel like everyone's looking at me."

"That's because they are."

Riley snorted a laugh. "Way to make a guy feel better."

Snow held up his hands. "Facts." But he grinned.

Carlos popped up from his seat. "Why doesn't pretty Snow dance with me now?"

Snow's eyes widened. "Did you see how badly I dance? I'll fall on my face."

"No, I'll teach you. There will be no falling." Carlos grabbed his hand.

Snow looked back at Riley as Carlos led him to the dance floor, but Danny was already waving his hands in what looked like an intense football discussion.

Carlos popped his head into Snow's line of sight and pointed to his own eyes. "Look right here." Snow instantly stared at his feet. Carlos laughed and tipped Snow's chin up. "Here." He smiled, and crinkles appeared beside his huge brown eyes. "Okay." He took hold of Snow's hand and waist far more firmly than Riley had and pushed Snow backward.

Snow stumbled. "Sorry."

"No sorry. Just relax and enjoy."

Snow managed to take about five steps before he stumbled again, but Carlos just kept dancing. Pretty soon, Snow was actually moving to the Latin beat.

Carlos twirled, and Snow made an attempt to follow. "You see. I knew you had potential."

"I'm a quick learner."

"Well, well. It's not enough to decimate the football team. Now you want to be the next Ricky Martin?"

Snow froze, almost knocking Carlos off his feet. "Hello, Ms. Popescu. Hello, Professor. This is my friend, Carlos Herrera."

She extended her hand. "I'm delighted. Any friend of Snow's is a friend of ours. But actually, he's incorrect. I'm not Ms. Popescu any longer. I'm Mrs. Kingsley. So happy to meet you."

Carlos must have felt Snow tense, because he looked at him sharply, then back at Anitra. "Encantado."

She fanned herself. "Oh my, Harold. Isn't that Spanish accent sexy?"

Professor Kingsley looked awful. Winded, gray, and now embarrassed and horrified. "I'm sorry not to have told you earlier, Snow. I was going to call you before the dance, but time slipped away." He frowned and looked even more confused. "We'll have a big wedding in the next few months, and you'll stand up for me."

Anitra laughed. "Yes, that will be lovely."

Snow gazed at his mentor. "Are you feeling well, Professor?"

Kingsley's eyes appeared glazed. "Oh? Yes, I think so. A bit tired. Not as young as I used to be. All this dancing."

Anitra pulled him closer. "You should have said something, darling. Let's go sit for a while—"

The microphone on the bandstand squeaked. "Just a quick break from the dancing, ladies and gentlemen, while we announce the homecoming queen and king." The noise level rose in the room as several faculty members filed onto the stage. Ms. Po—Mrs. Kingsley said, "Excuse me. I have to help out." She swept up onto the stage, causing another rise in the noise level and getting a half smile from the professor.

Snow took his arm. "Sir, are you really all right?"

"What? Oh yes, isn't she beautiful?"

There's your answer, idiot. Leave the man alone.

But—

Leave him alone.

The dean of students stepped up to the microphone, with Anitra beside him. "Being chosen homecoming queen and homecoming king is a special honor because it represents the approval and respect of your peers as well as requiring certain academic and extracurricular honors. We certainly had some splendid nominees this year. So without further ado, may I have the envelope for homecoming queen, please, Ms. Popescu?"

Anitra whipped an envelope from the man standing behind her and handed it to the dean. Obviously she was there for window dressing since the guy could just as easily have handed the winner's name to the dean himself.

The dean smiled and made a big show of opening the envelope slowly. "Gosh. Shouldn't we talk about the new academic offerings for next semester?"

On cue, everyone yelled, "Nooooo."

Finally he ripped the paper. "It's my pleasure to announce that your homecoming queen is a brilliant student and one of your very favorite cheerleaders. Are you ready? Courtney Taylor!"

Snow smiled and applauded loudly, since he knew how much she'd helped Riley. He glanced over his shoulder to see Riley beaming and clapping his hands. As Snow looked, Riley glanced up and flashed the dimples. Good. He was happy about Courtney. Plus, it seemed like a good accident that Snow stood in the middle of the dance floor, so he wouldn't be sitting beside Riley when everyone turned to applaud him as homecoming king. Less embarrassing for both of them—not that anyone had missed their dance.

Courtney laughed and giggled and got huge applause when she made it to the stage. "Oh, thank you so much. I'm very surprised. This means so much to me."

They handed her flowers and put a crown on her head. Then the dean smiled and said, "Stay right here while we deliver to you your king."

The whisper level rose as Anitra made a big show of collecting the envelope from the guy. She passed it to the dean with a flourish. He smiled, and the drummer from the band, clearly getting bored with the delay, did a riff.

The dean opened the envelope. "Ah. I see."

Anitra looked over his shoulder. Her eyes widened, she looked directly at Riley, then whispered something in the dean's ear. A short sotto voce conversation ensued. What on earth were they doing? *Announce Riley and get it over with.*

The dean leaned in to the mike. "Your homecoming king is Roget Brown."

A collective gasp. Then gradually people started to applaud, but different comments punctuated the noise.

"No way."

"Good one."

"What are they thinking?"

And the classic, "Show the fag he ain't no king."

Rog made his way to the podium, looking as shocked as anybody in the room. Snow glanced at Riley. His cheekbones gleamed pink, but the rest of his face looked pale. He'd plastered a smile on and applauded for Rog like the guy wasn't NorCal's chief homophobe.

Carlos didn't even bother to applaud. "What's going on? Danny told me Riley was a sure winner. And I know that guy who won is Danny's least favorite fraternity brother. What kind of fix happened here?"

Snow felt like he'd taken a board to the head. "No idea. Maybe the administration got word that he came out and wouldn't let him win."

Professor Kingsley grasped his own chest. "Oh no, that can't be. NorCal wouldn't endure a discriminatory policy."

Snow frowned. "Maybe Mrs. Kingsley knows what happened. She sure seems to be involved."

"Mrs. Kingsley? Oh, Anitra? Anitra."

Snow turned to run to Riley.

Stop. You'll just focus more attention on him at this moment of humiliation.

He has nothing to be humiliated about.

Tell that to the guy who's not homecoming king.

Snow looked back at the stage. Courtney stared at Rog like a large reptile had gotten loose in the country club. No matter their romantic fiction, she was Riley's friend. She wasn't going to like the guy who hated Riley. The dean handed Rog the king's scepter. Anitra gave him a big kiss on the cheek, after which she looked directly at Snow. Damn. That woman had something to do with this. But what? Why would she care?

Snow spun toward Professor Kingsley. "Sir, do you have any idea—" He stopped. The professor stood wobbling on his feet, with one hand extended toward Anitra on the stage and the other clutching at the tuxedo coat on his chest.

"Sir, are you okay?" He stepped closer and took hold of the professor's arm. "Professor Kingsley?"

Carlos came up beside the professor on his other side. "You okay?"

Suddenly, like a tall, thin rag doll, the professor crumpled to the ground. Carlos caught him before he could hit the floor too hard and lowered him gently. "Man, he's cold as ice."

Snow fell on his knees beside the professor. "Professor Kingsley. Help! Somebody help."

Riley slid up beside him, flopped on his knees, listened to the professor's chest, and started CPR. "He's not breathing much at all. Maybe his heart. Call 911, fast."

Carlos was already on his phone, giving directions to the ambulance.

Snow clutched the professor's icy hand to his chest. "Professor, don't worry. You'll be okay. You have to be okay." Tears slid down his face, but he didn't care.

The cool voice came from above him. "What on earth is happening here? What are you doing to my husband?"

CHAPTER 11

SNOW LISTENED to Riley's soft snores. He stretched his legs on the hard waiting room couch and snuggled his head deeper into Riley's lap. Jesus, only Riley's warmth kept him from dissolving into shards of ice. He glanced out the one window into darkness. Hours with no word. Of course, the hospital staff had let Anitra go back to see the professor as soon as he came out of lab tests. Snow couldn't go anywhere near him. He didn't qualify as family. No one cared that the professor was all the family Snow had.

More tears collected at the corners of his eyes, and he shook his head to free them. No way. He'd cried enough. He had to keep his wits. The professor might need him. If he still needed anything. Oh God, why wouldn't somebody tell him something? He dragged in a long, shaky breath.

"Hey." Riley petted his hair with a warm hand.

Snow turned so he looked straight up into Riley's face. "Hey."

"Sorry I fell asleep on you."

Snow raised a hand and touched Riley's cheek. "You had a rough evening."

"Not as rough as you."

"I can't believe they did some weird, homophobic, discriminatory play and named Roget homecoming king."

"Doesn't matter at all in light of real problems, does it?" Riley smiled sadly.

"It does matter. They shouldn't get away with stuff like that."

"Maybe Rog just had more votes."

"Bullshit!"

Riley really laughed. "I've never heard you say that before."

"It makes me mad."

"Have you heard anything about Professor Kingsley?"

Snow sat up. "Not a thing, and I'm about to run screaming into the critical care ward with an axe."

"Maybe I should make them aware of their impending doom, and they might give up a little data." He wrapped an arm around Snow's tense shoulders.

Snow shook his head. "I can't shake the idea that Ms. Popescu knows something about—well, everything."

"Mrs. Kingsley, you mean?"

"I guess."

Riley looked into Snow's face. "The professor seemed to verify that they're married, right?"

"Yes." He chewed the inside of his cheek. "But doesn't it seem weird that they rush out and get married and then—this?"

"These kinds of tragedies happen all the time. Maybe the professor sensed he was ill and wanted to, I don't know, reaffirm his youth or something."

"Maybe."

Riley tightened his arm. "I know this has to be so awful for you."

Snow nodded. *I'm not crazy. Or overreacting. That woman is weird.*

Like he'd manifested her, Anitra swept into the waiting room. "Oh, you're still here. How kind of you."

Snow leaped to his feet. "How is he?"

She tightened her jaw. "Unconscious."

"Oh God."

"There's a heart arrhythmia, which is affecting his breathing."

"That sounds bad."

"It is, I'm afraid." She walked over and slid an arm around Snow's shoulders, her brilliant hair brushing his cheek.

Don't tense. Don't tense.

"We have to help each other now. That's what he would want."

Snow nodded.

She released him. "Why don't you go home and get some rest? Come back tomorrow and we'll talk about—" She waved her hand idly. "—things. The future. You know."

"I'd rather stay here."

She let out a little sigh. Frustration? "I know, dear, but you have school."

"This is Sunday. Almost, anyway."

"Oh, is it? I'd forgotten. Anyway, you need your rest. I promise to call if there's the slightest change."

"Please—"

"Riley, will you take Snow home, please?"

"Yes, ma'am."

"Try to convince him it's for his own good."

Riley wrapped a big, warm arm around Snow. "Come on, sweetheart."

It was almost worth leaving just to hear Riley call him sweetheart.

As they walked down the hall, Riley murmured, "She's got all the power in here since she's his wife. We have to do what she says for now."

Snow paused and looked up at him. "So you don't think I'm a paranoid idiot?"

"I think you're the most brilliant person I ever met. If you think she's weird, then so do I."

Tears pressed out of his eyes, and he swiped at them. "Thank you."

"Come on. Let's go home."

"Home?"

Riley smiled. "My place or yours?"

"In my apartment, I like my rug. And my chess sets. But I like everything about yours." He managed to smile.

"In that case, let's stop at your apartment, get your chess set and some clothes, and then go to my place and settle in."

"Really?" Was Riley Prince inviting him to sleep over?

Riley wrapped his arm around Snow again and resumed walking. "No pressure. I've even got an extra bedroom with a really terrible futon, which I volunteer to sleep on because I have to practice my chivalry and shit." He looked down and grinned. Dimples popped out all over. Then he sobered. "I know right now isn't the best time for romantic encounters, but I don't want you to be alone."

Snow stopped walking, his head hanging.

"What? Are you okay?"

"How can you be so wonderful?"

"Am I? I'm inspired by you, I guess." He hugged Snow a little tighter. "I'm just a regular dumb jock who wants to live up to having you as my boyfriend."

"I'm just a freaky, weird nerd who talks to himself and doesn't even have the good manners to do it out loud."

Riley laughed. "Come on, my nerd. Let's go home."

ANITRA SLIPPED into the back door of the professor's house. Her house. She smiled at the shiny appliances and big granite island. *Mine.* She'd told Harold the condo she lived in was hers, but in fact she'd borrowed it from a friend for a small piece of the action. A debt soon to be paid.

She whirled. Jesus, she could smell the lube two rooms away. Tossing her purse on the counter, she hurried through the kitchen and dining room, then yanked the blinds closed in the living room. "Don't you do anything else?" Hunter lay on the couch wanking off to porn—again.

"I'm bored."

"Get a job."

"I've got a job." He sat and reached out, pulling her down onto his lap.

She wriggled back and pointed at his very erect and sticky penis. "I'm not sure there's room for both of us, plus, I don't want lube all over my clothes."

"I guess we'll have to find a place to put my cock so it doesn't take up so much room."

"That sounds good, but first I have to e-mail the people at the Anderson Chess Tournament and tell them that Snowden Reynaldi is too devastated to compete in the championships. I want it to be on their desks as soon as they get in tomorrow."

"Is it true? Is he too upset to compete?"

She stared at the window. "I'm going to see to it that he is."

IN THE shelter of Riley's good right arm, Snow walked up the front steps of the house and reached out to open the front door since Riley had Snow's stuffed backpack in his other hand.

The door flew open. *Whoops.* Mrs. Wishus grabbed Snow's arm and pulled him inside. "Oh, you poor dears, you must be exhausted. I heard about Harold. Awful. Just awful."

"You know Professor Kingsley, ma'am?" Of course, it wouldn't have surprised him to learn she knew the president of the United States personally.

"Yes, from way back. It seems so unlikely that he would have a heart condition. Always such a robust man."

Snow blinked a few times.

"Oh dear, I'm so sorry. You two head upstairs, and I'll bring you something to eat so you can go right to bed."

Snow's cheeks heated, but she didn't seem to think anything about it. She bustled into her apartment, leaving the blue door open.

Riley grinned. "Come on. Let's do as she says."

Snow stumbled as he climbed the steep stairs, and Riley held him up. "Easy, sweetheart. You're almost to a place you can rest."

Rest. Funny how half of him wanted to curl in a ball and never stop sleeping—and the other half wanted Riley to curl up around his balls and never stop sucking. Heat singed his ears. He was glad the staircase was dim.

In the apartment, Riley led the way down the hall to the inner reaches where Snow hadn't been before. Just as ever-so-slightly shabby and totally homey as the rest. He opened the door to a big bedroom complete with unmade bed and some very large sneakers in the middle of the floor, but otherwise pretty neat. He bustled over to the king-size bed. "Uh, sorry. I left kind of in a hurry. I'll get some fresh sheets."

Snow sat on the edge of the bed. "No. I like it just the way it is." It smelled so good—just like Riley.

Riley smiled at him and touched his cheek.

"Oh, boyyyyysss."

Riley glanced over his shoulder. "Coming, Eudora." He helped Snow up. "Come on, let's eat. She's an amazing cook."

"Don't know if I can eat."

"Try. Come on." He grinned like he had a secret.

In the dining area, Riley's table practically sagged under all the goodies. Two place settings with big bowls full of something steaming, a loaf of bread that looked homemade, and dishes of butter, pickles, cheese, and olives were spread out on the checked tablecloth. She smiled. "Sit down and enjoy."

Had to admit, it smelled amazing, like Riley said. Snow sat and leaned forward to peek. *Vegetable soup. Nice. No big thing.* Mrs. Wishus handed him a spoon, and he filled it up, blew, then sipped. *Holy cow.* Like every vegetable had its own unique flavor bursting in a different place on his tongue. But more than that, the broth had to be ambrosia, a gift from some random earth god. One more mouthful and he started shoveling soup in as fast as the spoon and moderately good manners allowed. Mrs. Wishus took the nearly empty bowl and handed him a big piece of bread, warm and dripping butter. "Take a taste of this while I get you more soup."

Riley grinned as he consumed soup at only a slightly slower pace than Snow.

The bread. Oh God, the bread. "This has to be manna." Crisp on the outside, soft on the inside, with pieces of grains he couldn't even identify—he stopped chewing. "These aren't nuts, are they?"

Mrs. Wishus set another full bowl of soup in front of him. "Oh no, dear. I'd never give you nuts."

He cocked his head at her as she bustled back to get Riley more soup. How did she know he was allergic? Maybe just because so many people were.

They both ended up eating three full bowls of soup, consuming the entire loaf of bread with chunks of some fantastic cheese, and shoving down a handful of olives. Snow tried not to talk with his mouth full. "Oh, thank you. I didn't know I was so hungry."

"My pleasure, cutie. Riley, dear, just put the dishes on the counter when you're done. I left you both some dessert and surprises in the bag." She pointed to a brown sack, rolled at the top. "Have a good night. Get plenty of rest. I know how horrible this is for you, Snow, but I want you to trust that good always prevails. It may not look that way, but truth can't be hidden forever." She walked to the door, waved, and was gone.

Snow shook his head. "So amazing."

"Yeah. She's like my second mom."

"Lucky."

"Do you believe what she said?"

Snow sighed. "About good prevailing? When I look around the world, I don't see truth all that often. Do you?"

"Maybe we just can't see it. Maybe truth looks like something else, you know, like waves and particles and shit." Riley shrugged. "You're the physicist." He pointed at the bag. "Shall I check on dessert?"

Snow nodded. *Truth having two forms. Looking like something else.*

Riley hopped up and grabbed the sack from the floor next to the door. With a snap he opened the top and peered inside. "Oh my God, Eudora's chocolate cake with lemon cream cheese frosting." Riley lifted out a plate with two huge slices of cake under a plastic wrap; then he started to laugh.

"What?"

He kept chuckling as he set the cake plate on the table. Were his cheeks really red? Riley shook his head. "She has a sense of humor."

"What is it?"

He pulled out a box of condoms and a large bottle of lube with a pushdown dispenser. He rotated the bottle so it faced Snow. "Vanilla flavored."

Snow dropped his head onto his arm. Had to hide his blush since obviously Mrs. Wishus had somehow intuited that he loved vanilla.

The bag rustled, and he looked up. Riley carefully placed the gifts back in the bag. "We'll save these for when you feel up to it. I mean, if you do, okay?" He set the bag aside and walked back to the table. "Let's have cake and then get some shut-eye. I actually have a game tomorrow."

"I'm so sorry. You need rest and I'm dragging you all over the county."

"I'm worried about the professor too. Besides, I'm used to no sleep. I have to study a lot to keep up my average, and with football and the fraternity, there's never enough time."

Snow nodded toward Riley's laptop sitting on the counter where Mrs. Wishus had probably moved it. "Can I borrow the laptop? Mine's in my backpack."

"Sure."

"Anitra said the professor had heart arrhythmia that was causing difficulty breathing, right?" He typed in the symptoms and searched. "There are a ton of links for heart arrhythmia, but they all seem to be related to atrial fibrillation and supraventricular tachycardia. Things like that."

Riley removed the plastic wrap, and the smell of lemon filled the air. "Easy for you to say."

"The weird thing is, I've known the professor for two years, and I've never seen a sign of heart trouble. Like Mrs. Wishus said, he's always been robust."

"But people have heart attacks all the time and they seemed really healthy before, right?" Riley sat in front of his cake.

"Yes, but that's a heart attack. This stuff usually has more symptoms. I don't ever remember him having shortness of breath. It's strange for this to have happened so suddenly."

Riley pointed with his fork. "You're not eating. You won't believe how good this is."

Snow carried the laptop with him to the table, picked up the fork, and took a bite. He dropped the fork. "Wow. What is that stuff?"

"I told you. If they sold this on street corners, it could replace the heroin trade." Riley took another bite while Snow dug in. The sweetness of the chocolate and the bite of the lemon married in perfect delight. Riley wiped at his lips with a napkin. "So seriously, what are you thinking? That something strange happened to the professor that caused this collapse?"

Snow pointed at the screen. "It says some medications can cause arrhythmias. Thyroid, for one. Maybe he was prescribed a medication that caused these symptoms."

"Surely that's one of the first things the doctors will ask about."

"But Ms. Po—Mrs. Kingsley won't know. I mean, she's only been around him a short time."

"Do you know anything new he was taking?"

"No. But I did notice him getting more tired and gray over the last week or so. If I went to his house, maybe I'd find something."

Riley waved a fork. "Snow, it's her house now. You can't just go in."

"Hell."

"When you go back to the hospital tomorrow, tell them what you saw. Maybe it will help."

Snow shook his head. "There has to be more. I need to find it." He wiped a hand over his head. "Before it's too late."

Riley got up and put their empty plates in the sink. "Chances are they're already exploring that angle. So don't worry." He ran a hand over Snow's neck. "Sorry, that's a dumb thing to say. But at least get some rest. There's nothing you can do tonight."

"Yes. I guess you're right."

Riley helped him out of the chair and walked him back to the bedroom. Snow's eyes strayed to the paper bag containing Mrs. Wishus's gifts.

CHAPTER 12

A HALF hour later, Snow lay in the big bed with the great-smelling sheets, staring at the ceiling. Riley had tucked him in, given him a kiss on the cheek, and gone to wash the dishes. The clanking and banging from the kitchen attested to the work in progress.

What could the professor have taken that could cause him to be so sick?

Go to sleep. You can't figure it out tonight.

Not really sleepy.

Maybe you need relaxing. A blowjob would be nice.

I don't think Riley's interested in another blowjob. Maybe I didn't taste good or something.

All guys are interested in blowjobs if they're getting them.

I shouldn't be thinking about blowjobs anyway.

Are you crazy?

This isn't the time.

You're in Riley Prince's house with a large bottle of vanilla lube. Somebody thinks it's the time.

Go to sleep.

He pulled the covers over his ears and focused on his breathing. The kitchen sounds stopped and everything got quiet.

You're not sleeping.

Shut up and go to sleep.

Where do you think he left the lube?

Riley's got a game.

All the more reason to relax him.

I don't know how to give a blowjob.

Fake it. How bad can it be?

"Hell." Snow sat up in bed. "I'm a terrible person. My best friend is dying and I'm thinking about sex." But those were the facts. He slid out of bed and padded to the closed bedroom door barefooted, his pajama bottoms falling low over his narrow hips and his half-hard cock. *Okay, I get it. You're in charge.*

The door squeaked and he froze. Quiet. Peering down the dark hall, he tried to see if the paper bag still sat by the door. No luck. He slipped out and crept toward the dining area, where he'd last seen the bag. *Man, dark.* Near the front door, he bent over and felt around the corner where he swore he last saw it. Nothing.

"Looking for this?"

Snow jumped up fast, stumbled backward, and fell right against Riley's very bare chest—and very hard cock.

Snow tried to regain his balance, but Riley held him, tipped his chin up, and planted his lips so firmly against Snow's that the pressure must have caused his brain to fly out his ears. He wrapped his arms around that hard body and ground himself against Riley's dick like it was giving injections of eternal youth. Strange mewling sounds poured out of his throat.

Riley walked him backward until his calves hit the edge of the couch, and he fell onto soft cushions with Riley planted on him from knees to chest, his big rod hitting Snow somewhere around the thighs. The best possible topping.

Snow opened his legs and grabbed the protuberance between them, then rubbed them together in his best caterpillar imitation.

"Holy shit!"

"Feel good?"

"Jesus, yes. Where did you learn to do that?"

"Made it up."

"Genius." He thrust into Snow's tight hold. "What do you want? Anything. I'll give it to you."

"No, it's your turn. You tell me what to do. Then you'll have to show me how. But I'll do it. I love vanilla. Want me to try to give you a blowjob? That's why I was sneaking around."

Still humping Snow's legs, Riley whispered, "That sounds good, but you know what I really want?"

"No, what?"

"I want you to fuck me."

"What? Oh God."

"Have you ever fucked a guy?"

"Jesus, Riley, I hadn't been kissed until you did it. When would I have gotten around to fucking?"

"Do you want to?"

His cock throbbed so hard it neared pain. "I want to do anything to you."

"It'll come naturally." He rolled off Snow onto the floor, grabbed the huge bottle of lube he'd dropped earlier, and pumped some into his hands. "Let me grease up that lovely cock." His breath came fast. He slipped Snow's elastic down and grabbed his penis. "So beautiful." He stroked the cool gel over it.

"D-don't I need a condom?"

"You're a virgin, and I haven't had sex without a condom in years." He shrugged. "I barely have sex, since I don't really get turned on by girls, and I have to go a long way away to find a guy who doesn't know me, so mostly I use my hand." He glanced at it. "No STDs. Plus, I've been tested."

Snow swallowed and nodded. The discussion made this whole thing very real.

Riley stroked more lube on Snow's penis.

"Oh God, don't do much of that, or I'll never do anything else."

"I want you in me so bad." He pushed onto his hands and knees and started shoving lube into his butt.

Snow swallowed. He might be terrified, but his cock knew right where it wanted to be.

Riley peered over his shoulder, the lubing still underway. "You understand the principle of fucking, right?"

"Uh, I believe so."

Riley pointed at Snow's now very erect penis with the lube bottle, then squeezed more into his hand. "You put that in here." He waved at his ass.

"Yes, I understand." The last word came out as a squeak. Suddenly that idea sounded so far beyond good he bobbed up on his knees and ripped the pajama bottoms down to the floor, then sat back and pulled them off.

Riley grinned. "I like your enthusiasm." His smile faded and he sat back on his haunches, which made his dick stick up like a lighthouse. "Am I rushing you? Maybe you don't want to take such a big step so soon? Maybe this isn't the right time? We could wait."

Snow stopped with his pajama bottoms in his hand and his cock bouncing against his abdomen. "Wait?" He pointed downward. "Speak to him."

"I could suck you instead."

He liked oral sex, no doubt. But Riley wanted intercourse. He'd said he could hardly wait. It had been Snow's intention to please Riley tonight. Plus— "I don't think Mrs. Wishus would have steered us wrong."

"There is that." The grin came back.

"Not many guys are virgins at twenty. It's time." His penis gave a hop, probably in protest of his lily-white condition. "Assume your position." Snow waved grandly.

Riley giggled and rocked back up to his hands and knees. Snow positioned himself behind on his knees. Gorgeous, rock-hard globes faced him, with a glimpse of a rosy pucker in between. "Wow."

"See something you like?"

"Oh yes. However, the limitations of physics are such that I am not going to be able to get this penis into that anus. You're simply too tall."

In one move, Riley brought his head down to the cushion and spread his knees, which had the effect of lowering his butt and also stretching open his hole so it gaped at Snow. *Right there. Put it right there.*

Frozen. This was it. A couple of inches and he could learn the secrets of sex. Drips of shiny liquid seeped out of the slit in his penis. *Do it. Do it.*

Suddenly that shiny pink bottom wagged. Just a little, but definite canine qualities. Snow burst out laughing, walked forward on his knees, lined up his penis with the opening that glistened shiny with lube, took a deep breath, and— "This won't hurt you, will it? You said you don't get much sex and—"

"Do it!" His bottom wagged back and forth emphatically.

Snow grabbed Riley's ass to hold it still, repositioned, and pushed. The pressure on his penis head felt wonderful—but that was all.

"Harder." Riley reached back with both hands, pulled his cheeks apart, and exposed a deeper layer of wrinkled flesh.

Snow grabbed Riley's arm with one hand, balanced himself with the other, and pushed as hard as he could.

Pop!

Holy—hell.

His mouth opened and closed. Heat rushed up his cock and seared his balls.

"You're in. Push."

He did. His cock slipped farther into the tight, steaming channel that embraced it, soft, silky tissue widening as he plowed through, then tightening around him like a—yes, like a lover.

"Now pull out."

Whole new experience. More drag than embrace, which stimulated every tiny nerve ending until it tingled, then shrieked with the desire to explode.

"Back in, Snow. Fuck me."

Whoa. No chance he'd ever expected to hear those words. Maybe the other way around, but this had to be a rare dream. He snapped his hips in and out. Riley mewled like a kitten. *How did I do that?*

He pumped again, so fascinated by Riley's reaction it took a little of the focus off his own throbbing penis. Thank God. He'd never last otherwise. In and out.

"Fuck! That's great."

Again.

"Yeah, oh yes. Bull's-eye."

Good Lord. Power. The power to give pleasure. He plunged his dick in deep and pulled it out to the tip, then back in again and again. Flashes of light lit up his brain with each drag on his overstimulated nerves.

"Sweet Jesus, Snow. I'm getting close. So close. Plant your feet and give me your hand."

Snow struggled to squat without taking his dick out, scooted to either side of Riley's bobbing butt, curved over his back, bent his knees, and thrust as fast and hard as he could. Saying it felt good won the award for understatement.

He balanced and wrapped a hand around Riley's hips. That hand got grabbed so fast he nearly toppled. Riley wrapped Snow's hand around his big dick and then closed his own paw over Snow's and started pumping. The whole operation took the coordination of a Cirque du Soleil star, but somehow he managed to stay upright.

But oh God.

Riley bucked and pumped under him, making sounds so primal they reached deep into Snow's most primitive places. His own cock squeezed in volcanic heat, and black spots floated in front of his eyes as flashes of pleasure zinged up his spine and spiked off the end of his dick. Couldn't be happening. How could anything feel so—amazing?

Riley threw back his head. "Oh, baby." His bucking stopped, his body went rigid, and hot, wet stickiness filled Snow's hand.

That warm wetness and the deep, musky smell triggered something in his brain—and his groin. *Holy—OH!*

A rocket blazed from his balls into his cock and hit his brain in a blinding flash. Each pump of semen had its own color, its own ecstatic tremble of pleasure. One. Two. Three. How could they keep getting better? His body froze, then shook in wave after wave. His feet quit and his legs crumbled. *Falling. Falling.*

Two bodies piled on the couch cushions in a heap of bliss.

Riley murmured something.

Snow raised his head an inch. "Can't hear you. Heart's beating too hard."

"How can a virgin be so great at sex?" Riley chuckled.

"Fast learner."

"I'll say. You can give up chess and physics. You've found your calling."

"Then you'll have to give up football, because I'm only inspired by you."

Riley chuckled. "They'll find our emaciated bodies, stuck together, humping like rabbits."

"What a way to go."

"I guess it's now officially later than hell."

"And you have to play tomorrow." Snow turned on his side and stared at the shine of Riley's golden hair—and his shining butt.

"No worries. But there is one rule you need to know."

"What's that?"

"He who tops gets the washcloth from the bathroom."

Tops. Good God, he was a top. He hopped from the couch. "With pleasure."

Ten minutes later, he'd cleaned them both up—a pleasure in itself—and lay in the crook of Riley's right arm. "I hope the professor is alive." He could barely say those words.

Riley tightened his arm. "Me too, sweetheart."

"I've got to try to get in that house."

"That could be scary."

"Yes."

Five minutes later, Riley's soft breathing rustled against the cushions. Snow stared at the ceiling.

CHAPTER 13

WHAT? WHERE? The ringing phone pierced his brain. Snow opened his eyes. *Didn't I just close them?*

Two facts. He was not on the floor in his apartment. A big, warm body snuggled next to him. Oh yes, and the phone was ringing in his pajama pants, which were somewhere he couldn't immediately identify.

"Umpff. Your phone?"

I'm on the couch with Riley Prince.

Duh.

Wow.

The phone quit, but Snow's heart took up the hammering.

Riley's lips grazed his ear. "Morning."

Snow smiled, warm and liquid. *Oh yes, I so remember.* "Morning."

"Your phone was ringing."

"I couldn't find it."

Riley chuckled. "You threw those pants so far I'm surprised they landed already."

"I was in a bit of a hurry."

Riley nibbled under his ear. "Sadly, speaking of hurrying, I better get up and power over to the stadium. You gonna come watch me play?"

"I—" The pants started ringing again. "I better answer. It could be about the professor." Snow leaped from the bed, located his pajamas, and fished in the pocket. "Hello."

"Is this Snowden Reynaldi?"

"Yes, yes it is."

"Grandmaster Reynaldi, this is Eleanor Turks from the Anderson International Chess Tournament."

"Oh, yes, ma'am." Thank God. Not bad news about the professor.

"I received an e-mail from a Mrs. Kingsley informing us of Professor Kingsley's illness."

Odd. "Yes, ma'am. He's very sick."

"I'm so very sorry to hear it. She told us that you are much too upset to compete and wish to withdraw from the competition."

"What? Withdraw?" He sank onto the floor, and Riley leaned off the edge of the couch, staring at him.

Riley mouthed, "Everything okay?"

Snow frowned and shrugged.

"Yes, that's what she said. But I'm calling you because I certainly wanted to be sure that it's your intention to withdraw. After all, it will change the nature of the contest considerably. I'm sure there are many players who would be delighted to hear that they don't have to beat Snowden Reynaldi in order to win. And a lot of spectators who won't bother to come if you're not playing." She gave a tight laugh. "I take it from your reaction that you may not have known this e-mail was sent?"

"Uh, no, ma'am. Mrs. Kingsley is a newlywed and, of course, is herself very upset. She doesn't know me well, so she might have assumed my reaction. In fact, I know for certain that the thing Professor Kingsley would want most is for me to compete. I wouldn't consider withdrawing."

"Ah, there's the Snowden Reynaldi I know. Good show, young man. We're proud of you. I'll disregard this e-mail and expect to see you at the tournament in a few weeks."

"Yes, ma'am. I'll be there."

"Brilliant. My best wishes for the professor's rapid recovery."

"Thank you." He clicked the phone and stared at Riley. "She told them I was withdrawing from the championships."

"Without even asking you?"

"Yes."

"What the hell is she thinking?"

"I'm not sure, but she's a chess player too. I wonder if she's entered?"

"That would be good to know." Riley sat up, looking yummy in his taut, shiny golden skin.

"I think I need to go over to the professor's house. If she's there, I can ask about this. If not, I'll go in and look for something the professor might have taken that could put him in a coma."

Riley frowned. "I don't want you to go without me. It might not be safe."

Snow smiled. "I kind of doubt she's going to attack me or anything. She's probably got some good excuse for trying to pull me out. I'll pretend to believe it."

"Can't you wait until after the game?"

"I have to get to the hospital as soon as I can. If I can find something that might help him, that would be best. I'm so sorry to miss your game."

Riley wrapped an arm around Snow's neck. "I'm just worried about you."

"Thank you." He wrapped his arms around Riley's neck and snuggled, trying to ignore the rise of his overanxious penis. Grinning, he looked down. "We'll get to you later."

Riley patted the head of Snow's cock. "That's a promise." He walked toward the bathroom. "I'll drive you."

A half hour later, Snow stared out the car window as Riley pulled to the curb a block from Professor Kingsley's house. "This is good. I'll walk from here."

"How will you get to the hospital?"

"My bike's at the physics building."

"Okay. But will you call me as soon as you get there and leave me a message so I don't go crazy?"

"Yes. As soon as I get there."

Riley took Snow's hand. "Be careful."

"Have a good game." Nerves jumping, he slid out of Riley's old car, waved, and started walking toward the beautiful old traditional home the professor lived in. Snow swallowed. Or used to live in. No cars on the street in front of the house.

He cut down the side of the neighbor's to check out the professor's garage, located just behind his home at the end of a long driveway. His classic Mercedes was gone, but an old, battered American car with chipped green paint sat outside the garage. Was that Anitra's? He'd never seen it before. He stared at the side door to the house. The one that led into the kitchen. *Here goes.*

He walked up the steps, took a deep breath, and knocked softly. *Don't be there. Don't be there.*

Quiet. Nothing.

He rapped again for good measure and then stuck his hand in his pocket for his key to the professor's house. As he drew it out, the door flew open, and Anitra stared out at him. Her red hair flew wildly around her face, lipstick smeared her cheek, and she gathered a floral kimono around her. "Oh, oh dear."

Snow stepped back, almost fell off the step, grabbed the rail, and managed to right himself. "I'm so sorry. I wasn't sure if you were here." He took his hand from his pocket.

"Yes, well, obviously I am. I came home for a quick nap and must have fallen more deeply asleep than I expected."

"I, uh, was on my way to get my bicycle and thought I'd stop to see if you had an update on the professor."

She glanced over her shoulder. "Nothing hopeful, I'm afraid. He's still unconscious."

"I just wondered if there was a chance he could have taken some medication that would cause a reaction."

She frowned. "That was the first thing the doctors asked."

"Yes. Yes, I suppose it would be." He stared at his tennis shoes. "Uh, I got a call this morning from the Anderson Tournament. They said you sent an e-mail withdrawing me from the competition."

"Oh. Well, I assumed you wouldn't be up to such a rigorous trial after this horrible shock."

"No."

She smiled. "Good, I don't want you overdoing."

"Excuse me, I meant no, I would never withdraw. The professor worked so hard to prepare me for the competition. I'd never let him down. I'll go through with it no matter what."

She raised an eyebrow. "Even if he dies?"

Tears flashed to Snow's eyes, and he blinked. "Yes, even then."

"I see. I had underestimated…." She trailed off. "Why don't you come in?"

"I really want to get to the hospital."

"Yes, well, I'll drive you. Or rather my, uh, cousin will."

"Cousin?"

"Yes. He just arrived when he heard of my challenges and heartbreak." She brushed her mane of scarlet hair back. "He's here to help, so he can drive you in his car, and I'll join you later. After I have, uh, some meetings I can't escape."

"I don't want to be any trouble." He backed away, teetered on the edge of the step again, and she reached out and grabbed his arm.

"Nonsense. No trouble. We're all family here." She pulled him into the kitchen.

Everything felt familiar—the shining appliances, butcher-block counters, neat line of spices—except the oddly musky odor and some knives usually on the large cutting block now lying on the floor.

"Hunter."

Snow looked up at her call and stared at the arched opening into the dining room as if it were the portal of hell. Through it marched a tall, rugged, and very handsome man with a sharp goatee and dark brown hair to his shoulders—just a little shorter than Snow's hair.

The guy looked as startled as Snow, with wide eyes and a slightly open mouth.

Anitra pulled Snow a step forward. "Dear, I've told you about my friend and student, Snowden. You know, the chess master?"

"Of course." He held out his hand, and Snow submerged his in it. Hunter held his hand more like a caress than a handshake and smiled. "You never described him. I was just startled at his beauty."

One of her carefully plucked eyebrows rose. "I want you to take Snow to the hospital and see if you can't get those infernal people to actually speak to him and perhaps let him see Harold."

Snow's breath caught. "Oh, can you really do that? I want to see him so badly."

"Well, if Hunter can't persuade them, I'm sure I can." She made a sweeping gesture toward the living room. "Please come in and sit down, Snow. I was just installing Hunter in his room since—" She looked up at Hunter with a direct stare. "—he just arrived. Let us get him unpacked, and then he'll drive you. And speak to the doctors, of course. Come, Hunter." She flicked her fingers toward the stairs and then walked to them with Hunter following.

Think fast. "May I get a glass of water, Mrs. Kingsley?"

She glanced back from halfway up the stairs. "Oh, of course, dear."

He waited until they were out of sight, then hurried to the kitchen. He took down a glass, filled it from the refrigerator water filter, drank a couple of swallows, and set the glass down. Very quietly, he opened the vitamin drawer and riffled through. Just the usual—men's multi, some vitamin

C, echinacea, and fish oil. A prescription bottle of medicine for erectile dysfunction stopped Snow. *Could that give you a heart attack?* He'd look it up later. He closed the drawer and peered into several cabinets, including the spices. Nothing unexpected.

Glancing over his shoulder, he tiptoed into the laundry room off the kitchen. *No noise from the stairs yet. Good.* He peeked in the cabinet above the washer. Just cleaning products. Under the sink, a whole raft of pest control and garden fertilizer lined the shelves. Snow shook his head. He'd told the professor this stuff ought to go out in the garage, but he'd never moved it. Some of it was poison. *Could he have accidentally ingested it?* Most of the lids looked old and rusted. Not like they'd been—*wait.*

He picked up a little brown stopper bottle nestled among the jars and boxes. Holding it against the light, he could see a small quantity of liquid still in the bottom. Somehow this looked newer than most of the stuff. The screw cap turned easily. He sniffed. *Odd.* Sort of a licorice smell. *He didn't remember—*

Voices. He put the bottle back in its place and stepped out of the laundry room. *Damn.* He'd left his water on the far counter. Quickly, he stepped to the window, put his face in his hand, and let his shoulders shake. Not hard to pretend he was distraught.

Footsteps sounded behind him. He raised his head and wiped at his eyes.

"Oh there, there. Things will be all right." Anitra put a hand on his shoulder.

He nodded, sniffed, then walked over and retrieved his water. "Sorry. I have no right to be acting like a baby when you're holding up so well." He drank the rest.

"Yes, well, Hunter is ready to take you." Hunter walked into the kitchen, looking at Snow with an expression of—what? He'd be inclined to say sadness. Maybe the guy really was concerned for his cousin.

Hunter tossed car keys in his hand. "Okay, let's do it." He walked out the back door.

Anitra had changed into a skirt and blouse, and her hair and makeup looked far less like she'd just gotten out of bed. "I'll join you later. If they let you see him, please tell him I love him and I'll be there soon, okay?" She smiled.

She's so convincing. Why can't I just get comfortable with her?

Maybe because, in the midst of her sadness, she took the time to withdraw you from the tournament. That might seem a touch suspicious.

You think?

"I'll see you later." Snow walked out into the morning sunshine and crisp fall air. *Cold today.* He shivered and wrapped his down jacket tighter around his shoulders. The old green car sat running in the driveway. Snow rounded the car and got into the front passenger side.

Hunter gave him a smile. "Buckle up."

Hunter had some music playing, so it cut down on the pure awkwardness of the situation. "Uh, so you're Mrs. Kingsley's cousin."

He snorted. "Yeah."

Was he being facetious or not? Couldn't tell. "She must be really upset. Just married and having this happen."

"Yeah, well, she's, shall we say, resilient."

How did he reply to that?

Hunter glanced over. "You sure are beautiful."

"Uh, thank you."

"Don't think I've ever seen a woman I thought was as pretty as you. Man." He shook his head and looked through the windshield as he made a turn.

Snow stared hard out the window. Where was this conversation going?

"You're gay, right?"

"Yes. That's pretty well-known. Are you?"

"Bi. I like it all ways." He laughed. "You ever been with a woman?"

"No. I don't have much experience, period."

"I generally like females better. Not so much of a battle for supremacy, you know? But lately—let's just say, I'd make an exception in your case." Another laugh.

Snow stared at his own hands. Long fingers. Always made him think of sea plants. "I, uh, actually have a boyfriend."

"Oh. Well, that's disappointing. Anitra didn't tell me that."

"It's kind of new. But why would she have been telling you about me anyway?"

"No reason. Just conversation."

Hunter slowed, seemed to stare out the window hard, then suddenly turned onto a side street.

"Uh, I don't think this is the way to the hospital. I go on my bike, but—"

"Yeah. I just have to stop at the drugstore. Need to get something to take to the hospital."

"Oh. Isn't that kind of coals to Newcastle?" He tried to laugh.

"Oh. Yeah." Hunter barked a couple laughs. "There's some candy thing that Anitra says the professor likes."

"Oh." Snow controlled his own frown. "That must be the chocolate marshmallow squares he loves."

"Yeah. That's it." He pulled into the parking lot, stopped, and turned off the car. "Why don't you wait here? I'll be right back." With a shove of his shoulder, he pushed the creaky car door open and got out, then slammed the door.

Why is he lying? The professor hates candy in general and marshmallows in particular. Maybe he plans something bad. He sure seems focused on you. He could be getting lube.

Damn! No, he wouldn't, would he? Mrs. Kingsley may not like me, but rape?

You should get out of the car and run.

Seriously. Maybe he's just buying liquor and doesn't want Anitra to know.

Run!

Snow slid out of the car, closed the door softly—hardly noticed the step up behind him before he smelled the acrid odor—and everything went black.

"STAY DOWN, fag. I hope I didn't get any on me."

The linebacker added an extra punch to Riley's midback as he lifted off the pile of bodies that had taken Riley to the ground on his last carry.

Slowly, Riley collected his parts and managed to pull himself to his feet. One of his guards lumbered up to him. "You okay, man?"

"Yeah." He didn't add, "No thanks to you."

"Sorry. I let him get through. I tried to stop him."

Riley cracked his neck in both directions. "If you plan to have a quarterback for the rest of the season, you might want to try harder." He laughed, but he couldn't have been more serious.

The guard patted his shoulder. Weird game from start to now. When he'd trotted out the cheers had been strange, like some people were yelling louder to drown out others who were hollering nasty shit. Rog had caught his passes with gloves on and made a big show of wiping his hands when he handed over the football, which got some laughs from the crowd and some boos. The score at the moment reflected the squirreliness. Twenty-four to twenty-one with NorCal ahead, but the other team would never have gotten that far if Riley's guys had been playing optimally.

Back on the line of scrimmage, he called the play. As the wide receiver ran out for the catch, Riley looked up in time to see a glance from his right guard, Junior Betz, full of humor—and hate. Betz and Rog weren't friends, but man, did the expression look similar. Betz stepped back just that little bit, and two huge linebackers headed straight for Riley. Thank God he saw them. He swerved, tried to get the pass off and failed, and braced for the impact, but still, nearly six hundred pounds of mean hurt like a son of a bitch. His body slammed into the ground, head hitting so hard his ears rang, face guard plowing into the earth, sending pieces of plastic grass flying. Then, oof. The weight landed on top of him, and air rushed from his lungs until he gasped for oxygen.

Shit, bad. Every bone felt compromised. His speed plus the talent of his linemen meant he seldom got his bell rung quite this hard. Vaguely he heard the time-out called. The ref ran over and knelt down. "You okay, Riley?"

Was he? Right at this second, it was tough to remember why he'd thought coming out felt quite so important. He took a deep breath. *Snow. Just think of Snow.* "Yeah, thanks. I'm okay."

CHAPTER 14

COLD. REALLY cold. Need more covers.

Snow reached out to grab another blanket. *Wet.*

Wait—wet. Why wet? Why—

Open your eyes, idiot!

As though great weights rested on his lids, his eyes barely flickered. *Open, dammit!*

Snow dragged his eyelids up. *Holy shit! Water. Everywhere. Where am I?*

Icy water hit his chest. He gasped. His heart rate spiked, and adrenaline shot through him like speed.

Holy shit, I'm in a car. River. In the river. Car in the river—I'm going to drown. No! Oh God. He thrashed against his seat belt and hammered at the passenger door beside him.

Water to his neck.

Gonna die! Die. Riley!

Wait. Stop. Take a breath.

What do you mean, wait? Are you nuts? Shit. Get out of here.

Snow inhaled deeply. His brain smoothed out like a big white cloud. *No point trying to get out until the water inside the car equalizes the water pressing on the door. Simple physics.*

But—

He took another deep breath. *Maybe it's not too deep.* Water to his chin. *Calm. Only seconds. I have a chance.* His fingers found the release for his seat belt. *Breathe.* He raised his head as the water neared his lips and filled his lungs again.

Water closed over his mouth and nose. *Calm. Stay calm.* He unfastened the seat belt, pressed his lips to the ceiling for one last lungful.

Don't panic. Wait.

The water filled the car. *Lungs. Pressure.* He pulled the handle and pushed against the door. Nothing. No movement.

Don't panic. Try again. He pushed the handle and shoved with his shoulder. A tiny squeak? His brain screamed, *Breathe!*

Don't listen.

Quickly he pressed his arms against the steering wheel and kicked with his legs.

Nothing—then—yes! It moved.

Lungs bursting. The door suddenly swung open like some cosmic doorman had pulled it from the outside. Snow shot out, relaxed, and let the water take him.

Must breathe. Must. His chest hurt like fire despite the icy water. The light got brighter but current carried him fast. He kicked hard with his legs against the force that dragged him in the same plane. *Must breathe. Must. Riley. Riley.*

A light beamed in his head. Music. A blue door. Peace.

One last kick upward.

Ahhhhhhhh. Light burst around him along with frigid air. He coughed, flailed his arms, and then sucked a breath into his lungs like elixir from heaven. Icy water dragged him in a swift current down what must be the local river.

Where am I? Besides freezing? He turned on his side and stared at the bank as it moved rapidly by. Trees, a couple of rooftops in the distance….

Couldn't last long in here. Too cold.

Wait. There. Ahead, he saw a house built on the banks of the river. He kicked hard, sending one of his tennis shoes flying off into the water. He twisted to catch it, and something hard bumped his elbow. *Damn. My phone.* He grabbed for it and missed as it sailed on the current far away. *Forget it.*

Stroking as powerfully as he could, he managed to cut diagonally through the fast current. He sailed right past the house but was closer to the banks now. Still stroking, he got near enough to grab a floating branch and stop his forward motion. The branch cracked with his weight and he grabbed another. His body bobbed, trying to pull him away, but he held on. Still, he couldn't reach anything else to pull himself closer. Jesus, he felt like a wind sock, swinging helplessly in a gale. A freezing gale.

"Hey, do you need help?"

Snow couldn't see where the voice came from. "Hell, yes. I didn't go swimming in the icy cold in my clothes on purpose."

"I'd watch the attitude unless you plan on staying in the river for quite a while." A short, stocky guy with a full beard and glasses peered around the edge of the bush Snow clung to.

He had a point. "Sorry. I just about drowned. I could really use some help."

The guy squatted down and surveyed the situation. *Don't hurry on my account.* Finally he seemed to come to some conclusion, stood, and disappeared.

"Uh, don't go, please."

Silence.

Well, damn. The fast-moving water ripped at Snow's pants, and the soaked down jacket managed to hold the cold against his skin just perfectly. His teeth chattered so hard they could break. *Maybe just let go. Float off down the river. Stop the cold. Stop.* Slowly, his eyes closed.

"Bring it over here, you guys. Hurry. He could have hypothermia by now."

The voices rattled in Snow's brain. *Help. Please help.* Had he said that out loud?

The bushes in front of him rustled and waved. *Oh, great. Make it harder to hold on.* But then a long pole of some kind stuck through the undergrowth.

"Grab hold."

What? Snow tried to get his hand to unlatch from the waving branch he held. *Frozen. Focus.* He stared at his fingers. *Move.* One at a time, they quivered until finally his whole hand began to straighten. *Funny. It didn't used to be blue, did it?* His hand unwrapped from the branch, and his body began to slide away with the current.

"No, dammit, take hold of the pole."

Oh, right. He grasped the lifeline with his right hand, then let go of the branch with his left and transferred it over. As soon as he had both hands on the pole, it began to move. *Oh!* Bushes and branches that stuck out of the water ripped at him, scratching his skin and tearing at his clothes.

"Hold on. Don't let go."

Easy for you to say. But his hands felt as locked to the pole as they had to the branch.

Suddenly his body, dragged by the pole and whoever was pulling it, burst through the dense reeds and bushes and hit ground. Wet, soggy ground to be sure, but not water. *Dear God, not water.* Vaguely he recognized some forms moving toward him. His eyes closed.

"SHOULD WE call a doctor?"

"I am a doctor."

"Not yet, you're not."

"He's fine. Trust me."

"Why doesn't he wake up?"

Snow forced his lips to move. "I'm 'wake."

"See, I told you he's okay."

"Looks like a drowned rat. But he sure is a pretty one."

"Where 'm I?" *Mouth not working. No pucker.*

"What did he say?"

A finger dragged Snow's eyelid open. Bright light shone in. Snow turned his head to the side. "Ouch."

"He wants to know where he is." The voice got closer. "You're in the Iota Pi fraternity house at Grimm College."

Snow focused and finally got a flutter. His eyes opened slowly. He lay on a couch of some kind, with blankets up to his chin. Two guys sat in chairs beside the couch—the stocky one he'd seen at the river and a tall, almost unbelievably handsome man maybe a year or two older than Snow. The handsome one smiled and the stocky one with the beard frowned. Both said, "How do you feel?"

"Uh, okay, I think. I haven't tried moving all my parts yet."

Bearded boy said, "Don't strain anything, but just tell me if I should call the cops."

"I'm not dangerous."

His frown deepened. "Not for you. How did you get in the water?"

Good question. "I'm not entirely sure. I was going to the hospital with this guy. The cousin of—anyway, he stopped at a drugstore. I got out of the car to, uh—so I got a whiff of this smell, and I woke up in the water inside the car. I waited for the pressure to equalize, pushed my way out the car door, and got carried by the current. I caught hold of the branch, and that's where you found me."

"What happened to the guy who was driving? The one who went in the drugstore?"

Snow shook his head, and it felt like water still lodged in his ears. "No idea, but there was no one in the car when I woke up."

"What seat were you in?"

"Passenger seat. Shotgun."

"Is there a chance the other guy was driving and got thrown from the car when it went over an embankment or something?"

"Not likely unless the door then miraculously closed on its own. Nothing was open." He shuddered and tried not to feel the water rising past his mouth.

The beautiful guy put a hand on the covers on top of Snow's leg. "It's a miracle you weren't killed. I'm Randy Romulus, by the way. People call me Romeo."

"I'm Snowden Reynaldi. Snow."

Short and stocky said, "The chess guy?"

"Yes."

"Son of a bitch. I thought you looked familiar. I'm Doc. Or rather, that's my nickname, since I'm in med school. My real name's Merchester, but that doesn't matter."

"Glad to meet you both." He pushed the blanket off his shoulders and sat. His skinny, bare chest shivered even though the big room was warm, so he pulled the blanket back around him. "I guess I better get up and start calling people. My phone's gone. Maybe I could use one of yours?"

Doc nodded. "Sure. We didn't see your phone. So what do you think happened to you?"

He shrugged. "I think someone drugged me and tried to kill me."

Romeo said, "No shit?"

"I know it sounds nuts, but I was getting out of the car when I smelled this acrid odor. Next thing I know, I'm more than halfway to drowning. I can't think of an accidental excuse that works."

Doc wrinkled his broad forehead. "No chance you had a couple too many and piloted your car off the bridge?"

"A. I can't drive."

"That might be a good reason for driving off a bridge."

Snow wrinkled his nose at Doc. "B. I was in the passenger seat like I told you and was belted in. C. I never had anything to drink."

Romeo took his hand. "Why would someone want to see you dead?"

"I'm not really sure. I'm not anything special."

"I wouldn't say that." Romeo smiled. Wow, he sure earned that nickname.

"Hey, Doc, can we meet the guest?" A tall, skinny guy with red hair leaned around the archway that led into the big, messy room where they were sitting.

"Sure. Might as well bring everybody in quick."

Five guys crossed into the room and stood staring at Snow. Doc waved an arm. "These are the Iota Pis. You met Romeo. This is Gormet." He flicked a finger at the tall guy. "Then there's BB, short for Ballet Boy, Lib, Hacker, and Bash." The last guy outweighed Riley by fifty pounds, all in his biceps.

Snow tried to smile. "Hi. I'm Snow."

The one called Lib, a delicate, attractive guy with dark hair, cocked his head. "You sure are pretty."

Romeo laid a hand on Snow's thigh through the blanket. "That's what I said."

Hacker chortled, "Watch out for Romeo, Snow. He could talk the ayatollah into homosexuality."

Snow stared at his hands. "I'm gay too, uh, but I have a boyfriend."

Gormet laughed. "Never stopped Romeo before."

Doc stood. "We better call the cops."

Snow shook his head. "I can't prove anything. Hell, I don't know anything."

"Still, we better."

"Okay, but can I use a phone?"

Romeo fished a brand-new phone from his pocket and handed it to Snow. It smelled like aftershave. Snow stared at it. How odd not to call Professor Kingsley first. He fished the digits out of his near-photographic memory and dialed.

"Hello?" Riley sounded tentative and worried.

"Riley, it's me."

"Oh my God, Snow. Oh shit." Was he crying? "Are you okay? Where are you?"

"Yes, I'm okay now. Somehow I wound up in a car in the river, but I escaped, and some guys helped me. I'm at Grimm College. In a fraternity house. They're calling the cops since I think I was drugged, so I'll probably have to be here for a while."

"Tell me where. I'm coming."

"I'm giving this to Ro—uh, Randy. He'll tell you. Oh man, I can't wait—okay, here's Randy." Snow handed the phone to Romeo and swallowed his heart out of his throat. "Would you tell my friend how to get here?"

The cops got there in fifteen minutes; Riley took twenty since Grimm was miles from NorCal.

The police officer had just asked, "So you didn't see anyone—" when Riley walked through the frat house door. The other fraternity brothers milled around in the hall, trying to look casual, but Riley still stuck up over most of them except Bash.

Snow didn't think. "Riley!" He leaped up and ran to Riley, where he got scooped into a huge hug.

"Oh man, I was so worried. Mrs. Kingsley called looking for you, and I just freaked."

Snow leaned back. "What?"

"Yeah, she called a few hours ago. Said her cousin had come home claiming his car was stolen. She thought you might have taken it, but I told her you couldn't drive."

The police detective stepped beside Snow. "Excuse me, but this sounds like something I should hear. I'm Detective Sanchez."

"Riley Prince."

"So who called you and what does she have to do with the owner of the vehicle?"

They sat down and talked for two more hours. During the conversation, another policeman called Detective Sanchez to say they'd located the car at the bottom of the NorCal River, a mile from the embankment where it appeared the car had entered the water.

Snow frowned. "Sir, can they tell if it ran off the road or how it ended up in the river?"

Sanchez talked for a few minutes. When he hung up, he said, "They think it was pushed. It doesn't appear to have been traveling at a high speed when it went into the water."

Riley's arm tightened around him. "God, that means it had to be done on purpose."

Sanchez nodded. "Possibly. We're reporting it as suspicious."

"Who in the world would want to kill me?" Snow shook his head and swallowed hard.

"Perhaps no one. There may be another explanation. Obviously robbery wasn't a motive. They took nothing and didn't even keep the car. Could it have been a prank gone awry?"

Riley tightened his lips into a line. "Some prank. It has to have something to do with chess."

Sanchez turned to Riley, notebook in hand. "Why do you say that?"

"Snow's this big chess champion."

"I know that."

"He's favored to win the Anderson Chess Tournament. Maybe somebody doesn't want him to play."

The detective dropped the notebook into his lap. "I hardly think someone is going to commit murder to up their chances of winning at chess."

Snow nodded. "I agree. Chess players are pretty rabid, but I don't think anyone would go that far."

Riley snorted.

Snow looked at Riley. "Do you think someone was trying to get to you through me? Like punishment for luring you?"

Sanchez frowned. "What do you mean?"

Snow turned toward Sanchez. "Riley came out to his football team as gay. A lot of people don't like it."

"Yes, I heard that. You think someone didn't like it enough to try to kill Snow?"

Riley shuddered. "Jesus, I hope not."

"Maybe they didn't think it would go so far? Didn't consider that he wouldn't be able to get out of the car?"

"I guess some jock could be that stupid, but man, that's tough to swallow." Riley wiped a hand over the back of his neck.

Sanchez leaned back on the ratty couch Snow had been sleeping on. The big room where the fraternity brothers lived contained a lot of chairs, two worn couches, and what seemed like a million laptops, TVs, and game controllers in many manifestations. "Has anything else unusual happened recently?"

"My mentor and coach fell ill. He's in the hospital. That's where I was going when this all happened."

Riley nodded. "It was his wife who called me."

"The cousin of the vehicle owner?" Sanchez jotted it down.

"Yes." Snow pressed a little closer to Riley and suppressed a shudder. "The cousin, Hunter, was the one driving me to see Professor Kingsley."

"Interesting full circle." Sanchez scratched a few more words and closed the notebook.

"You think it's significant?"

"Probably not. How did the professor fall sick?"

Snow glanced at Riley. "His heart, I think. It's interfering with his breathing. That's what Mrs. Kingsley says. They won't let me see him because I'm not family."

"I hope he gets better soon." Sanchez stood. "Don't go anywhere. We'll probably have to ask you more questions."

"I have two weeks until the tournament. Then I have to fly to Las Vegas."

"Stick around until then."

Riley stood beside Sanchez, pulling Snow up with him. "What if it was an attempt on Snow's life? Shouldn't you put a guard on Snow?"

"We're going to keep investigating, and hopefully we'll find some reasonable explanation for this whole thing soon. As you said, why would someone want to kill you?" He smiled and patted Snow's hand. "If you don't take any chances, I think you'll be fine."

"Isn't that taking a big chance with Snow's life?"

Sanchez shrugged. "We're a small-town police department, and I don't have the luxury of staff for guard duty. I think you'll have to be his guard, Prince, and something tells me you won't mind."

Riley shook his head. "Of course I'll protect him, but I can't be with him all the time. Sometimes I'm in class or on the field."

Snow held up a hand. "I'll be fine. Whoever this was took me by surprise once, but not again. I'll stay with people I know when I'm not with Riley."

Sanchez looked toward the front door of the fraternity house and gave a tight smile. "I'm guessing after the media circus this is going to create, no one will dare make a move against you."

Snow stared at the two news vans parked at the curb and the Iota Pis happily conducting interviews on the front lawn, pointing toward him with wild gestures. He heard words like "murder," "nearly drowned," and "hero."

His stomach hit his shoes. "Oh my God."

CHAPTER 15

"GOD DAMN them all to hell!" The newspaper flew through the air, scattering pages as it went. *Kill. Want to kill something.* Anitra grabbed the laptop and raised it over her shoulder.

"Hold on, Lady Macbeth. You'll be sorry later if you wreck that." Hunter grabbed the computer from her hands and carried it into the dining room.

She whirled and took a few steps after him. Yes, he was right. She didn't have the money to afford multiple laptops—yet. "If you hadn't blown this so thoroughly, our precious Snow would be fucking melted by now instead of being hailed as the hero of NorCal and half the state of California."

"I blew nothing. I couldn't kill him before he drowned. Coroners can pick that out. I've got no idea how he got out of that car. Hell, I drugged him first."

She gritted her teeth. "Obviously not enough."

"Again, I could only use what I thought would dissipate in his system quickly. Be reasonable, Anitra. I did what I was told."

He had a point. More importantly, he had a cock, and she needed one, and soon. She narrowed her eyes. "The higher that little twerp flies, the farther he'll fall."

For a flash, Hunter frowned.

Hmmm. Maybe he got sucked in by the little prick and didn't even try to kill him.

Then Hunter plastered on his easy smile. "What do you have planned next?"

"That's for me to know."

"You better not get too daring, dear. The police are already calling the circumstances suspicious. If you try again, they'll really dig in. Both of us could be implicated." He smiled tightly.

Yes, the bastard. If he gets caught, he'll sing like a bloody Wagnerian soprano. "I have many resources you know nothing about. I'll tell you when I need you. Meanwhile, bring your best feature upstairs. That I need now."

SNOW STARED down at the quiet, gray face with the breathing tube sticking out of his mouth. He squeezed the professor's hand. No response. At least it was warm. Someone had once said, "Where's there's life, there's hope."

He sat back in the chair at the bedside. They'd finally let him in to see Professor Kingsley because Snow was a "hero" who "was trying to get to the professor when someone abducted him and tried to kill him," and "he should be rewarded for his bravery." Whatever worked, although there sure as hell wasn't anything brave about self-preservation.

Snow stood, leaned over, and kissed the pale cheek. "I'm so sorry this happened to you. Of all people, you sure didn't deserve this. And no matter what, I'm going to go to Las Vegas and play. I'll win if I can. For you. Just for you."

"My, isn't that sweet."

Snow snapped up and turned to see Anitra standing in the doorway of the hospital room. He shrugged. "They say sometimes people in a coma can hear what's said to them."

"You're determined to play chess under such terrible stress?"

"Yes, ma'am. I think the professor would want me to."

"The chess club can't afford to pay for your ticket, you know."

He took a breath. What he knew was that money had been set aside last year for his trip, but why say that—to her? "I'll pay for it myself."

"Very well. I certainly wish you well. You set a fine example of determination."

He crossed his arms. "You mean stubbornness."

"You said it, I didn't. Let's just hope all goes well between now and then so there's no interference with your—determination."

Snow frowned. "What would interfere?"

"Oh, nothing. We'll just pray for an improvement in Harold's health."

"Of course." He looked again at the professor's quiet face. So not like him. He was always lively and smiling—until lately. Something had happened to make him change, and it couldn't be a coincidence that the change occurred when Anitra Popescu showed up. Snow shuddered. "Bye."

He walked out of the critical care unit. Man, it felt like he was dragging the building behind him. What a strange mix of feelings—anger, fear, exhaustion, sadness, plus that warmth that spread out from his heart and melted all those cold feelings whenever he thought about Riley.

He made it to the front door of the hospital and stepped outside. A young woman rushed over. "Hi, Snowden, I'm Haley with the *Daily Mirror*. Any idea who would want to kill you?"

He let out a little snort. "Sorry. Just not the kind of question a regular human expects to be asked."

She laughed. "I guess not. Still, the police might have played it down, but how else does a guy end up in a car underwater, if he wasn't driving?"

He sighed. "I honestly don't know what happened. The police are on it, and I have great faith in them."

She handed him a card. "If you learn anything interesting, will you call me? I'll treat the story honestly."

"Sure. Thanks." He glanced at the card, put it in his pocket, and looked up. Oh yes, there were those warm feelings. Riley stood on the sidewalk next to his car with Snow's bicycle beside him and a cute little smile curving his lips. *Sigh.* The man made gorgeous sound like a moderate adjective.

Haley laughed. Damn, he'd forgotten she was there. "So I gather all the stories about the chess champion and the quarterback are true?"

"Define 'all.'"

She raised her voice so Riley could hear. "Just that Riley Prince came out so he could date the beautiful chess master of Northern California University."

Snow glanced up. The crease between Riley's eyebrows vanished quickly, but still—Riley looked troubled.

Snow shook his head and stared at his shoes. What should he say? "Uh, Riley and I are friends."

"Does that mean you're not dating?"

Riley walked up and took Snow's arm. "Like he said, we're friends, and with people shoving him in the river, he needs somebody who's got his back."

"Ooh, the protector."

"Whatever. I need to get him to a place where he can practice for the tournament."

She took notes. "So despite all that's happened, you still plan to compete, Snowden?"

Snow looked up. "Yes, that's the one certain thing."

"Can I quote you?"

"Be my guest."

In the car, Riley took off like more than one lady reporter was chasing his ass. Snow glanced over. "You okay?"

"Yeah."

"Was practice all right?"

"Yeah."

"Is the square root of pi 1.77245385091?"

The corners of Riley's lips crept upward. "Yeah." He burst out laughing. "Sorry. It's just that it's tough, you know?"

"The impact on the team?"

"Yeah. Sorry, yes. My coming out has polarized the guys. Some are really on my side. Probably more than they would be if some of the others weren't so against me. But it makes for a lot of dissension, and that screws up our harmony on the field. We're playing like shit, and the championship is only a couple weeks away."

"Maybe you should have waited to come out?"

He wrinkled his nose. "That, my friend, is called Monday-morning quarterbacking. You should pardon the pun."

"Sorry. Things really are confusing." Snow blew out his breath slowly.

Riley wrapped his warm hand over Snow's. "Shit, listen to me complaining. You've got your coach and best friend in a coma, your own championship to win, and oh yeah, somebody trying to kill you."

"That doesn't make the upheaval in your life any less confusing or serious, Riley. I truly am sorry all this crap has happened at once. I'm just adding to your troubles, not helping."

He tightened his hand. "Actually, it helps me to think about taking care of you, which I plan to do right now." He pulled onto the road that led to his neighborhood. "I'm taking you home with me. Your building may be more high-tech, but I'd stack Mrs. Wishus up against any threat any day. I think you're safer at my place. We'll get a little of your stuff each day, but I'm guessing all you need are a toothbrush, a couple pairs of khakis and six chess sets." He grinned.

You're not going to let him railroad you into giving up your independence, are you?

"I'd love to stay with you if I won't be in the way."

"Seriously?" He laughed. "I made a bet with myself that you wouldn't give up your alone time without a fight."

Snow gazed out the window. "I've been alone enough for five lifetimes."

Riley's foot pressed the accelerator harder. "I've got to get you home before you change your mind."

Come on, Snow, don't be selfish. "But—"

"Uh-oh, here it comes." He pulled into his driveway and parked, then turned to Snow.

"My staying here could put you in danger."

"I'm a big boy."

Snow stared at his omnipresent shoes. "My staying here rubs your team's nose in the fact that you're gay. No one will forget it."

The frown flitted, then vanished. "They never come here. But more important, they're not going to forget it anyway. Eventually, maybe. If we win the championship. But until then? No way."

"*When* you win the championship."

"What?"

"You said 'if.' I said 'when.'"

"Thank you. I wish that was certain."

"It is."

He nodded, but the sadness under his smile ripped at Snow's heart.

They both climbed out of the car and started up the walk. Mrs. Wishus waved from the porch. "Hello, boys."

Riley waved back. "Hi, Eudora."

"Snow, I read about your awful experience. Tell me what you learned from it."

"What?" He laughed. Leave it to Mrs. Wishus to ask the unexpected. What had he learned? "Don't panic?"

"Seems like a good lesson to me. Remember it."

"Yes, ma'am."

Riley glanced at Snow. "I brought him here because I thought he'd be safer."

"Indeed, but there are many kinds of threats, now aren't there?"

"I suppose."

"How are your teammates accepting your homosexuality?"

Riley shuffled his feet like he wanted to run from the question. "Some real good. Some not so much."

"And how are you accepting it?"

His head snapped up. "Ma'am?"

"I know you've always been gay, Riley, but by not revealing it, you had the best of both worlds, in a way. You could have your little secret and not suffer the consequences. Now you have to own who you are. Never easy, my dear."

Riley's chest expanded like he was sucking down what she said. "It was hard being in the closet. Lying all the time."

"Yes. Remember that when some asshole decides to call you a fag."

"Yes, ma'am."

"Now get this poor boy upstairs and let him rest. Drowning is not fun."

Riley glanced at Snow as if he'd forgotten all about the near drowning. "Jesus. Right." He opened the door and held it for Snow to pass through. In the bright, airy apartment, he stopped. "Uh, shall I set up the guest room for you?" His chest didn't move. Was he holding his breath?

Snow smiled. "I think we passed guest room somewhere between the condoms and the lube." His cheeks got tight. "But I don't want to crowd your space."

Riley crossed his arms. "You don't? Planning on fucking me from far away?"

Snow sucked in his breath, and his cock hopped. He laughed. "I'm not *that* well-endowed."

Riley walked toward him. "You're not, huh?" His dimples flashed, and just like that, all the weirdness of the last twenty-four hours popped in a bubble and the whole world looked like Riley's smile.

Riley gathered him in his big arms. "You probably don't feel like making out, right? Too tired?"

Snow rose onto tiptoe and whispered, "I might be too tired fifteen minutes before I die, but until then, I'm ready."

"Oh, baby." Riley closed that perfect mouth over Snow's. His tongue explored Snow's mouth, then slipped inside and tickled the skin of Snow's upper lip. *Ummm. Wow.* Direct line from lips to penis. Riley leaned back and dragged his tongue across Snow's bottom lip—then licked the tip of his nose.

Snow giggled. "I'm so glad I learned kissing from you."

"You sure are one fast learner, beautiful boy."

"I try." He glanced down, then up to meet Riley's eyes. "Want to test me on my other lessons?"

"Oh yeah." Riley looked up studiously. "Let's see. Was that lesson about the square root of pi?"

"No. The square root of penis." He giggled.

Riley nuzzled Snow's ear. "Want to fuck me again?"

Snow swallowed. "I don't want to be a hog. I'll bottom if you'll teach me."

"Nuh-uh. That's a lesson for another day. My cock's not in the mood to wait."

Snow giggled. "Mine's a bit on the anxious side as well." He took Riley's hand and pressed it against his erection.

Riley smiled. "So now that you know what you were missing, you like it?"

"As a friend of mine would say—" Snow frowned and puffed out his chest to look more like a quarterback. "—'yeah.'" Then he laughed.

"Is that how I look when I'm being a pain in the ass?"

"No comment. But I certainly like the ass part."

"Then let's get this—" He squeezed Snow's hard-on through his khakis. "—in here." He turned sideways and stuck out his butt. "Race you." He took off like a giant football-carrying jackrabbit toward the bedroom. Snow gasped and ran after Riley. At the door to the bedroom, Snow slipped under Riley's arm and dove for the bed. Riley leaped after him and landed nearly on top.

"Ooof." Snow's lungs compressed and all the air *woosh*ed out, but *oh my*. The rest of his body loved the pressure, especially where that big bulge pressed into his thigh. He tapped Riley's forehead. "Aren't there linebackers who do that kind of move?"

"That would be me. Your linebacker of lurrrve."

Snow's laugh exploded, but that word still gave him a thrill. "You're wearing far too many clothes."

"Ah yes, let me change into uniform." Riley rolled on his back, skinned his jeans down over his interfering erection, kicked off his sneakers, and managed to bare his lower half, if you didn't count the socks.

Snow leaned on his fist. "Now that's what I'd call a tight end."

Riley grabbed his middle and shook with laughter. "Where did you learn that, sassy pants?"

"Watching you play."

"You watch my games?"

"No. I watch you. The games are incidental."

"Seriously, you've watched me play?"

"Of course. I've been lusting after you for a long time." He forced himself not to look at his shoes.

"You telling me that while I was plotting on getting you interested in me, you were mooning over my ass?"

"Please, I've never mooned anyone."

"Oh really?" Riley grabbed Snow's khakis and pulled them to his knees in one move, snagging his boxers along the way. They were so oversized he didn't even pop the fly button. He flipped Snow over and paddled his butt. Flashes of heat zipped through Snow's cock. Riley slapped, then rubbed, slapped again, and rubbed. "That's the prettiest full moon I ever did see."

"Uh, Riley."

"Yeah."

"I think somebody better fuck somebody soon, or I'm coming all over your bedspread."

Riley massaged across Snow's butt with his big, warm hand, then slipped between his thighs and tickled his balls.

Snow half giggled, half yelped. "That's not helping!"

Riley breathed against Snow's ear. "Come anytime you want, beautiful boy, but preferably in my ass." He flipped on his back, pulled his legs up beside his ears, and flashed his hole.

"Oh my God."

"Why don't you grab some lube and get busy on your homework."

Snow moved so fast he must have left speed lines in the air. He had lube in his hands and fingers in Riley's ass before he'd taken another breath. "If this is homework, I'd like to apply for an advanced degree, please."

"PhD in fucking?"

Snow stopped and gazed at that lovely face. "A doctorate in you."

"Oh yeah, let's start matriculating." Riley reached out and took hold of Snow's penis, slathered some lube on it, and pointed it at his own target.

Snow leaned forward until his cockhead pressed against Riley's pucker.

Riley's lips parted. "Do it."

"Do you like bottoming?"

"It's easier on the new kid." He grinned.

"But do you like it?" Snow pressed a little harder but didn't quite breach Riley's hole.

"Yeah. I do."

"How much?"

"Just fuck me, wiseass."

"Tell me how much." He gazed at Riley but didn't smile. Some deep instinct said Riley needed to say this. Needed to go there. "How much do you like it?"

"A lot."

"You like a penis inside you, Riley. You like me deep in your hole? Do you?"

"Fuck me!"

"Tell me."

"Yeah, I like it."

Snow pressed, felt the walls surrendering, and pulled back.

"Snow, dammit."

"You want me to fuck you? Push my cock in and out of you?"

"Y-yes."

"You want it badly?"

"Yes, yes!"

"Tell me."

"Fuck."

"Fuck you?"

"Yes."

Did he dare? "Yes, what?"

"Yes."

"And?"

"Please, please fuck me, Snow?" A mist filled his eyes like the request hurt—*good.*

"Love those fine manners." Snow pushed as hard as he could. *Pop.* In he went, and fire seared straight from his cock to his brain. "Holy shit." He threw his head back and started ramming in and out.

Riley's hips jackhammered up and down. "Oh God. Like that. Oh man, right there. Shit. So good. Love it. Love it so much. More."

Every word filled Snow's brain and heart like some mantra of passion until those declarations and his own heartbeat filled the room with sound. *Yes. Yes! YES!*

Riley screamed. An actual scream that triggered the promised big bang. Semen poured out of his cock and hit him in the eye, and then another spurt landed on his chin. Snow would have laughed, but his head exploded along with his groin as pump after pump of pure joy flooded Riley's insides.

It took a full minute for his body to stop shuddering in ecstasy. Finally he collapsed over Riley.

Quiet.

Maybe too quiet.

CHAPTER 16

SNOW SHIFTED so his softening penis pulled out of Riley. The sensation shot up his back from his too-sensitive dick. Riley didn't move. "You okay?"

Even the bedspread couldn't erase the edge in Riley's voice. "Of course. I'm fine."

Try not to ask anymore.

Snow sat up and ran a hand through his long hair to sort out the tangles. Suddenly Riley snapped upright. "Why wouldn't I be fine?"

Uh-oh. "No reason. I just didn't hear you breathing." He smiled. *What kind of nerves did I touch?*

"Next time we'll teach you how to bottom." Riley looked toward the window.

Ah, that was it. "Yes, I'm sorry I had to top twice. I really want to learn."

"Just need to get you ready. I wouldn't want to hurt you."

"Right. I hope I didn't hurt you. I mean, I know you must top all the time, so you don't get much practice—as a bottom, I mean."

"No, of course not." Riley got up and walked into the bathroom, returning with two washcloths. He rubbed one over his own genitals and handed one to Snow. "You're right, though. I do usually top."

"Of course." The smile tugging at his lips—he suppressed it.

Riley tossed the cloths back toward the bathroom. "Let's get some sleep. I have a big practice tomorrow."

Riley crawled in bed, and Snow curled up beside him with his head on Riley's shoulder. "Thank you for looking out for me. I really do feel a lot safer here with you."

Riley tightened his arm. "Good. That's what I hoped."

Snow sighed and snuggled closer. "I haven't had much chance to tell you. When I went over to the professor's house and saw Anitra—before I got pushed in the river—I snooped a little. I found something kind of weird in the laundry room in a stopper bottle, like it was drops of some kind. But I couldn't get a sample before she came back."

"How was it weird?"

"It looked like it might have been used recently, and it wasn't obviously weed killer or anything like that, which is what all the other stuff in there was."

"Could have been anything, don't you think?"

"I suppose."

"I mean, she's the one who called me looking for you, wondering if you took the car."

"Yes, I know, but there's a chance she was just trying to deflect suspicion. I can't imagine the professor never telling her I can't drive. Plus, that cousin of hers kind of came on to me before he went into the drugstore."

"Really? You never mentioned that to the cops."

"I didn't really think of it until now."

"Must not have been too serious."

"I told him I had a boyfriend and wasn't interested."

"Oh you did, did you?" He chuckled and his chest rumbled.

Snow smiled. "Yes. I had to discourage him somehow."

"Is that the only reason?"

Snow giggled. "Well, he is very good-looking."

Riley grabbed his side and tickled him mercilessly. "Just how good-looking would that be?"

"Help. No. I give. He's homely and ugly, and I told him my boyfriend is as beautiful as a Greek god."

"Okay, that's better." He stopped tickling and hugged Snow tighter. Snow's breath smoothed, and his eyes drooped. "Snow."

"Umm-hmm."

"Sorry I was an asshole about the bottoming."

Snow smiled, eyes still closed. "You weren't."

"Yes, I was. I love to bottom. I just don't let many guys in me, is all."

"Thank you."

"Why?"

"For letting me in. And for letting me see that you like it. And I guess for not letting many other guys in too." Snow grinned. It did give him a warm glow.

"I'm just a little weirded about the whole coming-out thing."

"I know. It's really hard, and I'm so very proud of you."

"Thanks."

"It's like Batman showing that he's Bruce Wayne."

Riley chuckled.

"Just remember, even when he's in a business suit, he's still a superhero."

Riley kissed his hair. "I'll try." They snuggled quietly. Riley took a breath. "If you think Mrs. Kingsley and her cousin are suspicious, then I do too. But it'll take some hard evidence to convince the police. She *is* his wife."

Funny how that didn't really make him feel better.

"HEY, SWEETHEART, I have an early lab, and I want to get to the hospital after that. I also need to get a new phone. Mine got drowned." Snow kissed Riley's ear and backed off the bed.

"Mff. Wait." Riley shook his head and then sat up, the sheet dropping off his bare and glorious shoulders to bunch in his lap over a very tempting morning erection. "What time is it?"

"Not quite seven."

"Give me a minute, and I'll take you to the lab. I've got practice at nine anyway."

"No, you need to eat, and I already did. I'll take the bike. It's not far to the physics building."

"I don't want you going to the hospital alone. She could be there, and if you're right about her, you're not even close to safe."

"She probably wouldn't try anything, but I'd rather go with you anyway. So I'll wait outside the physics building for you to get done with practice? I'll work on my chess moves until you get there."

"Deal. Watch yourself, okay? Stay near people you know and stuff."

God, it almost made him cry to think Riley worried about him. "I will." Suddenly Snow looked up. "Oh, wait." He crossed to the closet where he'd tossed his clothes from yesterday and searched the pockets until he found his epinephrine syringe. "Don't want to forget this." He shoved it in his pocket.

Riley cocked his head. "What is it?"

"For my nut allergies. In case I go into shock. Of course, this one went in the river with me, so I don't know if it's still good. I better get to the drugstore for a new one soon."

"What happens if you don't have it?"

Snow shrugged. "I die, I guess."

"Why don't I get you a new one?"

"Do you have time? It's at the NorCal Pharmacy."

"Yeah. The drugstore is on my way to the field. Can you leave me the label so I can show them what to refill?"

"Sure." He peeled off the paper label and put it on the dresser. "Thank you so much." He smiled, waved, and headed for the front.

Outside the apartment, he bobbed down the steep stairs. Mrs. Wishus's blue door stood open. *Must be out in the garden. Pretty cold for pruning or weeding.* As he approached the door to the outside, he heard her voice.

"I'm asking you all to please leave my yard. You have no business here."

What the hell? Should he get Riley? *Better see what's up first.* He opened the door, and flashes started going off in his face. Voices yelled at him.

"Hey, Reynaldi, what do you have to say about the allegations?"

"Is it true? Have you been running an illegal business out of your apartment?"

"Is Riley Prince your client? Or your business partner?"

Snow stepped back until his butt hit the door. "Mrs. Wishus, what are they talking about? What's going on?"

She grasped his arm. "They claim there's proof that you're a prostitute who has been scamming men at the college and running some kind of escort service."

"But… but, that's ridiculous."

"Of course it is, but they say there's evidence. You need to learn what it is and set this to rights."

Three of the reporters pressed up on the porch. Mrs. Wishus stepped forward. "Get off my property. Shoo. Snowden, get back inside."

Oh my God. He pulled the screen toward him and stepped in.

"Close the door, Snow. I'm calling the police."

With a shove, he slammed the door shut. How could this happen? He raced up the stairs. There had to be some mistake. *Oh crap.* He didn't have a key. He rang the bell again and again. Who could he call to find out where this ridiculous story came from? "Riley, open up."

The door opened, but no one was behind it.

Snow stepped inside.

Riley stood in the middle of the floor, staring at the television. The local news. A handsome guy Snow had met at homecoming was saying, "Yes, I paid him for sex and sent a couple other guys to him. Damned good too. I think he preferred athletes. He's got this innocent quality that's hard to resist."

The reporter said, "You're sure this was Snowden Reynaldi, the chess player?"

"Oh yes, ma'am. Not many guys look like that. See, I kind of like men and women, so he was a good bet for me."

Snow backed up. "How could this happen? How is it possible? I have to do something. Who can I go to for help? Can I use your phone? Maybe I can call the dean of students."

The reporter said, "Why would he do this?"

"Who can say? Maybe he wanted the money or sex. Probably he just likes the control."

Snow pounded a hand backward on the wall next to the door. "Riley. Can I use your phone?"

Riley turned, his golden eyes shiny. "Are you saying you don't know this guy?"

"What? Of course not. I mean, I met him with you, but—"

"Of course. That's Mike Henderson. He's the captain of the lacrosse team."

"But Riley, you're not asking me if I—if I charged him for sex?"

"Why would he put himself in this position if it's not true? My God, he'll be investigated for being involved in prostitution. Why would he?"

"Riley, listen to what you're saying."

He shook his head. "I know, I'm sorry. I'm just so confused. I don't understand why this is happening. And you're so good at it."

"Good at what?" Snow stared at Riley. *No. Don't say it. Don't.*

"Sex. You're so good at sex. If you're such a virgin, how come you're so good?"

Everything went cold. If a six-foot-six-inch cobra coiled in front of him, he couldn't be more horrified. "I see."

"I don't want to believe it. I don't." Riley shook his head again like he was trying to clear it.

Riley's phone started ringing from the other room. He walked into the bedroom with his shoulders slumped. Snow shook. He'd never be warm again. Riley walked back in and handed him the phone. Snow didn't even ask.

"Hello."

"Snowden."

"Yes."

"This is Dean Franklin."

"Yes, sir."

"There have been some shocking allegations made against you, young man. I want to see you as quickly as possible to hear your side of the story."

"Wait, how did you know to call me here?"

"I was told I might reach you through Riley."

"May I ask how this story happened to be given to the press?"

"I have no idea. I was appalled to discover it on the news."

"Who reported the story to you?"

"It's best if we don't discuss this over the phone."

Snow heard a familiar voice and looked up at the television. Anitra's cousin Hunter filled the screen, his handsome face looking deeply concerned. "Yes, I was with him on the day of his accident. He, shall we say, came on to me, suggesting that I might want to pay him for sex. When I told him no and recommended he get some help, he got quite irate. That's why I stopped at the drugstore. I thought if I got some medicine to calm him, he'd be well enough to see the professor. But when I came out, he'd taken my car and gone. I worried that he'd decided to commit suicide. Perhaps he tried and couldn't go through with it."

"Snowden. Snowden. Are you still there?" The dean's voice shouted through the phone.

Snow sighed. "Yes, sir. I am. I know who reported these allegations to you. I also know that I have no way to refute them. What can I do? Produce people who say I haven't asked them to pay for sex? What good will that do? Professor Kingsley isn't even here to speak for me." Tears pushed against his eyes.

On the TV, the reporter shook her head. "What an amazing story, right here in our town. Such a brilliant boy. What a shame."

Hunter flashed a small smile. "Sometimes the brightest are the most neurotic."

Slowly Snow hung up the phone.

Riley stood like a statue, not even looking at the screen. He just stared at the floor.

Snow said softly, "You don't believe him? Even if the other guy is confusing, you can't believe Hunter. You came to rescue me. You know I wasn't suicidal."

Riley's eyes flipped up to Snow's. "Can you drive a car?"

The idea of a person's heart breaking had always been metaphoric. Not anymore. Snow pushed off from the wall and opened the door. *Please, please say something.* No sound came from behind him except the TV reporter, who'd moved on to a story about a bear in someone's backyard.

Snow looked back. Riley stared at the floor with those shiny eyes. Slowly Snow descended the stairs, stepping on each tread with one foot, then the other. No one followed him. At the bottom, Mrs. Wishus's apartment door still stood open. He stopped and waited.

Please, stop me. Say you believe me.

If Riley doesn't believe me, how could anyone else?

He looked inside Mrs. Wishus's apartment. No one. She must still be outside doing battle with the reporters. He glanced around. *There.* A door in the back of the apartment, by the kitchen. *Maybe it leads—away.*

He crept in, dragging his body like it weighed a thousand pounds, glancing at the big front windows that looked out on the porch. Through the ruffled curtains, he could still see the outline of the TV trucks. He stayed back so the reporters wouldn't catch sight of him and circled the living room. Above the fireplace a framed piece of embroidery said "The truth is worth fighting for."

Snow swiped at his eyes. *I can't prove I'm innocent, and I'm about to be expelled. The only person alive who cares about me is in a coma and might die. That's the truth.*

Funny. He thought he'd been alone most of his life. He really hadn't known what alone was.

He slipped out her back door into the cold gray morning. His bike was in Riley's car. Good thing he liked to walk. Pulling his hoodie over his head, he stayed on the least traveled streets. Two blocks from his apartment, he stopped and watched the ATM at the local bank. *Nobody. Good.* He ran across the street and inserted his bank card, tapped in the code, then requested two hundred dollars.

Transaction Denied.

What?

He repeated the process.

Transaction Denied.

His breath poured from his lungs, and he fell against the screen. He didn't have credit cards. He'd always used cash. But he didn't have any. What little money he'd carried had gotten soaked in his pants pockets, and he'd left it to dry in Riley's kitchen. Sweet Jesus, he didn't have a cent.

A man in a suit walked up to the ATM, so Snow turned and hurried away. He had a little money in his apartment. That would hold him over until he could contact the executor of the trust and get some cash from him. Surely, no matter what the lawyer thought, he couldn't deny Snow his own money.

It took nearly an hour of slow trudging to get to his apartment. There they all were. From behind a tree, he watched the reporters outside his building. They must be coming in from all the surrounding towns, because there weren't enough local newspeople to fill one van, much less three. Damn being well-known.

How did they know to go to Riley's house to look for me?

Easy. The same way they got this whole story. Anitra Popescu. Or whatever her real name is.

What does she get out of this?

I suspect we'll find out.

Snow circled the building until he found the janitor's door. *Cross your fingers.* He tried the handle and the door slid open. *Yes.* The homeowner's association had chastised Mr. Olney, the caretaker, several times for being lax about the door. *Thank you, Mr. Olney.*

Snow sneaked through the basement and then took the stairs to the top floor. On the landing he slowly cracked the door open. *Holy God.* He closed it quietly. Police stood at the open door to his apartment.

Maybe I should just go give myself up to them. At least that way I can tell my story. Slowly he peeked out the door again.

A policeman in uniform walked out of the apartment door with an armload of stuff. He raised an eyebrow to the guard at the door. "Did you see this shit, man? I didn't know this kind of porn even existed. Jesus. Do guys do this to each other?" He shoved a magazine in the other guy's face. The guard's eyes widened.

Porn? What the hell were they talking about? Snow closed the door. Somebody had planted porn in his apartment? His breath came in gasps.

No roof over your head. No phone. No money. His mentor in the hospital. He'd even lost Winston's friendship. No one who didn't know the story of his imaginary shame. No Riley. His back hit the wall, and he slid down to the floor. Where could he go? A lawyer managed his family trust, but he only did financial stuff, not criminal defense. People thought Snow was a criminal.

He curled in a ball and let the tears slide down his face until his eyes closed on their own.

CHAPTER 17

WHEN SNOW'S eyes opened, the tiny bit of light that had filtered up the stairwell from the windows at the bottom was gone. Night? He moved and pain shot up his back. He was used to sleeping on the floor, but not a surface this hard. He pried his fingers into the door and opened it a crack. The door to his apartment had police tape over it. Still, he could sneak in and—

A burly sheriff wandered down the hall, looking bored. So much for that plan. Snow let the door close.

Alone with nowhere to go.

He took a deep breath. *Time to stop feeling sorry for yourself and do something.*

What?

Don't know, but something.

He stood quietly and stretched the kinks out of his back. *I have money, if I can figure out how to get it. Then I could leave here and go someplace else.*

What about the professor?

Jesus, he'd been so self-absorbed he'd nearly forgotten. *If I leave, he'll be at the mercy of that woman.*

He could already be gone.

No! He sucked in a breath. *Even if he is, I have to be sure she doesn't get away with it.*

With what?

Shut up.

He slipped softly down the stairs until he got to the basement and back to the janitor's exit. Interesting to find it locked. Someone must have realized the mistake. He opened it, made sure the lock was still fixed, peeked outside into the quiet night, then took a deep breath, stepped out, and closed the door behind him.

No going home.

That certainly expanded his horizons into the great unknown. He pulled his hoodie over his head and wrapped his windbreaker tighter against the cold. *Wish I had my warmer jacket.*

People in hell want ice water.

Where to?

The trees and foliage near the river would keep him hidden. Hard going, but hell, he didn't have a destination he had to hurry to. He slipped through alleys at the backs of buildings and down darker streets until he heard the sound of the river.

Taking a more rural road, he slogged along for another fifteen minutes until he saw the expanse of the river in the distance. He shivered. Not exactly the most pleasant memory. He pushed through some dense bushes and stared at the swift-moving black liquid. Liquid he'd nearly drowned in. If it hadn't been for—

Wait. What about the Iota Pis? They didn't live in Snow's town or go to NorCal. Maybe they wouldn't know about the story.

Hell, everyone knows.

But maybe they wouldn't care so much. Besides, if they did, at least he could steal some food from their garbage. Tomorrow he'd make his way to the office of the trust's executor, get some money, and figure out what to do next. He planted a foot into the wet, sucking dirt and moved forward.

Two hours later, he stopped and leaned against a tree. Branches had smacked and scratched him, and his tennis shoes, which actually belonged to one of the Iota Pis, had turned brown with mud. Their house was farther than he thought. In the water it had only taken a few minutes to get there.

Finally he recognized some of the features of the riverbank. *There's where they rescued me.* He could still see the big pole they'd thrust out into the current. The house had to be nearby. He didn't remember being carried far.

Maybe you blacked out.

Possible, but—no, there it was. That had to be it. The big, three-story farmhouse-style building stood tucked into some trees. Man, what a location. Isolated, with an amazing view of the river from the back. Unusual for a fraternity house to have such prime real estate.

All the windows but one were dark. *Makes sense. It has to be late.* The lighted window was on the second floor. A few big trees bowed gracefully near the house. Okay, he hadn't climbed a tree in years, but what the heck. Had to be like riding a bike, right? He scoped the tree nearest the window, took hold of a low branch, and swung up. After a few harrowing handholds, he made it high enough to look in the window. Doc sat at a desk, staring at a computer screen, with a large coffee cup beside him. Doc had saved him before.

Snow found a couple of hard berries growing on the tree. He picked them and tossed the first one at the window. Missed completely. Again. This one hit, and Doc looked up, but only for a second. Snow blew on his hands. Walking had warmed him up, but he was losing heat fast. He tossed another berry and then another immediately after that so it would seem less like an accident.

Doc cocked his head toward the window. Snow tossed two more berries. Doc got up and pressed his face to the glass. Suddenly his eyes widened. Snow let go for a second and waved, then grabbed the branch again. Doc disappeared from the window, and Snow started climbing down—carefully.

He was trying to figure out how to manage the six feet from the branch he was on to the ground when Doc's voice called, "Snow, is that you?"

"Yes. Hi." He looked down at Doc's upturned face.

"How come I always seem to find you clinging to branches?"

"Yeah, sorry." He stared at the ground, scooted on the branch until he could lower himself, then let go and dropped, but not without a huge splinter in his palm. "Darn." He sucked on his hand.

"Let me see."

Snow held out his hand to Doc in the near dark. "Splinter."

"More like a log. Come on, let's get that out." He walked toward the back door of the house, and Snow followed. Doc glanced back. "So, uh, why are you here?"

"I had some trouble. You might have heard."

"Haven't heard anything. Working on a huge paper. All I've done for the last four days is study and write. I disconnected my Internet so I wouldn't be distracted." Doc closed the door after Snow walked in, and turned on the light. Warm.

"Seems like I always come to your place to get warm." Snow smiled.

Doc turned and looked at him. "Holy shit! What happened to you? You look as bad as when I fished you out of the river. Worse. At least then you were clean."

"I walked here on the riverbank."

"Where's your car?"

"I can't drive, remember?"

"Oh, right. Why didn't you call us to pick you up?"

Snow stared at his muddy sneakers. "Wrecked my phone in the river and haven't had a chance to get a new one."

"Holy crap. Don't I remember a boyfriend? Couldn't he have brought you?"

"We broke up." It started as words and ended on a sob.

Doc put a friendly hand on his arm. "Oh man, you have got trouble. Come on. I think you need a shower and some minor surgery."

That barely covered it, but would be a good start. "C-could I have a drink of water?"

"My God, kid. When did you eat last?"

"Yesterday."

"Shit. Come on."

In the bathroom, Doc brought a glass, watched while Snow sucked down water, and pried the splinter out of Snow's hand without asking another question. Good. Snow really didn't want to answer. After his shower, Snow wrapped himself in some sweats Doc left for him and walked into the room about as big as a broom closet Doc had pointed to. A sandwich, some milk, and another huge glass of water sat beside the bed. Tears of pure gratitude slipped out of Snow's eyes. Doc didn't come back, so he wolfed the sandwich, drank the water until he was slurping the bottom of the glass, and fell onto the narrow daybed, sound asleep.

"YOU BOYS didn't lie. He is exceptionally beautiful. Reminds me of a friend from New York."

Snow rolled his head to the side to escape the voice. *Sleep more.*

"I'd sure believe he could lure anyone he wanted, so maybe the stories are true."

Damn. That was a different voice. Snow pried his lids open—and stared at the wall about six inches from his face. He flipped over and looked instead at the mass of people gazing down at him. He vaguely recognized them all—the fraternity brothers?—except for one tiny, elfin man in a brilliant red-and-yellow plaid suit. Just looking at him made Snow want to smile. The rest of them? Not as much. "Uh, can I help you all?" He didn't dare sit up, since the giant sweats he kind of remembered putting on last night seemed to have slid down to his butt.

The elf smiled. "How are you feeling, my boy? I understand from Doc that you came to us last night in difficult straits."

The biggest guy in the group—Bash?—jutted his chin forward. "Yeah, because somebody found out he was a whore and threw him out of NorCal."

Doc crossed his arms. "Sorry, Mr. P. I didn't know about any of it when I let him in last night."

Romeo smiled his beautiful smile in his beautiful face. "Why should it possibly matter to anyone if Snow is a professional? We all have to make a living."

Well, hell. Snow let the covers drop, grabbed the giant sweatpants, and pulled them up as he came to sit, a move that tangled him in orange cotton, but he finally managed to face his firing squad. "I'm not a damned whore. While I agree with Romeo that it wouldn't be anyone's business if I were, the fact is, someone who hates me for reasons I don't completely understand accused me. She's gone to a boatload of trouble to get rid of me. In fact, I think she was responsible for the whole drowning thing too, but I can't prove any of it. So thanks for the sandwich and the place to sleep, and if you'll get out of my way, I'll leave."

Mr. Elf crossed his arms like Doc. "Where will you go?"

Snow puffed out some breath. "I have some money with a trust executor. If I can reach him, maybe I can get it, and then maybe I can find someplace to live where they've never heard of me and—I don't totally know."

"And what will you do about the chess tournament?" The elf smiled.

Well, crap. There was another largely vital thing he'd pretty much forgotten. Snow looked at the little man. "Do I know you?"

"No, not yet, my dear. I'm Carstairs Pennymaker. I own this home the boys live in and visit them from time to time, although I live in the east." He extended his hand. "How do you do?"

Snow frowned but shook the offered hand. "I must confess to having been better, thank you for asking. And in answer to your question, I haven't thought much about the tournament in the last twenty-four hours. My life doesn't seem to be about chess anymore."

"Ah, my dear, I think you may find that your life is entirely about chess."

"What do you mean?"

"Why don't you arise, dress in something the boys can provide that fits a bit better, and we'll feed you breakfast."

The brother called Bash glowered at Mr. Pennymaker. "I don't want anything to do with no stinking prostitutes."

Mr. Pennymaker smiled. "*Any* stinking prostitutes, Bash, and what about the young woman you paid for sex only two weeks ago? Would you condemn her for the very act you took advantage of?"

"Aw, Mr. P." He stared at the carpet.

"Don't be a hypocrite, my boy. The world has far too many of them already." He started making a shooing motion. "Besides, Snow is not a professional sex worker."

Romeo grinned. "Damned shame."

Mr. P. raised an eyebrow and laughed. "In that case, Romeo, you get to make breakfast."

Fifteen minutes later, Snow sat in the big homey kitchen of the Iota Pis, wearing some jeans and a sweatshirt from Lib, the smallest of the IPis, downing scrambled eggs with tomato and feta cheese—a Romeo specialty. A couple of the guys had left for class, but the other five hung around, along with Mr. Pennymaker.

Snow chewed. Hard to talk when the food was so good, but— "Sir, what did you mean that my life is all about chess?"

Mr. P. smiled inscrutably. He nodded at Ballet Boy, who was standing closest to the old television they kept in their kitchen. "BB, will you turn on the local news?"

Just as the channel flickered on, the local female newscaster was saying, "I think this will be brilliant for the sport of chess, don't you? Such a beautiful woman. And such a force in chess, I'm told. Wouldn't it be great if she won the Anderson Tournament?"

A video of Anitra with her brilliant hair floating around her head, bent over a chessboard with a serious—and seriously contrived—expression, flashed on the screen.

Snow's mouth opened. *What?* He closed it.

Mr. P. said, "You look surprised."

"Uh, my coach—"

"Her husband, I believe."

"Yes. He said she wasn't that good. That she had talent but hadn't really been tested. I'm just surprised that she's entered." Well, maybe not that surprised.

The TV cut to a live interview. Anitra looked seriously at the camera. "After the terrible disappointment of Snowden Reynaldi, I feel that it's my responsibility to represent NorCal with honor and skill."

Snow's fingers closed on his fork. *Don't throw it. Don't.* No more appetite.

Mr. P. looked back at Snow. "Now do you understand?"

"I don't quite get it."

"When you said someone hates you and has falsely accused you, who did you mean?"

He pointed toward the TV. "Her."

"And now she intends to take your place in the tournament. Are those facts not connected?"

"But—the prize money for the tournament is only $100,000. I mean, it's a lot for chess, but not worth killing for—even if she could win."

"When was the last time chess had a beautiful female Grandmaster?"

Snow shrugged. "There aren't many."

"As beautiful and charismatic as Anitra Popescu? The answer is never. If she wins, she'll get club money, book deals, and above all, product endorsements. We're talking millions."

"She could get a lot of that even if I won."

Mr. P. shook his head. "Quite honestly, Snow, it's not likely. You're not only talented at chess, you're exceptionally beautiful."

Romeo snorted. "You got that right."

"If you show up at the championships and win, I think she fears she'll be eclipsed."

"So she'd go to these lengths? The professor? Me?"

"I didn't say she wasn't disturbed. She's smart, ruthless, and crazy. A very dangerous combination. We need to be careful."

"We?"

"Of course, my dear. We're all going to help you with your future."

CHAPTER 18

"OKAY, USE this phone. Do you know how to access your phone messages?" Hacker handed Snow an old smartphone, then went back to fiddling with the computer he'd half taken apart on the desk in his room, frowning behind his nerd glasses.

"Yes." Snow called the number that let him access messages from alternate phones. When it answered, he put in his code.

"You have seventeen messages," the service reported.

"Oh man."

"Bad?" Hacker typed in stuff on the computer so fast Snow could barely see his fingers.

"Just a lot." Snow hit 1 for the first message.

"Snow, where are you? I'm so worried. I can't reach you." Riley's voice stabbed at his heart. He must have left this message when Snow was in the river.

Snow played it again.

Get over it.

But—

Move on.

He clicked 4 to erase and sighed.

The next message was from a local reporter asking about the championships. Snow erased it.

Another reporter wanting to know about the accident. Erase.

Another. Erase.

And another. Erase.

Then the reporters' voices changed. "Please call me regarding these allegations. I want to tell your side of the story." Erase.

"Call me as soon as you can." Erase.

And another and another.

"Snowden, this is Dean Franklin. Please call me at once." He'd left a number. Erase.

"Grandmaster Reynaldi, this is Eleanor Turks with the Anderson Invitational Committee." Snow took a breath and pressed the phone tight to his ear. "I need to speak with you right away. Please call me at your earliest convenience." She'd left her number. Snow stared at the phone.

Hacker looked up. "Something wrong?"

"A call from the tournament. Probably to tell me I've been disqualified."

"So you really aren't what the press says?" Hacker peered at a circuit.

"A prostitute? No. Funny. I've only ever had sex with one person." Snow's chest hurt just saying it.

"Where's that person?"

"He believed the stories."

"Sounds like a stupid guy."

"No, not stupid. He gave up a lot to be with me, and the stories are pretty convincing. I think it freaked him out that he changed his life so much and then I wasn't who he thought."

"Sounds stupid to me." Hacker grinned, which made his thin face cute.

Snow smiled back. "Thanks, I think." He looked at the phone. "I guess I should get this over with." He dialed.

After two rings a voice said, "Eleanor Turks."

"Hi, Ms. Turks, this is Snow Reynaldi."

"Snow, thank God. We've been pretty worried about you."

"You have?"

"Yes. We hear all this bullshit about you from the new head of your chess club, but we don't hear from you."

"Sorry, my phone got wrecked. So I'm not disqualified?"

"Why would you be?"

"All these stories about my being a—you know?"

"Darling, unless you set up a sex shop at the tournament, all we care about are your chess skills, and the last I knew, those were impeccable."

"Thank you, Ms. Turks. Things have gotten a little complicated here. The stories aren't true, by the way. But I still plan to be there."

"Good. That's all I needed to know. I didn't want to have to announce that you weren't playing. My God, all this publicity will probably double the size of the crowd."

Snow snorted. "I guess publicity has its ups and downs."

"We'll make sure they spell your name right."

"Uh, ma'am, I see that Mrs. Kingsley entered the tournament."

"Yes. It appears she's been hiding her light under a bushel. She's quietly amassed a string of impressive wins that she apparently achieved while in some kind of disguise. Anyway, she more than qualified. I saw that she told the press she was taking your place. That's why I called in such a panic. We certainly don't want to lose you. I can't think of anything better than the two of you meeting in the finals of the tournament. What a media show that will be. Of course, we'll have to see if she's actually that good." She laughed. "See you soon."

"Yes, ma'am."

She hung up. What a weird shift of fate. Was he actually going to meet this wicked woman across a chessboard?

Hacker gave him a nudge. "Doesn't sound like it went so badly."

"Apparently they don't care if I'm a prostitute, as long as I'm a whore who plays chess." Snow held up the phone. "Now I need to get some money to pay for my trip to Vegas." He dialed the executors, and a receptionist answered. "Can I speak to Martin Southwick?"

"Who can I say is calling?"

"Snowden Reynaldi."

"Oh. Yes, I'll tell him." Hold music took her place for a moment. "Uh, Mr. Reynaldi, Mr. Southwick said to tell you that they've frozen your accounts until it's determined if you owe fines and damages."

"What the hell? Who are 'they'? Let me speak to him."

"Uh, I'm sorry. He's in a meeting." The phone went dead.

Hacker frowned. "I gather that one didn't go so well."

"No. Which is bad, because I don't have a dime without that money, and I need tickets and a place to stay in Las Vegas."

Mr. Pennymaker stuck his head into the room. "Ah, there you are, my dears. Ready for your makeover, Snow?"

"Makeover? What do you mean?"

"We're preparing you to go to the tournament with style and verve. No one who sees you win will ever forget it."

"Win? Jesus, Mr. P., I can't even get the money together for a plane ticket."

Mr. P. fluttered a hand as he perched on the edge of Hacker's bed. "Nonsense. You're our investment. We plan to see that you not only win, you capture more endorsements and sponsorships than any chess champion in history."

"How are you going to do that?"

"I'm not. You are." Mr. P. beamed and sprang to his feet, brushing imaginary lint from his black-and-white striped suit, which managed to make him look like a bundle of licorice. "Now, here's the plan. Bash will teach you self-defense, Gormet shall make you a connoisseur of food and wine, BB will instruct you in dancing, Hacker will equip you with the latest electronics, Romeo will perfect you in the arts of love, Lib and Doc will challenge you at chess, and I—" He bowed slightly. "—shall teach you the elements of fashion."

Snow's brain had exploded somewhere back around the arts of love. "Sir, I can't let you do this. I don't even know why you'd want to."

Mr. Pennymaker gave Snow a level look. "Good must defeat evil in this world, Snowden, and why shouldn't good have style?" He laughed as he led Snow from the room.

RILEY WALKED off the field and waved as the fans leaned down to try and get autographs. Didn't feel like stopping to chat. Felt like crap.

Rog trotted by. His face softened from its usual glower, and he gave Riley a nod. Man, that was fucking different. Why didn't it make him happy?

Danny jogged up beside him and bumped his shoulder pads. "Good game, man."

"Thanks."

"Looked like a well-oiled machine again today."

"Yeah."

"That catch Rog made was one for the books. Keep that up and the championship is yours."

"Hope so." Funny how his head always seemed to feel heavy these days. He stared at his shoes as he walked.

"I guess they quit giving you shit about being gay? Is that why the team is working so well again?"

Riley sighed. "They don't like it, but they figure I got sucked in by a prostitute and lured and it wasn't my fault."

"You're shitting me."

Riley frowned. "No. That's what they think."

Danny slowed his steps, and Riley cocked his head to look at him.

Danny turned down a side hall and leaned against the wall. He waited until Riley followed. "I guess what matters is what you think. Do you believe that shit?"

Riley stopped. When had he ever thought Danny was a dumb jock? A dumb gay jock. He looked around. "I'm pretty confused."

"Why?"

"The guy who accused Snow is kind of credible. I mean, I know him, and I can't imagine he'd make up a story like that."

"More credible than Snow?"

Riley lowered his voice. "It's just that—" He took a breath. "—Snow claimed to be a virgin, but he was pretty accomplished in the sack, you know?"

"No, I guess I don't know. But I never kicked somebody out of bed because they were too fucking good, man."

Riley wiped a hand over the back of his neck.

"Snow ever ask you for money?"

"No. But maybe he was working up to it."

"I heard the guy had some kind of trust fund."

"The police say that may just be the proceeds from his escort service."

"Oh yeah?" Danny pushed off from the wall.

Riley slapped a hand against the wall. "Jesus, Danny, I changed my whole life for him."

"Really? I thought you changed your life because it was the truth."

"Shit."

"And I'll tell you something from an outside observer. Snow Reynaldi's one of the most beautiful guys I ever saw. If he's selling that on the open market, why the fuck did he pick a no-money asshole like you?" Danny laughed and walked toward the locker room with that slow, loose-limbed gait.

Riley just shook. He'd asked himself that question twenty times. No good answer. But the police kept telling him the story appeared true. Jesus, pornography in Snow's apartment. *I don't want to believe it. I don't. I don't.*

He dragged himself into the locker room. A lot of the guys were already changed. He peeled off his uniform and took a quick shower. *Don't think.* As he pulled on his clothes, Roget and two of the other players walked by. Rog glanced back at Riley. "Helluva pass today, Prince."

"Thanks."

"Heard any more about the whore?"

Riley just kept dressing.

"If he comes back to this campus, I'll sure as fuck see he never gets his fag hands on any other good men again. I'll call you so you can join the lynch mob."

Riley's head snapped up, but Rog and his buddies were already walking away.

That's what I'm making possible. That's the logical conclusion to this story.

He yanked his sweater over his head and grabbed his jacket.

I don't want to believe that Snow's guilty.

He could practically hear Danny's voice ringing in his head.

You don't want to believe it, asshole? Then don't.

SWEAT POURED off Snow as he danced back and forth from foot to foot and jabbed at a large punching bag.

"Remember, when you're fighting a bigger opponent, it's all about evasion. You can't fight him toe to toe, or he'll wipe you out. Jab, jab. Not bad, Reynaldi." Bash put a hand on the bag to steady it. "Okay. Stop for a minute."

Snow dropped his hands to his knees and tried to catch his breath. Mr. P. insisted he had to learn self-defense. Said his life could depend on it.

"The other thing to remember is if somebody attacks you, fight dirty. Grab whatever you can and use it as a weapon; kick them in the balls, head butt to get out of a hold. Okay?"

Snow nodded but kept breathing.

"Let's try a few moves. Then you have your lesson with Romeo."

Holy wow, Romeo. Snow tried to concentrate for fifteen more minutes of punching, grabbing, and kicking. "Thanks a lot, Bash."

"You're not near as hopeless at this as I thought you'd be. Couple more lessons and you might actually be able to hold up in a fight."

Snow gasped. "That would be great."

"Probably need a shower before you go see Lover Boy." Bash laughed, went to the bench press he had set up in the IPi garage, and lifted some astronomical amount of weight from his chest. Snow hurt just looking at him.

He staggered up the stairs to his shared bathroom and showered, then went to his tiny makeshift room and dressed in the jeans and sweatshirt Lib had loaned him. Mr. P. planned to take Snow shopping the next day so he'd be able to return the clothes. Not sure how he'd return Mr. P.'s money or his kindness.

Next lesson. Holy crap, his hands were shaking. What exactly did they mean when they said Romeo would teach him about the arts of love? And why did he need to know? Not like he had anyone he wanted to practice on.

Here goes. He walked down the hall to the room he knew was Romeo's and knocked.

"Come in." Romeo's silky, soft voice was a lesson in sex all by itself.

Snow opened the door. *Whoo boy.* Romeo sat on the bed, the blinds behind him mostly closed and several candles burning in the room. The place smelled like oranges and some other good stuff. *Wow.*

Romeo himself embodied the art of love. He wore loose-fitting black pants that hung low on his narrow hips and a shirt that had to be silk. It begged to be petted. His bare feet managed to be ridiculously sexy. "Come in and be comfortable."

Snow pressed back against the bedroom door he'd just closed. "Uh, Romeo, what exactly are we doing? Because the stories about me aren't true. You know that, right?"

"Yes, dear, sadly I do. What we're going to do is make you a bit more like that image than you are now, so you are positively irresistible in bed."

"Why should I be?"

"Why not?"

Had him there.

"What does it have to do with winning at chess?"

"Everything. A winner is someone with confidence. As Mr. P. says, a dash of positive arrogance. You need to know you can function optimally in every situation. Love is one of those situations."

"I don't know."

"There's no reason not to be romantic, is there?"

Snow shrugged but couldn't keep the frown from his face. "One of the reasons the guy I liked believed the stories about me was that I was more, uh, accomplished than he thought a virgin should be." Everything about the thought hurt.

"Your boyfriend sounds like he isn't very experienced himself."

"Probably not. I mean, he was in the closet for all of college."

Romeo waved to the chair beside the bed, all cushy and deep with pillows. "Come sit."

Snow crossed to the chair and sank into it.

Romeo sat cross-legged, propped his elbows on his knees, and cupped his chin in his palms. "For thousands of years, stupid humans have played this ridiculous game. Women have been required to be virgins. If they show enthusiasm, they're branded whores. Then, when they have no experience or expertise in bed, their men leave them at home while they seek more satisfying companionship elsewhere. It's a construct so that men can have it their way, which is nonmonogamous. It's the worst kind of bullshit."

"Wow, I never thought about it."

"Yes, well, you're gay. You didn't have to—until you got treated the same way."

Snow stared at his feet. "I don't think he expected me to be a virgin."

"No, but he liked that you were."

"I guess."

"Because that made you 'his,' right?"

"I suppose so."

"Well, you're not his, Snow. You're yours."

Snow looked up, and his mouth gaped open. How could such a simple statement hit so hard?

"Your affection has not one particle more or less value because it's inexperienced. What has value is your decision, your choice to care about someone, not some imaginary hymen in your asshole."

Snow snorted out a laugh. "Graphically put."

"So let's get to work making you sexually irresistible, and let your boyfriend grow up on his own."

"I, uh, think you're really gorgeous, but I don't want to—"

Romeo whipped a large pink dildo covered in a condom from behind him on the bed. "Thank you for the compliment, but this is your practice tool." He handed the slightly obscene object to Snow, then tossed him a plastic squeeze bottle of lube.

Snow blushed and laughed. "Thanks."

"All right, let's start with hand jobs. Grab your lube."

Snow swallowed hard and did as Romeo said.

"Each aspect of physical love has its own expression, its own beauty, its own qualities. Your mouth has warmth and wetness and a remarkable capability for suction. Your ass squeezes and tightens on its own. Plus it has the psychological value of supreme intimacy—literally entering the body of another." He held up his hands, long-fingered and graceful. "But the hands have their own unique value. They have dexterity that the tongue doesn't possess and more control than your ass. So let's put them to work."

Romeo applied his lube-slicked hands to a dildo similar to the one he'd given Snow. "Let's begin with the basic grip and twist. Hold the shaft firmly at the base with one hand. Slide upward with a firm squeeze, grasp with the other hand at the base as the top hand twists the head. Grip, slide, and twist, grip, slide and twist."

Snow practiced until his hands moved effortlessly. *Oh my, hard not to imagine this dildo being Riley's warm flesh.*

"Good. Now let's make some fire, Boy Scout style. Put both hands at the base of the cock on opposite sides, and slip them together like you're twirling a fire stick."

"Really? Does that feel good?"

"Yes, quite amazing as long as your partner isn't too close to orgasm. Then he may be too sensitive for that much stimulation."

"Fascinating."

Romeo smiled. "You see. Just one more science for you to master." He stood the tall pink cock flat on the bed in front of him. "Now, let's add the mouth—"

CHAPTER 19

RILEY TOWERED over Mike Henderson, leaning in to emphasize the six-inch difference in their height. "Tell me what happened, and I swear to you, I'll know if you're lying."

Henderson held up his hands. "You know what happened. I told the press. I told the police. Why should I tell you?"

"Because they weren't planning to leave you bloody for lying, you asshole."

"Come on, Riley. I heard he did it to you too."

"Who did what to me?"

"Snowden Reynaldi got you to pay him to have sex."

Riley clenched his fists and narrowed his eyes. "You heard wrong. I never paid him anything—and neither did you. In fact, I strongly suspect you never even had sex with him. Unless you forced him. Is that what happened, Henderson? Did you try to rape him?" He raised a fist. No need to tell the asshole he'd never use it.

"Hell, no! I never—"

"You never what? Tell me, Mike. What did you like best about Snow?"

"He was great at, uh, you know, oral shit."

"Gives great head?"

"Right. Fantastic. A real pro."

"Yeah. That tongue stud of his really does a number on your cockhead, right?"

"What? Oh yeah. It does."

Riley grabbed the neck of Mike's hoodie and lifted. "He doesn't have a tongue stud."

"Yeah, I mean, he does sometimes. He takes it out."

"Tell me the truth, Mike. How much did they pay you to lie? Tell me now, or I'll make every day of your life hell, even if I have to follow you to the end of the fucking earth to do it."

"Shit, Riley, they told me you'd go along."

"Go along?"

"I mean, that it happened to you—uh, too. That's why I agreed. They said he did it to you."

Riley tightened his grip. "Do I look like I'm going along?"

Henderson tried to swallow, which had to be getting harder. "I'd, uh, never have done it if I knew it would piss you off, Riley."

"How much, Mike?"

"Hell, Riley."

"How much?" He screamed the words in Henderson's face.

"Ten thousand. I needed it. My dad's sick and can't pay for college."

"Didn't this phony confession make you an accessory to a crime?"

Mike tried to shrug in the stretched hoodie. "You know how they are about guys and prostitution. They said I'd get off if I cooperated."

"Have they paid you the money yet?"

"Half."

"Who hired you?"

"Don't know. Just a voice on the phone and money dropped in my mailbox."

Shit. Riley loosened his grip by half. "If I speak to the police, I expect you to come through with the real story."

Tears filled Mike's eyes. "They'll take back the money, Riley. Maybe hurt me."

"We'll figure out something. But you are going to tell the truth when I ask you, right? Because otherwise, it's going to be way worse for you than having to go to a cheaper college. Got it?"

"Yeah. Okay. I wouldn't normally do something like this. You gotta believe me."

Sadly, that's why he had believed him. "Just be ready when I ask you to tell the truth. For now, keep going along."

"Okay. Seriously, I only did it—"

"Don't care, Mike. We all make mistakes, but we have to fix them if we can."

"Okay. Yeah. I'd like that."

Riley took a breath and adjusted the recorder under his sweatshirt.

"BLOODY FUCKING hell!" She hurled the newspaper as far as it would sail, then picked up a coffee mug and slammed it against the granite countertop until it shattered.

"What is it now?" Hunter looked up from the idiotic adventure novel he was reading at the kitchen table.

"Look." She gritted her teeth as she pointed at the pages lying on the floor.

He sighed. "Where?" He leaned over the newspaper.

"Am I boring you?"

"No, of course not. I just don't know where to look."

She stalked the few steps to the center of the room and turned one of the newspaper pages with her foot. She stepped on it, then back. "There."

He twisted his head, then frowned. "Well, shit."

"Yes, shit. Double shit. Shit to the hundredth power. Do you realize what this means?"

Hunter examined the headline of the full page ad, which read, *NorCal's Own Snowden Reynaldi Leads the Pack at Anderson World Chess Tournament, Las Vegas. Get Your Tickets Now.*

He pointed far down in the copy. "They mention you."

"Thank you for sharing." She kicked at the paper. "He's obviously still in the tournament."

"Yeah. They must not have cared about his terrible reputation."

"Are you making fun of me?"

"Of course not, just an observation. So, you're still in the tournament. All you have to do is beat him. That will double your triumph and your endorsements."

She stared out the window. "Yes." Slowly she turned to Hunter with her nails digging into her palms. "Do you, in your wormlike brain, have the slightest idea what it would take to defeat Snowden Reynaldi at chess?" She stepped toward him and he cringed back, which made her smile. "No, of course you don't. Your intellect isn't even on the same planet with Reynaldi. You couldn't grasp what he can do on a chessboard if you harnessed the best thoughts you've ever had in your brain and rode them like Ben-Hur's chariot. Of course I can't defeat him, you idiot!"

"But you said you were good."

"Yes, I'm good. Maybe even great. Reynaldi is another matter."

The doorbell rang.

"What the hell?" She looked at Hunter. "Are you expecting someone?"

"No. Nobody."

She looked around the kitchen, then walked to the mirror on the wall near the back door and checked her makeup. *Gorgeous.* She gathered her hair and fastened it in a knot at her neck. The grieving almost-widow. That was another source of irritation. Kingsley was still alive. Oh well, it wouldn't be long. "Pick up the fucking newspaper, you idiot." She strode to the front door and looked out through the peephole. *What?* Riley fucking Prince. What in the hell could he possibly want? *Look as defeated as possible.* Slowly she opened the door. "My, what a surprise. How are you, Riley?"

"Doing okay, ma'am, considering."

She placed a hand on her cheek. "I know just how you feel."

"I don't mean to intrude."

She waved a hand. "Of course not. Life goes on."

"I became very fond of Professor Kingsley when I was being tutored in physics."

"How nice."

"I was thinking I'd like to stop by and see him."

What? "Uh, no one but family is allowed."

"I know. I thought maybe you'd give me permission to visit him, just for a moment. If there's anything you need to go to the hospital, like flowers, or if he has a favorite book you like to read to him, I could do it for you. I know this has to be so hard on you, with all your responsibilities."

She gazed at him. Such a handsome boy. Why would he want to go spend time in a smelly hospital? "Of course, how very thoughtful of you."

"Maybe you could write a note saying it's okay for me to see him?"

"Yes, of course. And your idea about the book. How nice. Please come in."

He followed her into the vestibule and then the living room. Hunter sat forward on his seat. She glanced at Riley. "You know my cousin, Hunter?"

"Uh, no." He stuck out his hand. "Hey, man."

Hunter half rose, nodded, and shook his hand. "You're Snow's friend."

Riley shrugged. "He tutored me in physics. But I think calling him a friend now would be pretty weird. Sorry about what happened to you. I saw it on TV."

Hunter shrugged. "I'm not hurt. Just the loss of an old car. At least he wasn't killed. That's good."

Riley nodded. "I guess."

"Yeah, I guess."

Anitra put a hand on Riley's arm. "Let me get you that permission slip, shall we call it?" She smiled. My, he was good-looking.

"And the book."

"Oh, right."

"Ma'am—"

"Just call me Anitra."

He grinned and dimples popped out in his cheeks. "Anitra, could I get a glass of water? No telling what they'll have available in the hospital."

"Of course. Hunter can show you."

Riley held up a hand. "Don't bother. I don't want to interfere with your reading. I loved that book." He nodded at the paperback Hunter had set aside. "I'm assuming the kitchen is straight back."

She nodded. "Yes."

"I'll just be a second."

He headed toward the back of the house. She watched his flexing ass. She'd heard he was gay. Maybe she could change his mind. He wanted a book. Oh hell, which one could she logically say Harold loved? She glanced at the shelves. Nothing. Maybe in his study. She looked at Hunter, who'd gone back to his reading. The novel probably had pictures based on the cumulative intelligence of these two boobs. "I'll be right back."

He nodded.

It took her five minutes to write the note and find a copy of a Hermann Hesse novel she felt comfortable claiming was a favorite of Harold's. When she walked back downstairs, the TV was on and both men were staring at some horrible football thing. "Here you are, Riley."

He stood instantly. At least he had manners. "Thank you so much, Mrs. Kingsley. I hope my visit can take some pressure off you."

"That's very kind."

He shook her hand, and she kissed his smooth, postadolescent cheek. What a yummy boy. Once again, she admired the movement of muscle in his perfect posterior as he crossed the street to an old, beat-up vehicle.

Hunter's chuckle woke her from her reverie. "You're thinking a bunch of stuff you shouldn't be thinking."

"I am not." She smiled. "And what if I am. He's not underage."

"Yeah, well, if you want a three-way, let me know. I wouldn't mind a piece of that."

"What a charming idea." She stared back at the pile of newspapers beside Hunter on the couch. "We have to pack for Las Vegas. And I have to perfect a plan."

A HALF hour later, Riley Prince walked into the chemistry lab, where he met his friend Josh Froder. "Hey, man, thanks for meeting me."

"No problem. What do you need analyzed?"

Riley held out the small brown stopper bottle he'd taken from the laundry room at Professor Kingsley's house. "If you could get on this right away, I'd appreciate it. I'll be back in an hour. I have to go visit someone in the hospital."

SNOW WALKED around the big living room of the Iota Pi house, making a move in each chess game, one after the other, and slapping the timers. Mr. P. had set it up so he could play every IPi brother who had any knowledge of chess all at the same time. Only Doc, Hacker, and Lib had real skill. The others just made for background noise, but still, it was good practice. When he'd beaten them all in less than twenty minutes, Doc rocked back in his chair. "Shit, man, you are awesome. And I don't use that word lightly."

Snow stared at the brand-new, beyond cool shoes Mr. Pennymaker had bought for him. "Thanks. All you guys were great."

"Snowden!"

He looked up at Mr. P. striding in the front door. "Hello, sir."

"Snow, your modesty is charming, but I want you to practice a modicum of arrogance. It's needed and expected in a Grandmaster. Try again."

Snow took a deep breath. He looked directly into Doc's eyes and extended his hand. "Thank you for the compliment. You were an excellent opponent." Then he snorted, and both he and Doc burst out laughing.

Mr. P. smiled. "Much better. Until that last part, of course." He clapped his hands together. "Have you tried on all of your lovely new clothes?"

"Yes, sir, but—"

"No buts. You're going to require most of the wardrobe in Vegas. After all, you have to look the part of a champion. Ask any actor. They'll tell you, half the performance is just in the wardrobe." He looked around at the IPis. They tended to gather when Mr. P. was around. Apparently he'd done some special service for each of the brothers. He'd taken Romeo off the streets and saved him from being a rent boy and was paying a big part of Doc's tuition since his family was dirt poor. People had assumed Bash was stupid until Mr. P. revealed he had a genius IQ, and he'd bailed Hacker out of jail. Twice. All the IPis loved him immensely. "Now, boys, get packed. We leave early tomorrow."

Snow stepped forward. "Sir? Everyone's going?"

"Of course. You don't think one of us would miss an event like this, do you? Gormet has a big van we can all fit in."

Wow. They all wanted to go with him. He grinned. "Are you kidding? My wardrobe will take up a whole van by itself."

Later, after dinner, he sat in the study, staring at a book of chess moves.

"Doesn't look like your eyes are moving, my dear. Not much reading going on, is my guess." Mr. P. stood in the doorway, a red flower in the buttonhole of his checked suit.

"Just thinking."

"May I join you?"

"Please do."

He sat on the couch next to Snow. "What's on your mind?"

"Just wondering how good she is. Most of the other players are known quantities. Some of them are very good and, under the right circumstances, a few can beat me. But I don't know about her."

"Yes, she's stayed well hidden."

Snow blew out a long column of air. "And win or lose, when I finish, nothing's changed. The professor will still be in the hospital—or worse. I'm still expelled and being investigated by the police. I have no money I can count on to repay you." He didn't say, "And I still won't have Riley."

"We'll cross all those grand bridges when we come to them."

"Yes, sir, but I want you to know that I plan to get a job to pay you back." He breathed in. "I've been thinking. I'm a pretty damned good physicist, and tech companies need people with my skills. I figure they'll overlook a police record to get them." He laughed.

"Now there's the arrogance I was looking for."

"Oh no, sir, I didn't mean—"

"Snowden, quit while you're ahead."

Snow looked the little elf in the eye. "Yes, sir. I will."

"MRS. KINGSLEY, welcome to the Five Diamonds. I hope your stay will be memorable."

"Thank you." Anitra smiled and adjusted her large-brimmed hat. She glanced at Hunter, who was standing with the bags just inside the hotel entrance.

The clerk checked the computer. "We have you in a two-room suite, as requested." He looked up. "For you and your cousin, I believe." He said the word "cousin" like they used the term "niece" in *Pretty Woman.*

She deepened her look of distress. "Yes, since my husband is so ill, my cousin has been taking care of me. Should my husband's condition change, I'll have to depart quickly, and Hunter will see that I make it back to California without injuring myself in my haste." *Hmm. Too much?*

No, the idiot fell for it. His expression changed instantly. "I'm so very sorry, and wish you great success in the tournament."

"Thank you." She took her keycard and walked slowly toward Hunter. A camera flashed. *Oh, good.* She turned and smiled.

A young woman crowded forward. "Are you Anitra Kingsley?"

"Yes. Yes, I am."

"Wow. You're even prettier than the pictures in the paper. I can't believe you're a chess champion."

"You must never assume a pretty woman is dumb, my dear. Look at yourself." *Lay it on thick.*

The woman clutched a hand to her chest. "Oh, thank you. Can I have your autograph?"

"Of course." She signed the girl's program for the tournament, then walked over to Hunter, who looked bored and impatient. She smiled at him like a cousin, then muttered, "Calm down. Getting people to pay attention to me is what we want, right?"

"I suppose. Let's get upstairs."

Before they made it to the elevators, two more people took pictures. *Hope they're reporters.* Finally they got to their suite on the fourteenth floor.

Hunter dropped the bags and looked around. "Not bad." It had a small sitting room with a nice view over the Strip and two doors leading to bedrooms.

She checked the blue couch and two chairs. "It's okay. I wanted a lanai suite by the pool. It would have been more impressive. But this one was all I could afford." She threw a pillow from the chair to the couch just for a little vent.

"When do you get the bank accounts?"

"Not till the old coot dies. I tried to get Harold to transfer over the bank account into my name, but I couldn't push too hard without him getting suspicious. We were only married a few hours legally, and I couldn't wait any longer or I would have had to have sex with him." She shuddered. "Anyway, his lawyers will only give me an allowance, since he never authorized the transfer. That's until he finally croaks and I inherit in our community property state. Then I'll have it all."

He chuckled. "And a whole lot more."

"Oooh, I like that as a motto. 'I want it all—and a whole lot more.' I think I'll have it embroidered on a pillow." Their laughter mingled.

She unpacked, and he put his things in the other bedroom so the maids wouldn't get suspicious. They'd have to hide the cum stains on the sheets. When she walked out, he was already dipping into the hotel's porn collection on the TV. "Save that. I need to go down and register for the tournament, then let people see me. You have to watch for Reynaldi."

He sighed. "Okay. Yeah." He flipped off the TV.

"You know what to do. Make it look like a robbery or something, okay?" Hunter nodded.

"Get it done, because my last line of defense is tricky. It's hard to pull off, and it might not work, even if I can do it."

"Yeah, sure, I'll get the job done."

She narrowed her eyes. "You didn't last time."

"Not my fault."

"It never is, Hunter." She slid on her sunglasses to add that air of mystery, and smoothed the slinky black dress that clung to her world-class ass. "I am going to win this tournament one way or another. My future depends on it. So does yours." She ambled toward the door, hips swinging.

"Great dress."

"Thanks." She pursed her lips in a mock kiss. "I'm in mourning."

CHAPTER 20

HACKER WAS at the wheel when they pulled into the driveway of the Five Diamond Hotel. It had been eleven hours, but with seven of them to drive—Snow didn't know how and Mr. P. was excused—they made it straight through with only stops for peeing and food. The tall hotel with its metal surfaces that shone like diamonds in the bright sun stretched above them.

As they waited for the valet, Mr. P. turned in his seat and looked back at Snow. "Ready to wow them?"

Snow exhaled long and slow. "I'll try, sir. It doesn't come naturally."

Mr. P. gave him a once-over. "Excellent job, Romeo. Quite natural. You look very lovely yourself."

"Thank you, sir." Romeo had "styled" Snow, trimming his ink-black hair, waving it, and brushing it to a high gloss. He'd even added a little eyeliner, mascara, and some lip color to enhance the whole picture.

Snow smiled. "You do look great." Romeo's hair was almost as dark as Snow's, though not as long or wavy. It had been brushed away from his stunning face, which was framed by a pure white shirt under a sleek black suit. "In that outfit, you could be a movie star."

Doc looked back. "Or a Mafia don."

Mr. P. raised a finger. "We shall keep them guessing. Some people will have read the stories about Snow, so seeing him escorted by a man so nearly his match in beauty will confuse them. It will also attract cameras and reporters. You know how to behave, Snowden."

"I'll try."

"Good. The rest of you too. Ready?"

"Ready, Mr. P."

The van pulled into the valet space. While not a limo, it was a very upscale Mercedes van, thanks to Gormet's upscale family, so Mr. P. had judged it impressive enough to create the needed impact.

"Good afternoon, sir. Welcome to the Five Diamonds." The valet opened the door, and as agreed, Bash stepped out. Clad in a dark suit and sunglasses, he carefully pressed a hand against his pocket, fingering a supposed weapon. He surveyed the group of fifty or so people gathered outside to see the chess masters. Doc climbed out behind Bash and took a spot on the opposite side of the door. Short but stocky, he still managed to look mean. Snow peered through the window and wanted to laugh, but that wasn't in the script.

Next, Gormet and Lib emerged. Told to look like "entourage," they whispered to each other, waved to imaginary friends in the crowd, and gazed back at the van in expectation. Hacker had given the valet the keys and walked around to join them in the act. By now, the crowd was muttering and people were hurrying from inside the hotel, apparently to see the entrance they were making.

Next came Mr. Pennymaker in a pink suit so elegant and outrageous, people literally stopped talking for a moment. He extended a hand to BB. Quite a beautiful guy in his own right, Ballet Boy raised the stakes on outrageous, wearing a silver jumpsuit just a fraction looser than a leotard on his lean, graceful body. Both of them stepped back to give full focus to the big arrival.

A gasp went up from the crowd as Romeo stepped out of the van. He ignored it and turned as if he couldn't wait for what was about to happen. Snow's hands shook so much he could barely adjust his sunglasses. With a deep breath, he emerged from the car, grasping Romeo's hand for balance. He looked up at the crowd, which had grown to what must be a hundred, removed his sunglasses, and smiled. All practiced, but he hoped it didn't show.

A little "ooooh" went up from the people. Someone yelled, "Hey, Snow, are you going to win?"

He didn't have to work hard to look shy. He glanced down at his elegant Italian shoes, then up toward the man who had shouted the question. "You tell me."

A couple of girls screamed, and Bash and Doc stood straighter, as if he might need protection from attacking teenyboppers.

Holding tight to Romeo's arm, he started into the hotel.

Romeo leaned down. "You're doing great, beautiful."

A woman with a microphone moved toward him as they neared the entrance. "Snow. Hello. I'm Kizzy Applegate from Chess TV. Can I have a moment?"

"Of course." He let go of Romeo's arm and stepped over to the reporter.

"My, my. This is kind of a new look for you, isn't it?"

He laughed, though his stomach flipped. "My friend Randy took me in hand and changed my style. Do you approve?" He did a little twirl.

"Very much. I've always thought chess needed some extra fashion sense."

He laughed at her joke.

"So I've heard that you had a bit of trouble back in California. I hope everything's all right now."

He frowned. "Yes. Sadly, I was falsely accused. It may be a mere misunderstanding." He waved a hand. "My lawyers are disproving it as we speak. But the tournament was kind enough to overlook this little dustup and insisted I attend anyway."

"Of course." She looked into the camera. "What would a major world chess tournament be without Snowden Reynaldi?"

Snow smiled. "I'm so glad you feel that way." He took a breath. "Apparently you're not alone."

"And now, with your new style and your, I must say, handsome escort, you'll be even more of an asset to the event."

"How kind of you to say so, Kizzy. I'll tell Randy your compliment."

She fluttered a hand in front of her face. "You're certainly proving that Grandmasters can be rock stars, Snow."

He laughed again. "I'm sure rock stars would be offended, but we'll give it our best." He leaned in and kissed her cheek. All the females in the crowd tittered or screamed while Kizzy blushed. Snow stepped back, waved, then took Romeo's arm and made it into the cool lobby before he passed out.

Hacker stepped forward with the room keys, Doc and the other guys grabbed the bags, and they headed to their rooms—a suite for Snow, Romeo, and Mr. P., and three additional rooms for the rest of the IPis, on both sides of the suite.

ANITRA WATCHED the entourage, trailing fans and reporters like pilot fish on a whale, climb onto the elevator. "What the bloody fuck?"

Hunter hissed, "Keep your voice down."

She wanted to hit him, but dammit, he was right. She whispered, "How could this be Snow Reynaldi? That mewling little pissant never met a pair of khakis he didn't love and couldn't hold a conversation with his best friend. What's happened?"

"I don't know. What he was wearing would buy a car, and that boyfriend is some world-class beauty. I thought he was in love with the quarterback."

"Whatever happened doesn't matter. It's just one more reason to squash that bug before he does any more damage. Come on."

She marched herself past Kizzy Applegate three fucking times before the stupid broad finally noticed her. "Oh, hello. Aren't you the new competitor, Anita—" She glanced at her paper. "—Kingsley?"

"It's Anitra. *Tra.*" She smiled. "Yes, I am." She turned her head so it captured the light under her hat.

"Oh yes, well, welcome to the Anderson World Tournament. It's so nice to have a lovely woman representing world chess."

"Thank you. We women must stick up for our right to excel at chess, mustn't we?"

"Yes, so nice that this tournament mixes men and women competitors so you can come up against the best of the best."

"I agree. Having women's tournaments, as if we were somehow intellectually inferior and must be grouped like chickens or something, is an archaic practice."

"Bravo, Anitra. And speaking of lovely, have you met Snowden Reynaldi? Have you seen his new look?"

Anitra dug her nails into her palms and tried to find an answer.

MORE THAN twenty-four hours later, Snow dragged himself off the elevator at the other end of the massive hotel floor from his room—again. He kept getting confused, the building was so huge. He looked at the room numbers on the wall and turned left. Almost home. Not home, just back to his room. But then, considering how little home he actually had, maybe this room was as good as any.

Long day. First round of the tourney. He'd played five games, won them all in under an hour each without so much as a draw, and then gone out for a nice dinner with Mr. P. and the boys. After that he'd had to spend a few minutes with the tournament organizers going over a fund-raising campaign for charity they wanted to sponsor. Now back to Mr. P. and the IPis. He trudged down the long hall with matching doors on both sides, the sameness marred only by an occasional room service tray.

God knew why they were all so kind to him, but if it took all his life, he wanted to repay that kindness—somehow. Of course, the guys would likely not have believed in him if Mr. Pennymaker hadn't—but he had. In a life short on family and friends, Mr. P.'s trust and confidence were a gift and a revelation.

The hall turned, and he turned with it.

Maybe he could—

He came up to another elevator lobby. Some movement made him look to his right. Hunter stood pressed against one of the walls.

Snow leaped back. *When facing a larger opponent, your first option is to run.* His feet started moving before Bash's words even cleared his mind.

"Snow, wait!"

Like bloody hell. He ran as fast as he could down the long hall. No idea where. A stairwell sign flashed ahead of him. Was that worse or better? *Shit!* Though the carpets absorbed sound, he could hear Hunter pounding behind him. If Hunter had only wanted to talk, why was he chasing? *Run fast!*

A door ahead opened. Yes, good. A man took a step out, saw Snow running, and retreated instantly, slamming the door. If Snow stopped to knock, Hunter would be on him—and the guy probably wouldn't open anyway.

His breath came in gasps as he turned another corner in the hall. He grabbed the new cell from his pocket and tried to dial. Fucking lock codes. Ahead, the hall ended. The bright stairwell sign shone over it. Decision. If he got in that stairwell, Hunter could kill him with no problem, and people wouldn't find his body for days. Wasn't a rational choice.

He whirled and dropped into a fighting stance.

Hunter's eyes widened, and he stopped a few yards away. Probably surprised by seeing Snow look like a fighter. Then he smiled. "You don't want to fight me, pretty baby. I'm bigger, stronger, and a hell of a lot meaner."

"So you think I should just let you kill me?"

Hunter looked a little startled but took a step forward. "Why would I want to kill you?"

"Because you failed the last time."

"No. That was someone else."

"Bullshit."

He cracked a little smile. "Shame you feel that way. I really do like you. If you just agreed to go away and forget the tournament and forget chess, I might even be able to find a way to keep you alive." He shrugged. "Of course, watching you would be a pain in the ass, so I better not consider that." Another step forward.

"However much she's paying you, I'll pay more."

Hunter frowned. "How could you do that?"

"Haven't you noticed my clothes and entourage? I have a benefactor who'll do anything for me."

"Hooked another one, huh?"

"No, it's not like that. He'd love to pay you to protect me."

Snow's back pressed against the window that looked out over Las Vegas. Hunter cocked a hip and crossed his arms. "Seriously?"

"Yes, he'd be quite generous." Snow took slow breaths to stop his heart pounding in his ears, and his fingers played with the phone in his hand.

It happened in one move. Hunter snorted. "Shit, she'd see me dead." He lunged forward to grab Snow. Snow's instinct, honed by six grueling lessons with Bash, struck. His knee came up and connected with Hunter's balls so hard they probably pushed into his stomach. Hunter screamed and grabbed his groin. Snow smashed at his nose with the phone in his hand, connected, and felt searing pain up his arm and heard the sickening crunch of bone crushing. Hunter howled again and fell against the wall. Doors down the hall started opening.

Snow ran far enough to feel safe, then turned. "He attacked me. Call security."

Someone said, "Oh my God, it's Snow Reynaldi. Someone call the cops."

Two young guys ran out of a room and grabbed Hunter, who was clearly not in much shape to struggle. Thank God for Bash's second lesson. When cornered, fight dirty.

Speak of the angels, Bash ran around the corner at that moment with Romeo, Doc, and BB behind him. "What the hell is going on?"

Snow sagged against the wall, and Romeo grabbed him into a hug. Snow snaked an arm toward Hunter. "He attacked me. He's the same guy who accused me."

Hunter held an arm over his nose but managed to gurgle out, "Lie. Is lie. He attacked me."

One of the young guys shook his head. "Oh no, he didn't. I saw the whole thing. I was just about to run out and help the little guy, but man, he sure took care of himself. He did some damage."

Snow smiled at Bash against Romeo's chest. "I learned my lessons."

"What's going on here?" Two hotel security guards trotted up the hall, beginning what was sure to be a long damned night.

TWO HOURS later he sat in his suite with Mr. P., Bash, Romeo, and Doc. The other guys had gone to bed. Mr. Policeman One—Snow was so tired, he'd forgotten his name—sat beside him, and Detective Ehrhardt, a tough-looking, broken-nosed kind of bruiser, sat opposite him. The two guys who'd helped him in the hall had just left.

"So the reason this guy Hunter attacked you is—" Ehrhardt made a circular motion with his fingers.

Snow didn't even try to suppress his sigh. The whole story was so unbelievable, and he couldn't prove most of it. "I told you, he doesn't want me to play chess, for one thing. He wants his cousin to win. Plus, he tried to drown me in a car back home in California, and he's afraid I'm going to figure out a way to prove it."

Ehrhardt looked at him like he was nuts but nodded. "I guess people get pretty worked up over this chess crap. A hundred K is a good-sized prize."

Suddenly the door to the suite opened, and Snow's whole body froze.

Anitra Popescu—he couldn't bring himself to say Kingsley—stood in the doorway, her red hair flying out of its clasp at her neck, the tight black dress, one of three he'd seen her in, looking a little rumpled. A policeman in uniform held the door for her. "Oh my God, Snowden. How horrible. I can't believe this has happened. How could Hunter have become so disturbed he'd go to these lengths?"

If he screamed "bullshit" at the top of his voice, would anyone mind? Slowly he rose to standing, staring at her like she was Medusa.

Mr. Pennymaker stood beside him. "Mrs. Kingsley, I presume?"

"Yes."

"I'm Carstairs Pennymaker, Mr. Reynaldi's mentor. Your cousin"—he said it like it tasted bad—"has caused great pain and suffering to Snowden and will be going to prison for a long time if I have any say about it." He smiled. "And believe me, I usually do."

For a second genuine fear flashed across Anitra's face—but maybe Snow imagined it. "I'm so horrified by my cousin's actions. He came to give me support in my tribulation and must have somehow felt so strongly that I have to win this tournament to restore my faith in life that he became unbalanced." She dropped her head in her hand. "It's just one more crushing disappointment."

Mr. P. raised an eyebrow. "So you'll be leaving the tournament?"

Her head popped up. "Oh no. I've given my word to the tournament organizers." She sighed noisily. "And like Snowden, I must do what I feel my husband would want."

Mr. Pennymaker spoke softly. "You believe your husband would want you to defeat his protégé, a boy who is like a son to him?"

Snow felt heat behind his eyes, but he clenched his jaw.

She smiled softly. "Of course not. I mean, how lovely it would be for the NorCal Chess Club to take first and second prize. I'm sure no one can beat Snow."

Snow grasped Mr. P.'s hand and squeezed.

RILEY STOOD on the front porch, staring down at Mrs. Wishus. Her hands planted firmly on her hips, she gazed up at him with her bright eyes. "Being a prince doesn't make you a hero, Riley. That's all about your values, your choices, and ultimately, your actions."

Riley nodded. "Yes, ma'am."

CHAPTER 21

SNOW STOOD in front of the mirror and felt his jacket pockets for all his needed stuff—key to the suite, phone, epinephrine, handkerchief. The gray suit looked amazing. Funny how Mr. P.'s fashion outrageousness only extended to himself. With Snow, his taste was impeccable. Such amazing kindness.

Breakfast. If he could get his stomach to digest anything but butterflies.

Nobody was in the halls. *Good.* He could put off his face-to-face with the public for another few seconds. Even the elevator stood empty. It was early, and Las Vegas was not an early town. But when the doors opened on the mezzanine where the restaurants were located, people turned and stared. A lot smiled, and one brave girl ran over with a napkin for him to sign. He wrote it to Margo as she requested. He grinned. "Do you like chess?"

She giggled. "Oh no, I just like you."

Wow, comments like that made him feel weird.

He stopped to sign four more autographs before he cleared the few yards to the breakfast buffet. When he walked in, Bash rose from the table where Mr. P. and all the IPis were congregated and came over to him. Bash had wanted to guard him all morning, but Snow had asked for a few minutes to gather himself—by himself.

"Everything okay?"

Snow nodded as he breathed deeply. "Yes. Just great." He walked to the table with Bash at his side, towering over him.

Mr. P. had saved a seat beside him. He flashed his bright smile. "We got food for you so you're not attacked by autograph seekers while trying to balance a plate."

"Thank you." He sat, happiest to see his tea latte beside his plate.

Mr. P. clapped his hands. "The big day."

Snow swallowed tea.

"As we predicted, Mrs. Kingsley is in the final four."

Hacker leaned forward to look at Mr. P. "She must be as good as she claims."

"Yes. One would not get this far in such rarified company without talent. I think we can assume that a tiny bit of manipulation of pairings has occurred, since I feel sure the organizers are quite anxious to have a showdown between Snowden and Anitra. It's hard to resist that much photogenicity." He laughed.

BB asked, "You don't think they cheated?"

"Oh no. Just selected starting partners so that she and Snow were unlikely to meet in the earlier rounds despite her lesser ranking. She had, in my opinion, far easier opponents to begin, plus she's benefitted from two disqualifications. I'm not entirely sure how those happened, but there you have it. Obviously the organizers chose wisely, as I expect they'll get their match."

Snow turned the cup in his hands. "Maybe I can't beat her."

"Ah yes, there is no certainty in chess. Too many variables. But the fact is, you *can* beat her six ways from Sunday, as the expression goes. We cannot say for sure that you will."

Snow glanced up and met Mr. P.'s gaze. His heart beat hard. "I don't even know how I can look at her across the table. I know she's tried to kill the professor. I know it. And me as well. I just can't prove it. And here she sits, like she has nothing better to do than play chess."

Mr. P.'s eyes looked deep as wells. "Don't look at her, my dear. Look at the board and look at your fans and admirers. And remember, she truly has nothing more important to do than play chess. She's desperate, grasping, and needy. You have a whole world of friends and future waiting for you."

Snow shoved his cup. "Sir, how can you say that? Because of her, my dearest friend is in a hospital bed. I have no school to go to, no home. People who used to at least tolerate me now despise me, and I might even go to jail. And I lost my—I lost a lot. It's all because of her." He banged his hand on the table, and the tea toppled, sending a splash of milky liquid all over his beautiful suit jacket. "Well, damn." Snow pushed back from the table and wiped at the rapidly spreading stains with his napkin.

"Don't worry, my dear. And don't rub. It just makes it worse. Give me the coat."

Snow pulled off the jacket. At least he hadn't ruined his shirt. Just what he needed.

Mr. P. extended the jacket to Romeo. "Will you take this to our suite and leave it for dry cleaning? Select the jacket you like best, but I think the teal should do the job nicely."

"Yes, sir." Romeo took the coat and hurried in that elegant way of his, as half the women and more than a few of the men in the restaurant watched him go with a sigh.

Snow shook his head. "I'm sorry. That was stupid."

"You're a physicist. You know everything happens for a reason."

He frowned. "Yes, and I also know that no person can see enough of the cosmic interaction to know what that reason is."

"What do you think the reason is?"

Snow shrugged and stared at the tea spreading across the tabletop. "To teach me a lesson, I suppose."

"You think the universe has it in for you?"

Good grief, had he implied that? Yes, he had. "Of course not."

"Right. So?"

"I meant there are things I need to learn."

"And what are those things?"

"I don't know yet."

"Why?"

"Because everything's still up in the air."

Mr. P. tapped the white cloth. "Ah, so don't be accusing the quantum reality of treating you badly until you've measured it."

Snow snorted. "The probabilistic interpretation of quantum mechanics is now being challenged by a more deterministic interpretation involving pilot waves."

"Pilot waves. I see. But you acknowledge we can't recognize the reality of this situation until it comes to rest. Until it's measured? Correct?"

Snow nodded.

"Good. Finish your breakfast—" Mr. P. grinned. "—and let's go make some waves."

Snow shoved some cooled scrambled egg into his mouth and sipped his new cup of tea until he saw Romeo cross toward their table, carrying his teal sport coat.

ANITRA STOOD in a small reception area outside the room where they'd play their last game. It had come to this—facing Reynaldi in the final match. Shit, if Hunter had done his job, she'd be meeting someone far less dangerous.

Now she was faced with the ultimate decision. No, not decision. She'd decided. It might not work, but if it did? Perfection.

The organizer, that shorthaired woman named Turks, approached her. "Will you surrender your cell phone please, Mrs. Kingsley? We don't want any chance of an accidental disqualification."

"Of course." She handed her cell, on mute, to the woman.

A few feet away from her stood Snowden Reynaldi. Anitra saw him pat his pockets, then look up at one of the officials. "Oh, I had to change coats. I left my phone in the other one."

The man nodded. Snow turned and studiously didn't look at her or acknowledge her. *The little shit.* Yes, she wanted the money, the fame, the unlimited future winning this tournament would guarantee, but she'd happily do this just to grind that obnoxious little turd to dust.

Ms. Turks pointed to a table set up at one end of the room. "We've provided some refreshments for you. It will likely be a while before you get to eat. Of course, we'll supply water to you periodically during the game."

"Oh great, thanks." *Perfect.* She walked to the table. Snowden purposefully stepped back and let her pass as he talked with the organizers. She surveyed the table. Fresh vegetables with dip, some string cheese, and—"Lovely."—some pastries. She loaded a few carrots and some hummus on a small paper plate and then slid a chocolate brownie beside it.

Casually ambling away, she munched a couple of carrots. The cake looked ideally gooey. She turned and made a big show of picking up the brownie and taking a bite. She laughed. "Oh my, I didn't do that gracefully." She dropped the rest of the brownie on her plate and tossed it in the trash. Licking her fingers ostentatiously, she stuck her hand in her jacket pocket and fished for a tissue, wiped the other hand, then put the tissue back, digging around some more.

Snow had sidled over to the table and was chewing on a piece of cheese. She smiled. Such a simple last meal.

SNOW'S MOUTH chewed, but his mind drifted. No light without darkness. No reality without measurement. Love. The one reality. Love for the professor. Growing love for Mr. Pennymaker. Love for—Riley.

How can you love him when he didn't come through for you?

We don't get to keep every gift.

That's pretty philosophical. He believed you're a whore, for God's sake.

Yes, but the evidence was damning. He barely knows me.

Still.

He taught me how to love, and I found out that when you love someone, it's not essential that they love you back.

But it would be nice.

Snow sighed. *Yeah. But you're a dreamer.*

"Lady and gentleman, it's time for the game to begin. Good luck to both of you." Eleanor Turks threw open the doors to the room, and flashes began to pop. Several camera crews had been allowed in the room. Unusual, but the Anderson Tournament attracted press. Turks raised a hand. "Ladies and gentlemen of the press, from this point on, you may record for posterity, but no flashes, no narration, no noise. Anyone disregarding these instructions will be asked to leave." The volume in the room instantly shifted to mute.

The official offered his hands to Anitra, and she tapped with her left hand, leaving her right in her pocket. White. First move. Some believed that gave her a slight advantage.

She extracted her hand from her jacket and offered a handshake to Snow. If he refused, it would be considered bad sportsmanship. He shook. Her palm had an odd grainy feeling, and her hand was cold. *Seems appropriate.*

He avoided her eyes.

They took their seats. *Just focus on the board and the audience. Don't look at her.* Trying to channel Mr. Pennymaker, he leaned back in his chair and looked out at the people gathered in the room. Mr. P. and the boys stood a row back, and Snow flashed them a grin. A pretty young girl pushed her way to the front row and pressed a hand to her lips when she met Snow's eyes. *Go on, do it.* He gave her a wide smile, raised his hand, and flipped his mane of hair off his shoulder. She squealed. Not loud, but enough for people to hear and start a giggle going. He glanced at Mr. P. and got a wink. Ms. Turks gave the girl a sharp glance, and everyone quieted again.

An official cleared his throat. "When you're ready, Mr. Reynaldi."

Snow nodded, then blinked. Odd. Felt like salt in his eye.

"Mrs. Kingsley?"

She tilted her head regally.

The official started the timer. Anitra, with a flourish, moved knight to f3.

He answered with knight to f6. His hair slid in front of his face, and he wiped it back with his hand.

They each moved pawns to c4 and g6. Snow cleared his throat.

Knight to c3, bishop to g7. *Is it hot in here?* He wiped a hand across his face, and it felt cold.

She moved her pawn to d4. He performed a king-side castle. Her soft gasp radiated across the board. He looked up and met her eyes. Hers narrowed, and her lips turned up ever so slightly. He wiped his finger across his sweaty upper lip.

Her finger slid her bishop to f4.

He reached pawn to d5, but his hand shook. *What the hell's going on—oh no!* The evilly familiar symptoms flashed across his brain as the tightness in his chest cut like an iron band restricting his airflow.

He ripped at his tie. *Have to get air. Have to. Worse than drowning.*

He stood, falling steps backward. His chair crashed to the ground as voices all around him yelled and screamed.

"Snow!"

"What's happening? Mr. Reynaldi!"

Above the melee, Anitra's voice cut through. "What's the meaning of this? A ploy to hide the fact that he can't beat me? I demand a forfeit!"

Snow raised his hand to his nose and smelled the sweet, oily, pungent aroma of peanuts—just a second before his body hit the floor.

"A doctor!"

"Is there a doctor?"

"Someone call a doctor!"

"I demand a forfeit!"

Snow groped at his pocket. Mr. Pennymaker landed on his knees at Snow's side. "What is it, Snow?"

Romeo held his head. "What's wrong, dear?"

"P-pea—" Needed the epinephrine. His fingers clawed. *Oh. Oh no. In my other coat.*

What the river didn't finish, a handful of peanut dust accomplished. His throat slowly constricted as cold climbed up his neck. His eyes closed.

A girl's voice whispered, "My God, he's so beautiful."

The voice reached a shriek. "I demand a forfeit!"

"GET THE fuck out of my way!" Riley raced through the crowd, bumping and shoving looky-loos with his larger body. "Snow. My God, Snow." He fell on his knees beside a doctor who was administering CPR. "It's his allergy. He's allergic to shit."

The doctor looked up. "Where's emergency? Be sure they bring epinephrine."

Riley sat back on his haunches and ran a hand over his windbreaker. Grabbing the syringe he'd gotten for Snow at the pharmacy, he stretched it toward the doc. "Here. He left it behind."

The doc motioned with his head to Snow's thigh as he continued CPR. "There."

Riley took a breath. "Don't die, baby." He stabbed the syringe through those great-looking gray pants and pushed the plunger. When it was all the way in, he leaned over the gorgeous body. "Wake up, my beauty. Please. I'm so sorry I ever doubted. I've been so dumb. I don't deserve you, but please, please don't leave me." He pressed his head against the cool, still neck and prayed for a pulse. "I love you."

Thump.

Riley gasped. "I love you."

Thump, thump.

"I love you, Snow."

A gurgle next to his ear brought Riley's head up. "He breathed. I'm sure of it. Do it again, baby."

"Nggghhh. Ri—"

Riley pressed a short kiss against the rapidly warming lips. "Hey. Breathe for me."

A short, strangled gasp popped from Snow's beautiful lips.

"Music to my ears. Again."

This breath sounded half normal. Riley laughed and looked up, only to come eye to eye with that gorgeous guy he'd seen at the frat house who took care of Snow. He still knelt at Snow's head and raised an eyebrow as he looked at Riley.

The emergency techs pushed through the crowd with a stretcher.

Some funny little man in a bright plaid suit dropped to the floor next to Snow. "Are you all right, my dear?"

Snow managed to nod his head.

The woman's voice cut through the noise and confusion. "Well, this is all lovely, but he shouldn't be taken anywhere until he forfeits the Anderson Tournament to me."

A few people in the crowd booed.

Riley looked up. "Officers."

Lieutenant Rex Cocher stepped out of the crowd. Riley nodded at Anitra. Rex stood in front of her. Her eyebrows rose.

"Anitra Kingsley, you're under arrest pending extradition to the state of California for attempted murder."

"Murder? Like hell." She glanced over her shoulder and took a step back, but two of the IPis caught her.

Riley looked at that beautiful, wicked face. "Yeah, I did a little snooping and found the aconite you fed to Professor Kingsley."

"You're crazy. You'll never prove I did anything like that."

Snow raised his hand to Riley. "What?" Snow moved the hand to Riley's nose. "What the fuck?" He looked up. "Peanuts." He pointed at Anitra. "Check her pockets."

Before the police could agree or deny, the big guy from the frat house had shoved a hand in Anitra's pocket. He pulled it out with a scowl. "She's got ground-up peanuts in there."

She sniffed. "That's hardly a crime."

Riley held Snow close. "It is if you know a person will go into anaphylactic shock with just one whiff of peanuts."

"How would I know that?"

Riley smiled. "As soon as the professor has fully recovered, I'm sure he'll tell us exactly when he informed you about Snow's allergies."

Snow croaked, "Re-cover—?"

Riley petted his lovely hair. "Yes. As soon as I found the aconite, the doctors were able to hone in on an antidote and treatment. He's really weak but conscious and getting better with every breath."

Snow's head dropped against Riley's hand.

A young medtech stooped over Riley. "Excuse me, sir, but we need to get him to the hospital. He needs additional treatment and observation after this kind of reaction."

"Can I go with him?"

The tech looked around. "Is anyone here family?"

Riley, six frat boys, one romantic lover, and one little old elf all raised their hands.

CHAPTER 22

SNOW GIGGLED as Romeo fed him soup. "I really can feed myself."

Romeo grinned. "The docs said you shouldn't exert yourself."

"Maybe if I only lift three noodles instead of five, I can manage it." He opened wide and accepted another spoonful.

Ballet Boy tucked the afghan around his legs on the old couch, and three of the other guys stared at their computers in various parts of the big frat house living room. They seemed to make it a practice to hang around with him whenever they weren't in class. He was half in heaven and half uncomfortable. For someone who spent most of his time alone, living with the IPis and, more particularly, being the center of their attention, was unnerving—and delightful.

He opened his mouth for more soup.

"Uh, hi."

Snow's head snapped back, and he managed to spill soup all over the napkin Romeo had wrapped around his neck. Behind him, in the archway from the front door, stood Riley. He stared at his shoes. "Sorry. The door was open. I, uh, brought someone who wanted to see you."

Snow tore off the napkin and turned. "Mrs. Wishus!"

He started to leap up, but Romeo stretched out an arm. "He's not supposed to exert himself."

Snow pushed against him. "Romeo, I'm doing fine."

Mrs. Wishus held up a hand. "Nonsense. I'm coming to you."

All the guys stared and grinned. Good reason. She brightened the room with her flowered dress and matching teal-blue hair. BB pushed a chair beside the couch for her, and she smiled as she sat, then took Snow's hand. "Hi, cutie."

"Hi, Mrs. W."

"Hear you about got killed—again."

"I guess so." He shrugged.

He could almost ask the question for her. "And what did you learn, cutie?"

"Eudora, are you bedeviling my protégé with life-altering questions, you enchanting goddess, you?"

She gasped, leaped up, threw her arms wide, and ran like she was sixteen, not seventy, toward Mr. P. "Carstairs! What a delightful surprise." She swept him up in a hug that nearly lifted him from his feet, since she boasted a good six inches on him. When she stepped back, she made a twirling motion with her finger. "Let me look at you." He turned without a hint of self-consciousness. "Sartorial splendor, as usual."

Mr. P. had outdone himself in a red-and-white candy-striped shirt, yellow slacks, and a plaid vest, all of which somehow managed to go together on him. He pointed at her hair. "A new look, I believe?"

She patted her waves. "Yes, all the young girls are doing it. I'm not to be outdone."

"So, I interrupted at a key moment. Snow was about to tell us all what he learned from nearly dying twice." He escorted Eudora back to her seat, then looked over toward the door. "Riley, for heaven's sake, my boy, come and sit. This is all about your future too."

Riley seemed to swallow hard but walked slowly over to a chair Doc had slid out with his foot and sat. He glanced at Snow, his eyes slid to Romeo, then he stared at the floor.

Mr. P. took a seat. "So, darling Eudora, you were saying?"

She waved a hand as if instructing the guys in the room. One more had come in during the grand arrival, so only Bash was still in class. "Typically when one experiences near death, lessons are learned. What were yours, Snowden?" She leaned her head on her hand as if waiting for a bedtime story.

Snow grinned at Mr. P. "I learned that the quantum reality isn't out to get me."

Mr. P. slapped his leg. "Good, my boy. Excellent."

"I learned what I should have known. That every event is just a potential in a far greater fabric and isn't inherently good or bad. It's a step to the next. What seems horrible may be glorious in the next moment and horrible again after that, until horrible and glorious mush together into a quantum whole."

Mrs. Wishus waved her hand. "Yes, yes, dear, that's all lovely and physicsy, but what did your heart learn?"

He looked at his hands. "I learned I'm not alone."

Riley sucked in a breath, and Mr. P. smiled.

Snow looked up and gazed at the top of Riley's golden head. "Forgive me, this won't come out the way I feel it, but I learned I'm not alone because I belong to myself." He looked over at Romeo and smiled. "Romeo taught me that."

Riley rocked back in his chair like someone had hit him, then glanced up.

Mr. P. leaned forward, elbows to knees. "So, Riley, what have you learned as a result of dramatically transforming your life?"

Riley looked surprised, since Mr. P. didn't know him at all. Snow shrugged. "Mr. P. just knows everything, don't worry."

All the IPis nodded.

Everyone stared at Riley. For a second he looked panicked. Then his face softened and saddened. "I learned that I'm too big an idiot to have the man I love."

Snow drew in his breath to speak, but Mr. P. held up a hand. "Always essential to learn one's failings, my dear. And why do you think you can't have this man?"

Riley fell back against the chair. "Because I don't deserve him. I had a chance to believe in him. To stand behind him in times of trouble, and I failed. Obviously, someone else filled that space." He nodded toward Romeo. "I can only hope he keeps up the good work."

Snow leaned forward. "Riley, where have you been since I left Las Vegas?"

"Meeting with the police."

Snow nodded. "The police of both Las Vegas and here, right?"

"Yeah."

"Because you found the evidence that put Anitra in jail along with Hunter and saved Professor Kingsley's life."

"Yeah, after Hunter sang like a birdie, confessed to trying to drown you, and to Anitra's peanut scheme to save his own skin."

"Seems to me like you're my hero. You saved me."

Riley shrugged. "I never would have found the aconite if you hadn't told me where to look."

Snow smiled. "Okay, then we make a pretty good team."

For a second his face lit up; then he frowned. "But I blew it. Whoever heard of a hero not believing in the goodness of his love?"

Mrs. Wishus smiled. "Every man has to grow into his herohood."

Riley sighed. "But Snow said he wants to take care of himself."

She propped a finger on her chin. "Hmm. I didn't hear him say that."

Snow smiled. "I said I know I belong to myself. I never have before, Riley. I was always so stuck on being alone, all I wanted was someone to belong to—a family, a team, a lover. I forgot that I can be a part of those things, but they don't own me. Still, that doesn't mean I don't want a family or a team, or—a lover."

Riley looked up, his gold eyes connecting with Snow's. "What about him? Romeo?"

Snow cocked his head. "Romeo, will you tell Riley whether or not we've had sex?"

Riley held up a hand. "No. I don't want to know that. I just want to know if you love him."

Romeo laughed, and Riley frowned. "I wish, lover boy. Snow made it very clear that despite my considerable charms, he was in love with someone else."

Snow nodded. "I love Romeo dearly, and all the IPis, but I'm in love with you."

Riley's eyes widened. "Me?"

Romeo snorted. "Yeah, even though I told him you were an asshole who didn't deserve his love, he wouldn't listen." Romeo stood and stretched his lean, graceful body, then leveled his gaze at Riley. "But just remember, if you treat him badly, I'm the one waiting in the wings." Languorously Romeo left the room, flashing his beautiful ass to one and all. But in the ass department, there was only one winner.

Riley moved to the edge of the couch beside Snow. "Is it true? How could you love me when I treated you so badly?"

"Another thing I learned was that someone doesn't have to love you back for you to love them." He smiled. "But it's nice when they do."

"Hey, you guys, look!" Bash ran into the room, waving the newspaper. He stopped and pointed at the front page. "Two Murder Attempts Couldn't Stop Reynaldi From Taking Anderson Chess Championship." He laughed. "Hey, Snow, you won. Listen. 'Two murder attempts by known felon Monica McGillicutty, aka Anitra Popescu Kingsley, on NorCal's own Snowden Reynaldi couldn't stop the young Grandmaster from taking the trophy and $100,000 winnings at the Anderson International Chess Tournament.'"

Snow shook his head. "I never dreamed they'd call it a default. I better remember for the future that prostitution may not disqualify you from chess, but murder does." He laughed.

Bash rattled the newspaper. "Listen to this. 'Thanks to the intervention of local hero Riley Prince, police collected sufficient evidence to hold McGillicutty and her accomplice Hunter Borders for attempted homicide, not only on Reynaldi, but also on Professor Harold Kingsley. Kingsley, who has been in a coma for several weeks, is recovering after Prince's sleuthing demonstrated he'd been poisoned.'" Bash grinned. "Is that cool or what?"

Gormet yelled out, "Hey, Snow, are you going to transfer to Grimm?"

Snow shook his head. "It's really tempting, but I only have half a year to go until I graduate. Besides, the dean called this morning and apologized for being taken in by Anitra. I'm not expelled anymore."

"What about the money your trust idiots wouldn't give you?" Hacker asked.

"I haven't talked to them, but I expect they'll see things differently. Actually, I'll be twenty-one in a few months, and then it's all mine anyway. They'll be so fired."

Bash laughed. "Hey man, who gives a shit? You just won a hundred thou."

Mr. P. clapped his hands. "And when we're finished, those winnings will be a mere dribble compared to all the products and services that will benefit from association with your beautiful face."

Snow just shook his head.

Gormet said, "Even if you won't transfer, you can still come live with the IPis."

Mrs. Wishus waved her arms. "Oh no you don't. He's coming with us, and we're installing him in his new apartment—upstairs from yours truly."

Snow looked at Riley. "Really? You want this?"

"I thought it would be, uh, you know, good for you to, uh, have somebody looking out for you and all." He actually scuffed his sneaker.

Mrs. Wishus put a hand on Riley's arm. "You're blowing this, darling. Tell Snow how you feel."

He whispered, "He knows I love him. I said it about twelve times when he collapsed."

"Riley! He was unconscious."

Snow smiled softly. "No, I wasn't. I heard every word." He looked in Riley's golden eyes. "Every time you said 'I love you,' I felt more alive. I barely needed the epinephrine."

Riley's face lit like a summer sunrise. "So would you want to move in and live with me—and Mrs. Wishus, of course?"

Snow blinked hard. "It would be almost like having a mom."

Mrs. Wishus rocked back in her chair. "It will be exactly like having a mom when it comes to eating vegetables, getting sleep, and doing what makes you happy."

Snow wiped at the liquid that splashed his face. "Being with Riley makes me happy."

"It's done, then." She stood. "Riley, take your boyfriend home. You have a game to prepare for."

Snow slapped a hand to his mouth. "Oh my God, I forgot the championship game."

Riley shrugged. "No big deal. We'll either win or we won't."

Mr. Pennymaker laughed. "How very quantum of you, my boy."

"YOU SURE you're up to this?"

Riley gazed up at Snow, who leaned over him, naked and pale as the stuff he was named for. And just as beautiful. "Absolutely. I need some practice with my deep breathing. Are you sure you don't want me to start learning to bottom?"

Riley shook his head and pulled Snow's hand to his harder than hard cock. "This guy has been missing having you in my ass. I mean, really missing it."

"Ah yes, but I must first show you some of my newfound knowledge."

"Oh?"

Snow grinned and grabbed the lube. He squirted a dollop in his hand and took hold of Riley's cock with great confidence. Then that pretty little devil started giving him the hand job of the century—hand over hand with a twist at the top. "Holy crap! That's incredible. Don't do too much or I'll come too soon."

"Hey, you're only twenty-one. Who says you can't come more than once?" Snow laughed, and the happy sound dove straight to Riley's cock, along with the amazing flashes of fire sparking into his balls.

Snow put his slender hands on either side of Riley's upright cock. Riley grinned. "What are you up to?"

"Watch." Snow started rubbing his palms on either side of Riley's dick like he was making fire.

"Jesus!" A shock of pleasure soared up his cock, into his balls, through his spine, and set off fireworks in his brain. "Oh, oh. Oh shit!" Going, gone. All determination be damned, cum flew out of his cockhead like Snow had succeeded in starting that bonfire. "Oh my Gooooood." His hips thrust on their own, froze, and shuddered through the near painful pleasure of the release.

Finally his trembling stopped. Eyelids fluttering, he managed to look at Snow, who gazed at him with undisguised delight and pure cat-in-the-sun satisfaction despite his cock being stiff as a fire pole. Riley tried to smile. Too much effort. "Wow. Where in hell did you learn that?"

"From Romeo."

Riley was ashamed, but he tensed. *Relax. Not like you're a virgin, asshole.* "Obviously he didn't get his nickname by accident." He laughed, and it sounded halfway genuine.

"Yes, he showed me that move on a bright pink dildo. He was quite proud of its size and girth, so I didn't disappoint him by saying you're bigger." Snow grinned and fireflies danced in his brilliant eyes.

"Uh, dildo? Pink?"

"Yes. You didn't want to know if I'd ever had sex with Romeo, but I didn't. He was my tutor in the romantic arts, just as Bash taught me self-defense. But we had no personal contact."

Riley slid his hands behind his head and let Snow's satisfaction flow though him as well. "I heard you brought that Hunter dude down like a lioness on a gazelle."

"More like the gazelle turned and kicked the shit out of the lioness."

"So I guess I shouldn't hate Romeo, right?"

Snow stalked across Riley's body like that lioness and stared down at him. "I think you should love him, darling, because we're about to move on to oral."

RILEY STOMPED into the locker room, already in full uniform. The guys were mostly dressed and ready to play, horsing around nervously as they got ready to face their toughest opponent and biggest potential reward. Riley stepped into the middle of the room and yelled, "Listen up!" The guys turned and faced him. Every kind of expression crossed every kind of face—admiration, fear, hatred, derision on white, black, brown, and beige. "Gather around. I got something to say."

One of the linebackers, Oesterman, called, "You gonna lead us in prayer, Prince?"

"You better pray I don't kick your ass down the hall. Now get over here."

The guy frowned, then looked at Riley, who was smiling. He started to laugh. "Let me know when you're big enough, little man." But he walked over, still laughing.

"First off, I'm sorry I missed the last practice. I, uh, had to go to Las Vegas for something."

Fred Furness said, "Yeah, to bust up a ring of potential murderers, from what I heard. Good job, man! The alumni are gonna shit, they'll be so proud."

That wasn't what he'd expected. "Thanks." He glanced at his shoes, then up. "Look, I don't care what you think of me. I'm gay, I lied about it, and I'm sorry. About lying, not about being gay. That part I like. I like being who I am. And in case you were thinking I got lured and tricked into being gay, forget it. I'm in love with a guy, so if you don't like it, fuck off.

"But here's the thing. No matter how you feel about me, this game is more important than your bullshit feelings. Not because it's any big deal in the grand quantum reality, but because for some of you, it could mean hella shit for your future. Like you, Rog. I'm not good enough for the NFL, but you are, man. If you let your hatred of me keep you from catching my passes, then a lot more's going to get blown here than some cock. Same with you, LeRoy. And others, who may not be looking at sports careers, still want to say they were on a championship team. I can't make you play well. You gotta do that by yourself and for yourself."

Danny slouched against the locker. "Hey, Riley, what are you going to do after you graduate?"

He smiled. "I hope I can be a college football coach. I used to not think I was smart enough, but somebody changed my mind."

McMasters's voice came from behind him. "I hope I was one of those who changed your mind, Riley. You know you've got my support and recommendation. This team has never had a better leader." He looked around the group. "I hope what Riley said sank in. You've all got a choice. When you walk off this campus, you're going to have to get along with all kinds of people. Work with them. Live with them. If you look at Roget and all you see is black or Riley and only see gay, then your chances of being happy are pretty much zero. This game is just one chance out of many to show the world who you are. Take advantage of it." He stuck his hand in the center, and they all piled on top. "Go NorCal!"

SNOW STOOD in the tunnel, waiting for halftime to begin, so freaking excited he might barf. He leaned down to that dearest of ears on that dearest of men and said, "Are you sure you're warm enough, Professor?"

Professor Kingsley leaned back in the wheelchair. "Snowden, you have me so bundled up I may never find my own balls."

Snow barked out a laugh. "I see near death has increased your wit."

"And increased your confidence. I'm so proud of you, Snow." He wrapped his hand over Snow's on his shoulder. "I truly am sorry to have been such an old fool and put you in danger from that evil woman."

"We all had lessons to learn, sir."

A cheer went up from the crowd. "NorCal seems to be wiping up the field with Southern."

"Yes." The grin spread all over his face as shrieks of "Riley, Riley" and "He's our Prince" resounded off the walls of the stadium. Snow pushed the chair a bit closer to the tunnel entrance so they could see better. Riley grabbed the ball from the big guy who threw it through his legs. He ran backward about three steps and then he passed the ball. It sailed and sailed like an eagle in flight far down the field and there, as if planted by some good fairy, ran Roget. The guy held out his arms, and the ball fell into them as he leaped across the big finish line, and the crowd went apeshit.

The professor half rose from his chair and yelled, "Touchdown!"

The band started to play, whistles sounded, and the cheerleaders ran on the field. A guy came up behind Snow and the professor. "It will just be a few minutes now. The dean will say your names, okay?"

Snow nodded and smiled. It looked like Riley might have his win, and no matter what, everyone would see how brilliant he was on the field.

People milled around in the stadium, buying food and going to the restrooms. As the general hubbub started to die down, a singer came on stage and performed. When she was done, the dean walked onto the platform in the middle of the field. Snow gave the professor a short hug.

The dean's voice rang out over the sound system. "Ladies and gentlemen, we at NorCal are celebrating a lot today, and one of the things we're most grateful for is the presence of two of our dear friends and hometown heroes. Some of you may know that these two have literally been to hell and back lately. So today's game, win or lose, is dedicated to these inspiring men—Professor Harold Kingsley, head of our physics department and coach of the championship NorCal Chess Club, and Grandmaster Snowden Reynaldi, who we might say recently wiped up the chessboard with the evil queen."

Snow pushed the professor out on the big, vast field. The crowd went nuts, laughing and cheering. He looked up. *Wow.* Off to one side, near the front of the stands, stood all the IPis and Mr. Pennymaker alongside Mrs. Wishus. Seeing Bash with tears on his face was definitely scary.

As they got to the platform, the dean said, "It seems fitting that to present our dedication, we've chosen the prince of NorCal, our own quarterback, Riley Prince."

Riley trotted out from the NorCal tunnel, carrying a plaque. When he got to them, he accepted a microphone. "Thank you. It's my honor to dedicate this game to Professor Harold Kingsley and Snowden Reynaldi, two people who have personally inspired me beyond my power to express." He presented the plaque to the professor and handed him the mike.

The professor dabbed at his eyes. "I can only say I'm very happy to be seeing all of you, because it wasn't a sure thing there for a while. But I didn't do any of the work." He pointed to Riley and Snow. "These two heroes did, and I couldn't be prouder of either of them." He handed the microphone back to Riley and wiped his cheeks.

Riley looked out at the crowd. For a moment, everything was nearly quiet. Then he lifted the mike. "Please excuse me for using this moment for a personal event, but since you've all shared in our lives—both good and bad—lately, I think you should be in on this."

Snow cocked his head.

Riley went down on one knee, and Snow gasped for breath. "I know we both have to finish school, but I also know that I can't imagine spending a day of my life without you. And since you've escaped death twice in the last month, I figure I better not waste time. Snowden Reynaldi, you make me feel smart. Will you marry me?" He opened a velvet box. The simple gold circle glistened.

Snow slapped a hand over his mouth as tears squeezed out of his eyes. The whole stadium held its breath. At the peak of quiet, Mrs. Wishus's voice rang out. "Say yes, cutie."

Snow laughed. "Riley, you've made my life a fairy tale. It's easy to forget that fairy tales have gorgeous princes and knights in shining armor, but they also have witches and ogres and near misses with evil. That's what makes them so important. Yes, I will marry you." He threw his arms around Riley's neck, and they hugged. A stadium full of football fans might not be quite ready for a kiss. Snow looked up and whispered, "I've learned that I'll never be alone again."

IN THE stands, Hacker said, "They're pretty young. A lot can happen before they even graduate. Do you think they've got a chance at happy ever after?"

Mrs. Wishus leaned over and gave Mr. P. a nudge. "Oh dearie, only their fairy godmothers know for sure."

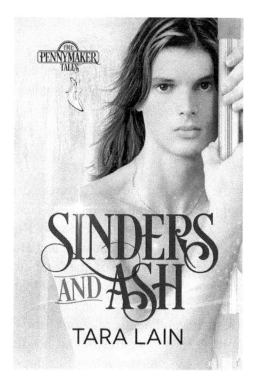

A Pennymaker Tale

Housekeeper Mark Sintorella (Sinders) works diligently at a resort hotel while designing clothes anonymously, hoping to get into fashion school. Then his carefully planned life is upended with the arrival of Ashton Armitage, son of the fifth richest man in America—and the most beautiful guy Mark has ever seen. Ash must find a wife or he'll lose his grandfather's inheritance, and he settles on Bitsy Fanderel. But secretly Ash is gay, and the guy who cleans the fireplaces sets his heart ablaze.

Further stirring the pot is the little elf of a man, Carstairs Pennymaker, who has Mark wearing his own designs and masquerading as a girl to impress the fashion investors in the hotel. When the clock strikes twelve, two beautiful princesses line up for the wedding—but one isn't a woman. Will the slipper fit? Only Mr. Pennymaker knows for sure.

www.dreamspinnerpress.com

TARA LAIN writes the Beautiful Boys of Romance in LGBT romance novels that star her unique, charismatic heroes. Her bestselling novels have garnered awards for Best Series, Best Contemporary Romance, Best Erotic Romance, Best Ménage, Best LGBT Romance, and Best Gay Characters, and Tara has been named Best Writer of the Year in the LRC Awards. Readers often call her books "sweet," even with all that hawt sex, because Tara believes in love and her books deliver on happy-ever-after. In her other job, Tara owns an advertising and public relations firm. Her love of creating book titles comes from years of manifesting ad headlines for everything from analytical instruments to semiconductors. She does workshops on both author promotion and writing craft. She lives with her soulmate husband and her soulmate dog (who's a little jealous of all those cat pictures Tara posts on FB) in Laguna Niguel, California, near the seaside towns where she sets a lot of her books. Passionate about diversity, justice, and new experiences, Tara says that on her tombstone it will say "Yes!"

E-mail: tara@taralain.com
Website: www.taralain.com
Blog: www.taralain.com/blog
Goodreads: www.goodreads.com/author/show/4541791.Tara_Lain
Pinterest: pinterest.com/taralain
Twitter: @taralain
Facebook: www.facebook.com/taralain
Barnes & Noble: www.barnesandnoble.com/s/Tara-Lain?keyword=Tara+Lain&store=book
ARe: www.allromanceebooks.com/storeSearch.html?searchBy=author&qString=Tara+Lain

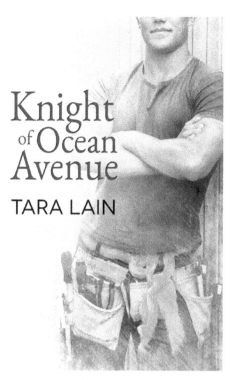

Knight of Ocean Avenue

TARA LAIN

A Love in Laguna Novel

How can you be twenty-five and not know you're gay? Billy Ballew runs from that question. A high school dropout, barely able to read until he taught himself, Billy's life is driven by his need to help support his parents as a construction worker, put his sisters through college, coach his Little League team, and not think about being a three-time loser in the engagement department. Being terrified of taking tests keeps Billy from getting the contractor's license he so desires, and fear of his mother's judgment blinds Billy to what could make him truly happy.

Then, in preparation for his sister's big wedding, Billy meets Shaz—Chase Phillips—a rising-star celebrity stylist who defines the word gay. To Shaz, Billy embodies everything he's ever wanted—stalwart, honest, brave—but even if Billy turns out to be gay, he could never endure the censure he'd get for being with a queen like Shaz. How can two men with so little in common find a way to be together? Can the Stylist of the Year end up with the Knight of Ocean Avenue?

www.dreamspinnerpress.com

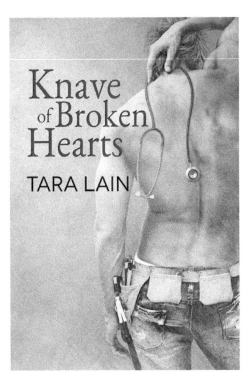

Knave of Broken Hearts

TARA LAIN

A Love in Laguna Novel

Jim Carney has a full time job—running from himself. Since he walked out on his wealthy family at sixteen because he'd wrecked his best friend's life over some yaoi graphic novels, Jim has lived a macho, blue-collar existence of too much booze and too little responsibility. Then Billy Ballew, the man Jim most admires, gives Jim a chance to come through as his construction supervisor. For once, Jim is determined to make someone proud. Then Jim goes in for a physical for his new job, and his yaoi dream comes to life in the form of cardiologist Ken Tanaka. Jim discovers he has two heart problems—a wonky mitral valve and a serious attraction to his doctor. But Ken is a major player, and Jim might be just a notch on the doc's stethoscope. To Ken, Jim is unforgettable—but the living embodiment of his traditional family's worst nightmares. How come the minute Jim decides to be responsible, he finds himself taking care of his kid brother, getting a proposal from a wealthy woman, making a deal with the devil, and winding up in the hospital—when all he really wants is the Knave of Broken Hearts?

www.dreamspinnerpress.com

A Novel in the Long Pass Chronicles

Will Ashford lives in two closets. He meets his wealthy father's goals as both the quarterback for the famous SCU football team and a business major, but secretly he attends art school and longs to live as a painter. And he's gay. But if he can win the coveted Milton Scholarship for art, he'll be able to break from his father at the end of his senior year.

In a painting master class, Will meets his divergent opposite, Noah Zajack. A scarred orphan who's slept on park benches and eaten from trash cans, Noah carefully plans his life and multiple jobs so he has money and time to go to art school. Will's problems seem like nothing compared to Noah's. Noah wants the scholarship too and may have a way to get it since the teacher of his class has designs on him, a plan Will isn't happy about.

www.dreamspinnerpress.com

A Novel in the Long Pass Chronicles

Six foot seven inch, 300 pound Jamal Jones loves football, so when he finds out the ultra-conservative owner of his new pro football team fired their current center because he's gay, bisexual Jamal decides to stay in the closet and hang with the females. Then, at a small drag show, he comes face-to-face with his sexual fantasy in the form of Trixie LaRue, a drag queen so exquisitely convincing she scrambles Jamal's hormones—and his resolve to nurse his straight side.

Trevor Landry, aka Trixie LaRue, hides more than his genitals. A mathematician so brilliant he can't be measured, Trevor disguises his astronomical IQ and his quirk for women's clothes behind his act as a gay activist undergrad at Southern California University.

To Trevor, Jamal is the answer to a dream—a man who can love and accept both his personas. When he discovers Jamal's future is threatened if he's seen with a guy, Trevor becomes Trixie to let Jamal pass as straight. But Trevor risks his position every time he puts on a dress. Is there a closet big enough to hold a football pro and a drag queen?

www.dreamspinnerpress.com

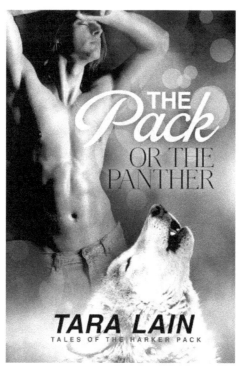

Tales of the Harker Pack: Book One

Cole Harker, son of an alpha werewolf, is bigger and more powerful than most wolves, tongue-tied in groups, and gay. For twenty-four years, he's lived to please his family and pack—even letting them promise him in marriage to female werewolf Analiese to secure a pack alliance and help save them from a powerful gangster who wants their land. Then Cole meets Analiese's half-brother, panther shifter Paris Marketo, and for the first time, Cole wants something for himself.

When Analiese runs off to marry a human, Cole finally has a chance with Paris, but the solitary cat rejects him, the pack, and everything it represents. Then Cole discovers the gangster wants Paris too and won't rest until he has him. What started as a land dispute turns into World War Wolf! But the bigger fight is the battle between cats and dogs.

Sequel to *The Pack or the Panther*
Tales of the Harker Pack: Book Two

Socialite Lindsey Vanessen wants someone to love who will love him back—an impossibility for a gay, half-human, half-werewolf. Too aggressive for humans, too gay for wolves, and needing to protect the pack from human discovery, Lindsey tries to content himself with life as a successful businessman. But when someone starts kidnapping members of wealthy families, Lindsey meets tough cop Seth Zakowsy—the hunky embodiment of everything Lindsey wants but can't have.

Seth has never been attracted to flamboyant men. What would the guys in the department think of Lindsey? But intrigue turns to lust when he discovers Lindsey's biting, snarling passion more than matches his dominant side. It might mean a chance at love for a cop in black leather and a wolf in Gucci loafers.

www.dreamspinnerpress.com

Tales of the Harker Pack: Book Three

Winter Thane was raised on the two cardinal rules of werewolf existence: don't reveal yourself to humans under penalty of death, and there's no such thing as a gay werewolf. It's no surprise when his father drags him from his wild life in remote Canada back to Connecticut to meet his old pack in hopes it will persuade Winter to abandon his love of sex with human males. Of course Dad's hopes are dashed when they come face-to-face with the gay werewolves in the Harker pack.

Winter takes one look at FBI agent Matt Partridge and decides bird is his favorite food. Partridge is embroiled in an investigation into drug dealing and the death of a fellow agent. He can't let himself get distracted by the young, platinum-haired beast, but then Winter proves invaluable in the search for clues, a move that winds them both up in chains and facing imminent death. Winter quickly learns his father's motives are questionable, the pack alphas are a bunch of pussies, humans aren't quite what they seem, and nothing in the forests of Connecticut is pure except love.

www.dreamspinnerpress.com

Betrothed
A FAERY TALE
THERESE WOODSON

JACOB Z. FLORES

BLOOD TIED

THE WARLOCK BROTHERS OF HAVENBRIDGE: BOOK TWO

Cardinal
Sins
LISSA KASEY

FEARFUL
SYMMETRY

FRANCIS GIDEON

www.dreamspinnerpress.com

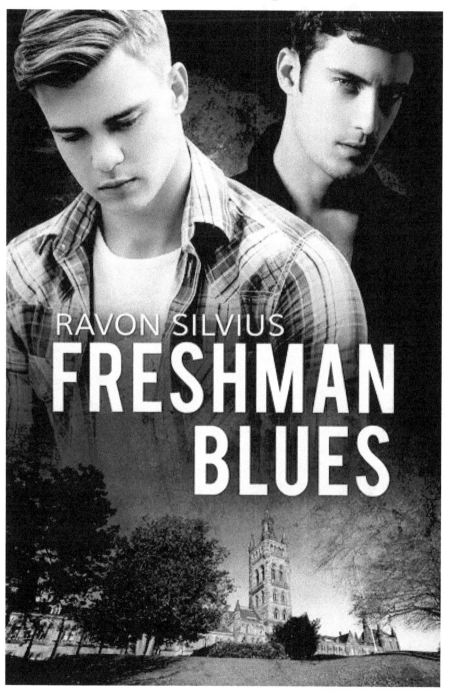

RAVON SILVIUS
FRESHMAN
BLUES

CPSIA information can be obtained
at www.ICGtesting.com
Printed in the USA
LVHW040339090420
652756LV00013B/351

9 781634 766180